THE TRUTH WON'T HELP THEM NOW

THE TRUTH WON'T HELP THEM NOW

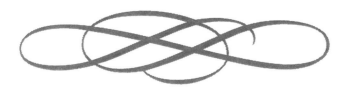

Joan Hunter
and
Steven Cobos

THE TRUTH WON'T HELP THEM NOW

Cover artist L. Ray Bingham

iUniverse books may be ordered through booksellers or by contacting:

iUniverse
1663 Liberty Drive
Bloomington, IN 47403
www.iuniverse.com
1-800-Authors (1-800-288-4677)

ISBN: 978-1-4917-8958-2 (sc)
ISBN: 978-1-4917-8959-9 (e)

Library of Congress Control Number: 2016905323

Print information available on the last page.

iUniverse rev. date: 05/25/2016

To my good friend Evelyn George. Thank you for the help and encouragement.

—Joan

To my wife, Rose Ann, with love.

—Steven

ACKNOWLEDGMENTS

Writing a book of fiction is a challenging endeavor. No labor is successful without the help, expertise, and encouragement of friends and family. We want to acknowledge these people in particular:

Evelyn George read successive drafts of the book. She found errors, made suggestions (gently and otherwise), and was a wonderful help to the overall work. Norman Castle, an expert on fishing, shared suggestions on landing the big one. Pam Smedley, coach at the Writing Gym, offered welcome encouragement. Rose Ann Cobos put up with Steven's crazy writing hours. Ray Bingham produced our striking book cover. Carolyn Bingham contributed ideas and makes a cameo appearance in the book. Robert Cobos, a former Los Angeles County deputy sheriff, provided insights into the world of law enforcement. Nicholas Veronico, author of numerous works, shared ideas for sales and distribution.

Many others helped in other ways, and we thank you all.

AUTHORS' NOTE

This is a work of historical fiction. However, the authors have included actual family members and family friends as characters. While the overall narrative is fiction, many of the circumstances are true. For example, Richard Woolfolk was a dealer on the *Rex*, Zoe Woolfolk was an astrologer in Santa Monica, and Cliff Thoms was a Los Angeles County deputy district attorney.

CHARACTERS IN *THE TRUTH WON'T HELP THEM NOW*

Luis "Lou" Gomez—Santa Monica Robbery/Homicide detective

Delores "Lola" Gomez—Lou's wife

Francisco "Paco" Gomez—Lou's son

Guadalupe "Lupe" Gomez—Lou's daughter

Randy Williams—Santa Monica Robbery/Homicide detective and Lou Gomez's partner

Dr. Davis—coroner for the City of Santa Monica

Dr. Jenson—assistant to Dr. Davis

Fletcher Bowron—mayor of Los Angeles

Buron Fitts—district attorney for Los Angeles County

Clifford "Cliff / the Chinaman" Thoms—deputy district attorney for LA County

Lucille Thoms—Cliff's wife

Mary—Cliff's secretary

Scott Squad—special squad headed up by Cliff Thoms investigating a series of murders

Frank Wallace—a detective on team one; Harry Clark's partner

Harry Clark—a detective on team one; Frank Wallace's partner

Bill Wright—a detective on team two; Ray Sanchez's partner

Ray Sanchez—a detective on team two; Bill Wright's partner

Lewis and Lopes—the detectives comprising team three

Dr. Yashida—a coroner for Los Angeles County

Fred Tsheppe—LA County probation officer and brother of Marie Woolfolk

Zoe Woolfolk—a business consultant and psychic astrologer

Richard Woolfolk—Zoe's son and a card dealer on the *Rex*

Marie Woolfolk—Richard's wife

Bobby Woolfolk—Zoe's son and younger brother to Richard

Clarence Woolfolk—chief accountant on the *Rex* and husband of Zoe Woolfolk

Lenny "Lefty" Green—gangster owner of illegal gambling establishments

Robbie Willows—Lenny Green's attorney

Dorothy Green—daughter of Lenny Green

Helen Burke—friend of Dorothy

Virginia Reed—friend of Dorothy

Carlota Gonzalez—Dorothy's maid and nanny to her child

Jack Dragna—head of the major crime family in Los Angeles

Pietro "Pete the Snake" Mara—associate of Dragna

Anna Mara—wife of Pietro

Tony "the Hat" Cornero Stralla—former bootlegger and owner of the gambling ship the *Rex*

Ricardo Stralla—son of Tony Cornero's cousin and assistant to Clarence Woolfolk

A. J. Barnes—attorney for Tony Cornero

Daniel Roberts—assistant to Clarence Woolfolk on the *Rex*

Earl Warren—attorney general for the State of California

Michael Robinson—Warren's bodyguard

Jerry White—Warren's chief of security

Barbara Scott—tenacious searcher for her missing sister

Mary Scott—younger sister of Barbara and sorority member

PART 1

CHAPTER 1

Santa Monica, California
Saturday, June 3, 1939

Fishermen arrived before dawn where Route 66 ended and the Santa Monica Municipal Pier began. Looking down its length, they saw the pier's overhead lights illuminate the fog as it rolled in off the sea, white over white, heavy in the air, and damp on the skin. Smells of gutted fish and salt air mixed with diesel fumes from the water taxis. The billowing fog gave the pier a dreamlike quality of washed-out colors and ghostly shapes in the distance.

As the fishermen prepared their lines and bait, the crabbers, who had spent the night on the pier watching their nets, the ocean, and the sky, checked their hoop nets for the last time and began to pack up for the trip home.

Drawing the rope attached to the nets hand over hand, the crabbers pulled up their nets. One net, its metal hoop measuring a yard in diameter, was unusually heavy.

"Think you caught yourself a car tire," one fisherman joked.

The straining crabber kept pulling on the rope, hoping not to tear the net. "Something big," he grunted. Both men looked

1

over the railing and, through the fog, could see something large and dark just below the water's surface.

"Damn, a black sea bass," the angler said, shaking his head in amazement. "That son of a bitch is as big as a man!"

A small crowd began to gather and watch as the dark form broke the surface. The crabber, fearing that the net would tear if the catch was lifted out of the water, tied off the rope on the railing. Then, together with the crowd, he looked down upon his prize. As the darkness receded and the fog lifted, it gradually became apparent that the form was not a black sea bass but a man's body. The crabber, who had spent the night sitting alone on the pier checking his lines and watching the stars and the tides, was sickened by the sight and angered, maybe a little, that this stranger's death had intruded on his cherished solitude.

The call came in to the Santa Monica Police Department at 5:40 a.m. A police powerboat was dispatched, and officers soon had the body out of the water. They docked at the west end of the pier and carried the dead man to the upper surface of the pier by six. The corpse was wearing a suit but was missing his tie and both shoes. He was about thirty and white with a slender build. The officers from the powerboat kept curious anglers away from the body. In a short time, two homicide detectives arrived.

The air felt chilly and damp as the men walked onto the Santa Monica Municipal Pier and past the adjoining shorter but wider Pleasure Pier to the south. The Pleasure Pier had once been covered by amusement rides, but since the start of the Depression, only a carousel was left in operation. The carousel was housed in a large building. A second building, a dance hall that had failed in 1934, was now used as a convention center and headquarters for Santa Monica's lifeguards.

The ocean was calm, but the detectives could hear the water lapping against the pilings as they walked along the long, narrow Municipal Pier. The sun, still low in the east, illuminated the heavy cloud cover that was common for June mornings. In spite of the cold, a few more fishermen had joined the early birds and were setting up along the railings. As the detectives walked toward their destination, a slight breeze stirred trash on the pier.

Lou Gomez, the senior of the two detectives, was a short, stocky, brown-skinned man in his early fifties. He was proud that while his parents spoke the uneducated Spanish of Mexican dirt farmers, he spoke excellent Spanish and English, and he had put himself through junior college. Despite his age, he still had a muscular build but was starting to get a paunch. His black hair was thinning and shot through with gray. Lou was self-conscious about letting others see him wear reading glasses, but he slipped them on anyway and squatted down beside the body to take a closer look.

His partner, Randy Williams, was over six feet tall, balding, and prematurely gray. He was only in his midforties, but fighting in the trenches in France during the Great War had exacted a price. Randy stood back a few feet and looked over Lou's shoulder. "How long has he been in the water?"

"Hard to tell. The fish got to him a little, but other than that, he's in pretty good shape. He's not in full rigor, so he's either going in or coming out, but he hasn't started to bloat. If I had to guess, I'd say no more than ten hours. Get closer; take a look at his hands."

"I can see fine from here. Soft hands except for the callus

on his right middle finger. That's from writing with a pen or pencil all day. So what do we have, a bookie?"

"No, the suit is too nice," Lou said. "It's something you would wear to meet the public."

"So a clerk or a bookkeeper or an accountant. Anything in his pockets? Anything that identifies him?"

"No, nothing. The powerboat boys did find a book of matches. We'll have to let them dry out before we can read the printing."

"Someone wanted him dead in the worst way. From where I'm standing, I count two shots to the head and at least one to the torso. What you think? A .38?"

Lou looked back over his shoulder at Randy. "I think if you were closer, you could enjoy the smell along with me," he said with a faint smile. "Yeah, either a .38 or a nine millimeter. A .45 would have taken off the back of his head."

"One of the lab boys should be coming with the meat wagon. They should be here soon. I'll tell the uniforms to keep the tourists and the damned reporters away. We don't need this getting in the papers."

The squad room at the Santa Monica Police Department was cramped. Lou and Randy had their desks pushed together facing each other. When they returned from the pier, Randy left his gun in a desk drawer and went downstairs to the cafeteria for breakfast. Lou went straight to the morgue to pester the coroner, Dr. Jenson, to rush the autopsy. Jenson had agreed to complete the autopsy that morning but asked Lou to leave the room so he could work without the detective's incessant questions.

The coroner called at 9:00 a.m. He was ready to review his preliminary autopsy report with the detectives. Lou popped up out of his chair when the call came and was ready to go by the time he hung up the phone. Randy continued to lean back in his chair with his feet on his desk. He was already on his third cigarette of the morning. He leisurely swung his long legs around and stood up. Together they made their way down to the basement, where the morgue was located. Dr. Jenson met them at the morgue entrance. He read from his notes:

"White male, twenty-eight to thirty-three, five foot ten inches tall, well fed and well groomed, no significant scars. Cause of death was three gunshot wounds: one to the chest, entrance one inch under the left nipple, and two to the head, one to the right temple and one to the jaw just in front of the right ear. The head wounds were both through and through with some small fragments recovered, while the bullet to the chest ended up lodged in the spine. I recovered it, but it's smashed pretty bad. Looks to be a .38. The composition of the fragments from the head wounds are consistent with the recovered bullet, so it looks like they all came from the same gun. From the lack of decomposition, the stomach contents, and the fact that only now is he going into full rigor, I'd say your guy was killed last night between nine and one o'clock. There were no powder burns on the decedent's shirt, so the shot was from at least a few feet away. My guess is that the guy was shot in the chest first and then the killer put two in his head, a coup de grâce, as it were."

"Well," Randy offered, "that was thoughtful of the killer." He reached for his cigarettes, looked at Lou, and then returned the pack to his shirt pocket. "Did you find anything we missed to identify this guy? Any laundry tags? What about that matchbook cover? Could you read it once it dried out?"

"Yes, it was from a gambling ship, the *Rex*. They have, what, two thousand customers a night? That narrows it down. I managed to get a clear set of the guy's fingerprints, but it will take some time to get word back on the identification. But"—the coroner walked over to the examination table where the body lay—"take a look at these." The dead man's naked body was covered by a surprisingly white sheet from the waist down. The man's torso was exposed, and the detectives could see that both shoulders were crudely tattooed in charcoal-colored ink. On his right shoulder was "13 1/2," and on his left shoulder was "SHELLQ."

"A foreign language quiz and a goddamn fraction problem. Okay, I see you smiling," Lou said. "You've got it all figured out, haven't you, Doctor."

"Not quite," Jenson said, still smiling, "but I can tell you with some degree of certainty that these are jailhouse tattoos, and I know what thirteen and a half is."

"Okay," Lou said, "I'll bite. What is it?"

"Twelve jurors, one judge, and half a chance. It's been around for years. I see it most often on men from the South."

"What about Shell Q?" Lou asked.

"That's a new one to me. It may not even be English. Does that mean something in Spanish?"

"Nah. Can't say that I've ever seen it before either," Lou said, peering closely at the tattoo. "I see what you mean about the tattoos. They aren't professional. 'Well fed and well groomed,' that's what you said, right, Doc?"

"Yes."

"So it stands to reason that he's been out of jail or prison for a while, right?"

"Yes, yes, that makes sense. Several months at least."

"Randy, any ideas about Shell Q?"

6

"No, and it doesn't look like an English word to me. Maybe we can get some language expert to look at it."

"I think I know someone who can help. Thank you, Doctor. If you think of anything else, be sure to give me a call." Lou started for the door and then suddenly stopped. "Oh, any idea how long our friend was in the water?"

"Most of the night, I imagine."

"So he was shot and dumped in the bay pretty soon afterward?"

"He was dumped soon after being shot, but he would have sunk and couldn't have drifted far. No, I'd say he entered the water just a few yards from where he was found."

"Interesting." Lou made a note to have police officers interview fishermen on the pier starting at eight or nine at night.

Lou flipped through the address book at his desk. He couldn't find the name he needed, so he just called the main line for the Los Angeles County probation office. "Hello, this is Detective Luis Gomez from Santa Monica Robbery/Homicide. May I speak to Fred? I don't remember his last name, but he is a PO and speaks German and Russian, I think."

"Sure, you want Fred T. You know, he also speaks Spanish and French. I hear his Russian isn't so good, but no one seems to complain. You realize it's Saturday morning. I'm only here to make up some time. I went to a funeral on Wednesday and—"

"Can you get me Fred's home number? I'm trying to conduct a murder investigation."

"Right, sorry. Okay, I can't give his number, but I can have him call you. So what's your number?"

"Good morning, Detective, this is Fred Tsheppe. How may I help you?"

"Thanks for returning the call, Fred. We met on the Philips case. You remember—he used the ten-gauge shotgun on his wife's boyfriend. We don't see ten-gauge shotguns much."

"Of course. How are you?"

"Fine. I have a language puzzle for you. We have a decedent, shot three times, white male, twenty-eight to thirty-three, looks like he has a desk job, but he also has what look to be prison tattoos. On one shoulder is a thirteen and a half; on the other shoulder is the phrase 'Shell Q.' We know what thirteen and a half is, but what is Shell Q?"

"Shell Q? Is that one word or two words?"

"One word, and it's in all capitals."

"I don't think it's a foreign word. Do you know what state he was incarcerated in?"

"No, but isn't the thirteen and a half a southern tattoo?"

"Not necessarily. The Q is baffling me. Almost always a Q is followed by a U. Maybe the Q is an initial or abbreviation. If your decedent was doing felony time in California, where would he have been incarcerated?"

"Folsom or San Quentin."

"San Quentin. SQ. And between those letters, h-e-l-l. Well, Detective, I think that's your explanation. The tattoo stands for 'hell in San Quentin.'"

"You're kidding. That's juvenile."

"We're not dealing with geniuses here, but it's not unheard of. I think you'll find that ancient peoples, especially the ones using nonphonetic writing systems such as hieroglyphics, would also make word plays based on the juxtaposition of their symbols."

"Nonphonetic juxtaposition. I was thinking the same thing. So our stiff did time in San Quentin—is that what you're telling me?"

"Yeah, that's most likely."

"Fred, how do you spell your last name? S-h-e-p-p-what?"

"Not a bad guess, but my name starts with a silent T. T-s-h-e-p-p-e. It's German."

"Oh, German. My partner, Randy Williams, was in the Great War. He is a little ... touchy about Germans. You understand, don't you?"

"Sure, but my family's been in this country for fifty years. I had a relative who fought with Teddy Roosevelt in Cuba."

"Thank you, Fred. I'll run this down with the folks in San Quentin and see if it gets us anywhere. I appreciate your help."

Lou contacted San Quentin prison but didn't expect much cooperation, not a little after ten o'clock on a Saturday morning. He got lucky. He spoke with that rarest of creatures, a bureaucrat who gives a damn. The clerk, Frankie J., understood that when a murderer kills one person, he often destroys a family. Lou told Frankie everything he knew, and Frankie promised Lou that he would work on the matter until he had an answer.

The telephone message was waiting for the detectives when they came back from interviewing witnesses on another murder case. It had taken Frankie only two hours to sort through the list of inmates who had been released a few months before and pinpoint their man. His name was Daniel Roberts, a white male, five foot ten inches tall, and born March 23,

1909. He had done time in San Quentin for embezzlement. Frankie was also able to provide Lou with the name, address, and telephone number of Roberts's next of kin: his parents living in Glendale. Lou called the parents and confirmed that they had a son named Daniel who was thirty years old. He broke the news to the couple about their son as gently as he could. The father went silent, and Lou could hear the mother sobbing in the background. He gave them a full minute before he spoke again. He asked them to come downtown, identify the body in the morgue, and provide information on Daniel's address, friends, and employment.

Daniel's parents arrived at the police department in the early afternoon. Lou and Randy went with them to the morgue. At first the grieving parents refused to acknowledge that the body on the slab was that of their son. They kept insisting that the face wasn't right. Lou explained twice what damage the bullets had done and how the fish later had fed on the exposed flesh. Mrs. Roberts broke down crying, and the coroner had to help her from the room and into a chair in the hallway.

Mr. Roberts watched his wife leave the room. Slowly he turned and looked Lou in the eyes. He surprised Lou by grabbing his wrist. In a soft voice, Roberts said, "The tattoos, I recognize the tattoos. I told him"—color had returned to his face and he had regained his voice—"I told him they made him look like a goddamn sailor. A goddamn sailor! He was my boy; how could I say a thing like that? God, look at him!" Roberts stared at his son. "I ain't seen nothing like that since the Great War."

Randy came around the slab, peeled Roberts's hand from

Lou's wrist, and put his arm around the older man's shoulders. Gently Randy mumbled something about the horrors he had seen in France.

"I know this is hard, but we need your help if we are going to find your son's killer," Lou said.

The father finally lifted his eyes off the body of his son, looked at Lou, and nodded slowly. "Mama and I will tell you whatever we know, but our son ... he didn't talk much about his work or his friends. We'll tell you whatever we know."

The parents didn't know much. They couldn't tell the detectives about the crime that put Roberts in San Quentin, and they didn't know about his friends, but they did know he had been working on the *Rex* as a bookkeeper of some sort for several months. He had been released from San Quentin between Thanksgiving and Christmas the previous year, and he had spent two months looking for a job. Danny, as his parents called him, had felt lucky to get a job so quickly and one that paid so well. Lou expressed surprise that Daniel could get a bookkeeping job after having been convicted of embezzlement. But, his parents explained, he was basically an honest kid who made a mistake. Daniel was good at his job and was able to come to an understanding with the owners.

After Roberts's parents left, Lou talked through what little he knew. "Tony Cornero owns the *Rex*, and word has it that Bugsy Siegel and George Raft put up the money to convert it into a casino. Roberts's parents said he had an understanding with an owner. So which owner, and what was the understanding?"

"My money's on Bugsy. Old Danny boy got caught with his hand in the cookie jar, and Bugsy's boys fucking elucidated the understanding to him three times. That Mickey Cohen and Hooky Rothman play rough," Randy concluded, jabbing the air with his burning cigarette to emphasize the point.

"Yeah, maybe. Let's radio the *Rex* and see what they can tell us."

CHAPTER 2

Tony Cornero had opened the gambling ship SS *Rex* in May 1938. She was anchored just beyond the three-mile limit on the open sea in Santa Monica Bay. The ship had been completely remodeled and was a first-class casino with good booze, good food, and honest games. The renovation reportedly cost $600,000 and was financed by Bugsy Siegel and the movie star George Raft. This beautiful, luxurious, moneymaking enterprise, grossing $300,000 a month, was a far cry from the *Rex*'s humble beginnings as a four-mast windjammer called the *Kenilworth* built in 1887 in Scotland and originally outfitted for shipping grain.

The *Rex*, which had no means of self-propulsion, was towed a little more than three miles offshore and opened for business. The ship's capacity was two thousand passengers; she had a crew of 350. There was an elegant dining room with a dance floor. The crew included the dealers, waitstaff, chefs, a full orchestra, and working girls. The casino offered craps, roulette, blackjack, chuck-a-luck, and faro. There were 150 slot machines along one wall of the casino. A room was set aside for betting on horse races and received race results via shortwave radio. There also was a four-hundred-seat bingo parlor. The games on the

Rex were honest, and Tony Cornero posted a $100,000 reward to anyone who could prove that they weren't.

The *Rex* had a constant stream of customers who were carried from the Santa Monica pier to the ship by water taxis. Customers arrived from all over Southern California. The pier was accessible by several major highways and the Red Car system. The Red Car system was part of the Pacific Electric Railway, which, in the 1920s, was the largest electric railway system in the world. Red Cars provided mass transit to the Los Angeles area—from Santa Monica on the coast seventy-five miles inland to the city of Redlands and southeast along the coast forty miles to Newport Beach.

The radio operator of the *Rex* called for his supervisor, who called for his supervisor, who called Tony Cornero. After conferring with his attorney, Cornero allowed his paymaster to provide Lou with information. Daniel Roberts had been hired full time as of Monday, February 6, 1939. His position was senior bookkeeper. He last worked on Friday, June 2. His shift ended at 8:00 p.m. His immediate supervisor was Clarence Woolfolk. The paymaster was able to provide Lou with Woolfolk's address and phone number.

Lou called Woolfolk's number several times. No one answered. Next Lou called the water taxi company that serviced the *Rex*. The man who answered identified himself as Rodolfo. After Lou identified himself, Rodolfo suddenly lost his mastery of English and told Lou in broken, Spanish-accented English that he didn't understand. Lou matter-of-factly told Rodolfo in Spanish that if he didn't cooperate with the police, Lou would personally come down there and beat him with a nightstick. *Nightstick* seemed to translate well. Rodolfo quickly found the taxi operator who brought *Rex* employees on the 9:00 p.m. run the previous night.

The taxi operator told Lou that he remembered bringing back four employees as well as some patrons. He knew the employees by sight since he saw them five days a week. There were two men from the kitchen and two from a room where the men got to sit and count money. The taxi operator thought that sounded like a dream job. He explained that the older money counter was the younger counter's boss, but the two men seemed to be on friendly terms. The older man was deaf or nearly so. The younger counter had to shout at the older man in order to converse. The operator was sure that all four employees made it off his taxi. The last he saw of them, the four employees were walking up the gangplank.

Lou again contacted the *Rex* and soon had the names of the two kitchen workers as well as the address and phone number of their rooming house. He spoke to both workers. They told him the same story. They got off work at eight, had dinner, and then waited around on deck for the nine o'clock water taxi. While they waited, they could hear the two counting-room guys talking with the older fellow's son. The son worked a roulette table and was on a break. The water taxi came, they got on with the counting-room guys, all four got off at the launch, and together they walked to the street. The kitchen workers caught a Red Car running southeast to Inglewood. As the Red Car pulled away, they could see the two counting-room guys standing at the edge of the parking lot near Pacific Coast Highway.

Lou again had the police department contact the radio room of the *Rex*. The ship's paymaster provided Lou with the address and phone number of Richard Woolfolk, Clarence's son. He was also able to confirm that Richard worked his entire shift and clocked out at 12:32 a.m. on Saturday morning.

"Lou, we can call," Randy told his partner. "We don't have to drive out there. We've been at this since six this morning, and it's nearly three."

"No. We have a father and son talking to the victim, and Dad was the last person seen with Roberts. It smells. Maybe Clarence didn't pull the trigger, but he'd be the first one to know if money is missing, and he is the logical person to finger Roberts for Bugsy's boys. We're going to Richard's house, and I'll have a car dispatched to sit outside Clarence's house in case he tries to run."

Richard and his wife, Marie, were in the living room of their small bungalow at the top of the first hill inland in Redondo Beach. Richard was singing along with the radio, dancing to some internal rhythm. He was medium height, slender, and normally light on his feet. This afternoon he was a little unsteady. Less than an hour before they had received the news about Danny. Since the first call, there had been three others, all with almost the identical expressions of grief and bewilderment: Have you heard? Isn't it terrible! Who could have done it? Richard coped with his shock and grief by pouring himself a water glass full of whiskey and then a second. After a pint of liquid therapy, he was able to smile and reminisce about his departed friend. Marie looked on, relieved that her husband had put the whiskey away, and continued playing a game of solitaire. Both of them were smoking Lucky Strike cigarettes, and each was nursing a bottle of lager. The front room was small and looked out on the front yard, such as it was, and on to the sidewalk and street. From his front yard, Richard could see the Pacific Ocean and feel the gentle breezes that flowed off the water and brought relief from warm summer evenings.

As a teenager, Richard worked a series of jobs near or on the beaches from Long Beach to Santa Monica for the company that owned most of the amusement concessions on the pier and along the beachfront. After Richard's mother, Zoe, married Clarence, Richard helped his stepfather, who was a barnstormer and a stunt diver. He rigged the parachutes, checked the airplanes, and helped with the recoveries.

Clarence's stunt-diving career ended one Saturday afternoon when there was turbulence in the air and in the water.

"Don't go up today," Richard pleaded, reading the weather signs.

"What's a little wind?" Clarence said dismissively. "Besides, that's what the people came to see, a little risk."

The biplane circled over Rainbow Pier at Long Beach. Richard was in a dory under the pier waiting to pick up Clarence after he dove from the plane into the sea. Richard always marveled at the perfection of the dives. That day, though, he could see the wind playing havoc with Clarence's steeled muscles as he executed an almost flawless dive. Only the practiced eye of an attendant could detect the slight change in muscle movement.

The wind blew Clarence off course. At the moment of impact, he failed to arch his back to create a shallow dive and dove too deeply. A huge searing pain exploded in his ears. When Richard picked him up in the dory, his ears were bleeding and the smell of blood was beginning to attract the sea scavengers. Richard hurriedly hauled his stepfather into the boat. Almost automatically, Clarence jumped to his feet and waved his arms over his head with his fists raised, showing his audience that he was fine. But ever afterward he had dizzy spells and could scarcely hear. That's when Richard started looking for a new line of work.

Richard had been working on the *Rex* as a croupier, a roulette dealer, from the day the gambling ship opened the year before. Since it was a ship, he had to have seaman's papers. Officially he was an assistant purser; all the croupiers and dealers on the ship were assistant pursers. He sometimes wondered if anyone in the maritime office ever asked why a ship needed forty assistant accountants. He felt lucky to have a job—a good-paying job—that didn't require hard labor, and he didn't mind working the odd hours. He enjoyed his work, which required him to quickly calculate payouts and watch for cheaters. Off duty he loved a good time and enjoyed playing little jokes on his fellow workers, all in good fellowship. It would be different now, now that Danny was dead. Richard knew the job couldn't last forever, not with Attorney General Earl Warren pulling all his dirty tricks to close down the gambling ships, but he had hoped that he and Danny would ... what? He didn't know. He didn't usually plan ahead.

Richard and Marie watched as a car drove up to their house and two men in suits strolled up the cement sidewalk. They could guess that the men were detectives there to ask about Danny Roberts. Richard turned off the music and met the men at the door.

"Richard Woolfolk?"

"Yes."

"I'm Detective Gomez. This is my partner, Detective

Williams. We're from the Santa Monica Police Department. We're investigating the death of Daniel Roberts. May we come in?"

"Yes, of course." Richard let them in and pointed to the loveseat in front of the window.

The detectives sat down uncomfortably close to each other. Lou quickly scanned the small living room: the wife playing cards and drinking a beer; the husband, unsteady on his feet, smelling of whiskey, and drinking a beer; a child's toy and baby bottle on its side on the floor. The voice of a small child came from a back room. *Judge not lest ye be judged*, he thought, *but Christ, it's the middle of the afternoon.* Pressing on, Lou asked, "What hours did you work yesterday?"

"My usual, four in the afternoon to twelve thirty. You know, I work in the main casino. I don't work with Danny in the counting room. My stepfather, Clarence Woolfolk, works with him."

"You were seen talking with Roberts and your father about eight thirty last night. What were you three talking about?" Lou asked. As usual, he was taking notes while Randy sat quietly, observing.

"Danny was telling us about the date he was going on. He wouldn't tell us the dame's name, just that she was young and pretty and rich. He was bragging that she had a foreign sports car that could go one hundred twenty miles per hour."

"Did your father and Roberts have some sort of disagreement? Witnesses said that they were shouting at each other."

"My stepfather is deaf. You have to shout at him so he can hear you. They weren't arguing, if that's what you're implying."

"When did you leave the ship?"

"About quarter to one. I rode the water taxi back to shore with some other guys from the ship and a few customers."

"Write down the names of the employees you rode the water taxi with," said Lou, handing his notebook and pen to Richard.

He wrote down the names of the three other employees. "I don't know their telephone numbers or where they live."

"That's okay. We can get it from the paymaster on the *Rex*," Lou said. "What time did you come home last night?"

"I got back to shore about 1:00 a.m. and drove straight home. I'm always eager to get home to my bride." Richard winked at Marie.

"Can you verify your husband's whereabouts, Mrs. Woolfolk?"

"Yes, whatever he said," she answered.

Both detectives looked at each other but said nothing. For the first time, Randy spoke. "Mr. Woolfolk, do you own a gun?"

"No."

"Does your ... did you say he is your stepfather?"

"Yeah. My parents got divorced around twenty years ago. My real dad moved away and remarried. Clarence is my stepfather. My brother and I started using his last name years ago."

"Does your stepfather own a gun?" Randy asked.

"Yeah. He has a Smith & Wesson snub-nosed revolver. I shot it a few times. He carries it when he has to carry around cash. Say, what are you getting at? Was Danny shot?"

"It's just a routine question. Does he carry the gun with him all the time?"

"No, I just told you. He only carries it when he has to carry around a lot of cash. He and Danny are friends. Clarence wouldn't hurt Danny. You're barking up the wrong tree."

"Cornero must really trust your stepfather to put him in charge of the counting room," Lou said. "And you said your stepfather sometimes carries around cash. What else does he do for Cornero?"

"Nothing. I don't know. He doesn't shoot people. My stepfather goes to work, comes home, sits with that stupid dog of his, and puts up with my mother. That's enough for one lifetime."

"Is your mother hard to get along with? Does she have expensive tastes? Does she ..." Lou paused, trying to sort out possibilities.

"My mother is a pill, but she makes her own money. She has high standards for herself and everyone in her family. Sometimes"—Richard looked over at Marie—"it's hard to live up to her expectations."

"Say," Randy began, "when was the last time you talked to your stepfather?"

"Last night when the three of us were shooting the breeze on the *Rex*. I was on my dinner break. I should go over to his house and tell him about Danny. He probably doesn't know yet. No one calls him 'cause he won't answer. He can't hear the phone ring unless he's standing right by it, and even then he doesn't hear well enough to talk on the phone."

"We'll break the news to him. We're going over there now. It looks like he was the last known person to talk to Roberts. We're hoping that he can give us information that will help us find the killer. Don't try to call him. We may have more questions for you later," Lou said.

"Thanks for your time," Randy added. He did not sound sincere.

Richard and Marie drank their beers and watched the policemen drive away.

The two detectives walked along the cement sidewalk toward Clarence Woolfolk's beach house. They could smell the sea air and feel the cool ocean breeze as they looked for the address they were given: fifty-one Navy Street, Ocean Park. The house was weathered, as were all the houses this close to the sea. The house was at one time a dark green, but now there were flakes of sand in the crevasses where the wind had sandblasted the paint over the last winter. When the homes on the street were built in the boom times of the twenties, they had been modern, beautiful examples of beach bungalows, but time and hard circumstances had started the subtle deterioration of the neighborhood. Lou and Randy climbed the stairs to the porch and were assaulted by the sound of a German shepherd vigorously barking to announce their arrival.

"Down, Polie!" came the command from inside the house. A rather tall, thin, balding man about fifty years old answered the door. He was dressed in a pair of casual slacks and a long-sleeved sweater. "There is no soliciting here," he said through the screen door.

"We're here to speak to Clarence Woolfolk," Randy said, flashing his badge.

"You'll have to speak a little louder; I don't hear very well," was the answer.

"I'm Detective Williams, and this is my partner, Detective Gomez."

"Mr. Woolfolk, may we come in?" Lou asked in a loud voice.

Clarence hesitated, slowly examining the two men. He saw that their suits were inexpensive without being cheap and their shoes were sturdy and well worn. The bulges under their suit coats, at the short man's left chest and the tall man's right hip, informed his experienced eye that both men were packing. Clarence had dealt with policemen for many years. In his experience, they were brutal, dishonest, and on the take; still, he couldn't keep them waiting for long. "What's this all about?"

"I'm afraid we have some bad news," Lou said, watching for Clarence's expression.

"Is my wife all right?" Clarence asked, concerned but baffled. A car accident? A robbery? Why would two detectives be sent instead of uniformed officers?

"She's fine." Lou detected some relief in Clarence's face. "It concerns Daniel Roberts."

"Is Danny hurt?" A car accident, no doubt. That damn foreign sports car.

"No, he's dead." Lou watched as Clarence's eyes widened.

It took a few seconds for Clarence to take it in. "Dead? What happened?"

"Someone killed him."

Clarence stumbled back a step and opened the screen door for the two detectives. He nodded to the dog to let Polie know there was no danger. Polie growled deep in his chest but remained still. Clarence led the detectives into the small front parlor and pointed to a threadbare couch. Lou sat down on a cushion that offered no support, and he felt himself sinking almost to the floor. Randy lowered himself carefully onto the cushion beside Lou. He too sank down. Clarence settled into an overstuffed chair. "When? Do you know who did it?"

"Last night, late," Randy said. "Our witnesses say you were the last person to see Roberts alive." The statement sounded more like an accusation.

"No, I saw Danny get in a car with a woman and drive off."

"Can you describe the woman?" Lou asked. His notebook rested on his knee.

"No, I never really saw her."

How can he be sure it was a woman driving? Lou wondered. "Well, what kind of car?"

"I don't know. Some foreign job."

"New? Old? What color?" Lou was starting to get impatient.

"It was new. I think it was black or maybe dark blue. It was hard to tell in that light."

"Do you have a gun?" Randy asked.

"Yes. A Smith & Wesson Terrier."

"That's what, a five-shot, .38-caliber revolver? A little gun. You could carry it anytime and no one would notice," Randy said, dropping his hands to his lap.

Clarence nodded his head at Randy. "Yes, very similar to the snubby you have on your hip, Officer."

"This," Randy said, fanning back his coat to expose his revolver, "is an M & P model. Six shots. A two-inch barrel like your Terrier, but it fires the .38 Special, not the .38 S & W like yours. The .38 S & W is a little unpowered."

"So where is it?" Suddenly conscious of the big Colt 1911 semiautomatic he carried in his shoulder holster, Lou was watching Clarence's hands.

"What?"

"Your revolver." Lou had set his notebook and pen on the arm of the couch and was easing his right hand under his suit coat.

"Oh, I'll get it," Clarence said and started to get up.

"No," Lou barked. "Just show me where it is—and keep your hands where I can see them."

Clarence led Lou into his bedroom. "There," he said, pointing to his nightstand.

Lou opened the drawer and retrieved the revolver, carefully touching it only with his handkerchief. He smelled it. It had neither been fired nor cleaned recently. He dropped open the cylinder. Five cartridges, none fired. Lou looked down the barrel as best he could. It was clean but slightly dusty. Lou was sure that the gun hadn't been fired for months and certainly not yesterday. He could take it to the station and have it test fired, but the bullet from Roberts's chest was too smashed up to match to a particular gun. The composition of the bullets could be matched, however. Lou arranged to take one of the bullets from Clarence's gun. Clarence, like any good accountant, demanded a receipt.

Lou and Clarence returned to the front parlor and took their seats.

Randy asked, "What do you do on the *Rex*?"

Clarence shifted his gaze from Lou to Randy and crossed his arms. "Well, *Detective*, you must have detected that I work in the counting room on the *Rex* with Danny every day."

"Just what do you do in the counting room?" Randy kept his eye on the German shepherd while Lou took notes.

"Strange as it may seem, we count the money as it is brought in from the gaming tables and the slot machines. That's why they call it the counting room."

Lou ignored Clarence's sarcastic tone as best he could. "Thanks for clearing that up for us. You said that you work with Roberts every evening. Exactly what hours do you work?"

"We work, well, Danny ... I work the eleven-to-eight shift with an hour for lunch."

"Do you know when Roberts left the *Rex* last night?"

"Danny and I finished our shift at the regular time, eight. He went into the locker room and did a quick shave. I remember he put on a clean shirt and a tie. He was wearing his nice suit." Clarence looked down at his dog and continued petting the animal as he recounted the night's events. "He came out of the locker room, and we were standing there talking, the three of us—me, Richard, and Danny. My son, Richard, was on his dinner break. Danny and I were waiting for the water taxi to take us back into town. We were shooting the breeze when Danny said he had a hot date with a real looker."

Lou asked, "Did you and Roberts arrive at the pier on the same water taxi?"

"Yes, and you should have seen the car that picked up Danny! It was a real beauty. It had to have been foreign because the driver was on the right. I couldn't see her, but if she was anything like her car, Danny was going to have a hot date."

Randy asked, "Did you see which way they went?"

"They were headed up Pacific Coast Highway toward Malibu was the impression I got. Where else would you have a car like that?"

"What time did the water taxi drop you off?" Lou asked without looking up from his notepad.

"It was a little after nine by the time we got on the dock."

"Did you go straight home from there?"

"Yes. My wife picked me up in the parking lot, and we drove straight home."

"Is she here now to verify that?"

"No. She's at work."

"What kind of work does she do?" The unexpected silence following this question caused Lou to look up from his notebook. "You do know what kind of work she does, don't you?"

"Yes, of course. She's a business consultant."

"Does she consult with Tony Cornero or Benny Siegel?" Randy asked. Lou had stopped writing and was watching Clarence struggle to frame his response.

"No. She's never even met those two. She advises people on investments and private matters."

"What kind of private matters?" Lou asked, but he could already anticipate the reply.

"If I told you, they wouldn't be private, would they?" Clarence smiled at his clever rejoinder.

"Were you there when they killed Roberts?" Lou asked as if inquiring about the time.

"You'll have to speak up."

"I said, were you there when they killed Roberts?" Lou was almost shouting.

Clarence looked genuinely surprised. "No, no. He was my friend. I had nothing to do with his death! How could you even ask that question?"

Lou and Randy exchanged glances. Lou returned to a conversational tone. "Why do you think anyone would want to murder Roberts?"

Lou's manner, accusatory one minute and civil the next, rattled Clarence. He struggled to regain his composure. "It's a very dangerous world out there," he offered. "Maybe…," Clarence's voice trailed off as the reality of Danny's death sank in. The dog's growl brought Clarence back from his ruminations. He petted the dog and suggested, "Danny had enemies from the old days. He had been in prison, you know. Maybe they killed him."

"Maybe they did," Lou said absentmindedly. Lou had put on his reading glasses and was studying his notebook. He glanced over at Randy, who continued to monitor the dog. "I know we've been over this before, but can you give us a fuller description of the car that picked up Roberts?"

Polie growled again. "I don't think my dog likes you. I'm afraid I can't be of more help right now. I need to get ready for work. I'm covering a shift for a family friend." Clarence stood up and started for the front door.

The detectives had more questions, but Clarence had given them new leads and they would need his willing cooperation in the future. Wordlessly, with the slightest of nods, they agreed to go. In unison they pushed themselves up from the depths of the couch. Before they left, however, they had Clarence give them his wife's work address.

As he dressed for work, Clarence's thoughts bounced from Danny to the cops to the why—why his assistant died. Last night Clarence had envied Danny, young, healthy, dating a beautiful woman; now there was just a body, still and cold, on a slab somewhere. Could those detectives, that Mutt and Jeff team, find Danny's killer? The white guy, tall and quiet, hadn't taken a single note, but the other fellow, short, dark, and intense, had asked a question that echoed in Clarence's mind. Clarence stepped outside and waited for his ride to work. He hadn't quite heard Lou's last name, but recognized his intelligence. Clarence wondered if the detective was Italian or Mexican. Mexican but educated, Clarence decided. Lou's question, why someone would kill Danny, was the question Clarence had been pushing away since learning of Danny's death. He didn't know who, but he knew why: cash—mountains of cash. The large amounts of cash made it easy to skim. Like taking cream off the top, skimming is taking a small percent of cash before a bookkeeper records it as income. The money is never accounted for in a business's official books, and it never gets taxed. It was necessary to take precautions when skimming—it was more likely for a gangster to go to prison for tax evasion than for murder—but if done with care, skimming could make a man rich.

CHAPTER 3

The office where Zoe worked was on the second floor of the building at the corner of Wilshire and Second Street in Santa Monica. She was casting an astrological chart for a longtime client, when the two detectives knocked on her door. She knew trouble was coming, so she steeled herself for an onslaught.

"Come in, gentlemen," she said sweetly. "How can I help you?"

Lou and Randy stepped through the door, removed their hats, and introduced themselves as homicide detectives. Zoe's smiling features were unchanged. Standing beside the men, she was a few inches shorter than Lou, but came up only to Randy's chest.

Randy looked down and asked, "Do you know a man named Daniel Roberts?"

"Of course, I have met him. He works with my husband on the *Rex*," she answered.

"Do you know of anyone who would wish him harm?" Lou asked as he pulled out his notebook.

"Daniel is, unfortunately, drawn to the wrong kind of

people. He sometimes drinks too much, and he has a weakness for women. Why do you ask?" Zoe responded.

Randy had stepped over to the back wall and was admiring a liquor cabinet with a stainless steel–covered fold-down shelf. "We fished his body out of the bay this morning," he explained casually.

"That's terrible!"

"We spoke with your husband. Randy, you have your notes from that conversation, don't you?" Lou asked, looking over at his partner.

"Ah, no." Randy made a show of patting his pockets. "I must have left them at the station."

"Well, no matter. What hours does your husband work, Mrs. Woolfolk?" Lou asked, looking over the top of his notebook.

"He works from eleven in the morning until eight at night."

"Monday through Friday?"

"Normally, yes. He is going in today. He's covering Ricardo's shift."

"Who's Ricardo?"

"Ricardo is the son of Tony Cornero's cousin. The dear boy is only twenty-three and is quite out of his depth in the big city. He's from Cucamonga and worked with his father in the vineyards. I, myself, am from a small town and know how it feels to be fresh off the farm."

"Ricardo's suddenly disappeared?"

"Oh, nothing like that. He called us a few days ago and arranged to have Clarence cover his Saturday shift. I believe that Ricardo has a lady friend he's meeting for the weekend."

"Is this normal for Ricardo?"

"Well, it's not the first time, but I wouldn't say it's normal. Ricardo, well, he fancies himself a ladies' man, but he lived a sheltered life in Cucamonga. Living in Los Angeles is still new and exciting for him."

"Did Roberts and Ricardo get along?"

"Oh, yes. Daniel is ... was ... an experienced bookkeeper. He was teaching Ricardo the trade. Ricardo looked up to Daniel and spoke of him often."

"Do you see much of Ricardo?"

"Not anymore, not since he got his own apartment. He lived with us for a few months. He is like a nephew to me. In fact, he calls me Aunt Zoe."

"What's Ricardo's last name?"

"Stralla."

Lou made a note to interview Ricardo on Monday. "What kind of car does your husband drive to work?"

"We have a Cadillac, but he doesn't drive to work. Sometimes I drive him to work, and sometimes he gets a ride with another employee from the *Rex*. I pick him up when his shift is done. That's usually eight thirty or nine o'clock. It depends on when he gets on the water taxi."

"How about last night? Did you pick him up?"

"Yes."

"What time?"

"A little after nine."

"Was he alone?"

"Yes."

"You mentioned that Roberts saw women. Where did he meet them?"

"I don't know."

"Well, do you know if there was some special woman? Did he have a steady?"

"Not that I know of."

"Did you or your husband ever see Roberts with a woman?"

"I think"—Zoe cocked her head and stared off for a second—"my husband saw Daniel go off with a woman last night. Oh, that's why you're asking. Of course, yes, my husband mentioned that Daniel got into a car with a woman after they got off the water taxi. He was quite impressed by the car. I gather it was an expensive foreign model."

Lou's attention was drawn to the chart on Zoe's desk. "What kind of work do you do?" he asked, edging over toward her desk. Lou stood over Zoe's desk and tried to make sense of the chart. "Say, what is this?" he asked, jerking his thumb toward the chart.

Zoe ignored the second question. "I'm a business consultant."

"Randy, come here and take a look at this."

Randy walked over to the desk and examined the chart. "What kind of business did you say you're in?"

"If you must know, I'm an astrologer, and I figure out what is going on in the business cycle by consulting the astrological charts of the individual clients," she said.

"Isn't that fortune-telling?" Lou asked sharply.

"Of course not!"

"Hey, Randy, maybe we should call the fraud squad. I think they'd be interested in this."

"I have done nothing illegal," Zoe asserted vehemently.

"Well, well, well, the little lady has a temper after all," Lou said, smiling and nodding. "The fortune-telling stuff can wait. We have some more questions about the Roberts murder."

"Well, I have no more answers for you. If you want any more information from me, you'll have to deal with my lawyer."

"We'll get back to you and your lawyer—if you have one," Lou said.

"You know, Lou," Randy said, turning to his partner. "We don't have to report this ... astrologer business to the fraud squad. Maybe she'd like to make a contribution to the policeman's widow fund."

"Yeah, a successful business consultant who drives a Cadillac. Yeah, she can afford a contribution. What do you say, Mrs. Woolfolk, would you like to stay in business a little longer?"

Zoe puffed herself up to her full height and said in a firm voice, "You two gentlemen are going to have to leave, now."

"We'll just do that," Lou said. And the two of them headed for the door.

When the men were gone, Zoe sat down at her desk to assess the meeting. Her biggest problem was Roberts's murder. The police could turn their attention to her and her family. Zoe had no sense of who was truly behind the murder, but she was positive that she could not trust the two vultures to impartially seek the true killers. Innocence was not a defense in this town. Her second and more immediate problem was that practicing astrology or fortune-telling was against the law in California. It was unavoidable: she needed a lawyer. He would have to be a good lawyer, of course, but he needed to understand the underworld and have the political connections to protect her from the police. Zoe decided to call a friend of hers, one of the women she met while she was working at I. Magnin, a fashionable and expensive department store. Her friend's husband was a deputy district attorney who handled private clients on the side. Once she picked up the telephone and dialed the number of her friend, Lucille Thoms, she knew it was the right decision.

After Lucille listened to Zoe's concerns, she said, "Why, of course, Cliffy will be able to help you. We're friends after all."

Mayor Fletcher Bowron was heading up the meeting in the big conference room adjacent to his office. Around the long conference table sat the heads of departments; the senior city attorneys; Buron Fitts, district attorney for the county of Los Angeles; and Fitts's senior deputies. They were expecting a guest, Wayne Munson, an organized crime expert from New York City. Every man in the room considered himself an expert on corruption. They had all lived through the administration of Mayor Frank Shaw. Shaw had run a spoils system where criminals—men and women who ran gambling dens and houses of prostitution—paid the police for protection. It was said the police did not prevent crime; they managed it. Nearly all the officers on the vice squad were on the take; they were bagmen for payoffs and bouncers in bordellos. Despite years of efforts by reformers to expose the corruption and rot in city government, it was only after ordinary citizens saw the attempts of the Shaw administration and the LAPD to slander, intimidate, and kill their opponents that the people of Los Angeles recalled the mayor in September 1938 and voted in Bowron as a reformer. Bowron was working hard to keep his promise to uproot the tangle of corruption that had threatened to undermine the very legitimacy of city governments throughout Los Angeles County. This Saturday morning presentation by a New York expert was just one more effort.

Munson walked in. He was about fifty, heavyset, and carried a large, battered leather briefcase. The men around the table wordlessly examined the cut and material of the expert's suit. It was one thing to see the magazine ads, but it was another to be in the same room with a man wearing the latest fashion from New York City. Munson began his presentation on the nature of organized crime. He talked at length about how organized crime could infiltrate and manipulate city officials. The men assembled around the conference table soon realized that corruption in New York had a different face but bore a family resemblance to corruption in Los Angeles. Crime in New York was more cohesively organized. Not only did each faction—Italian mobs, Jewish mobs, Irish mobs—have its own structure, but they were also coordinated as a whole by an umbrella organization called the Syndicate. The men around the table knew that in LA, in contrast, the criminal groups were smaller and more fragmented. The New York expert pointed out something that his audience was only slowly coming to appreciate: local mobsters Jack Dragna, Guy McAfee, Lenny "Lefty" Green, and Tony "the Hat" Cornero were under increasing pressure from East Coast mobsters such as Meyer Lansky and Charles "Lucky" Luciano to get organized, or else. Benjamin Siegel, called "Bugsy" behind his back, had been sent to Los Angeles to organize crime East Coast style. LA mobsters who resisted had their businesses ruined and their lives threatened. Those who cooperated had new partners and fresh funds to expand their businesses.

As Munson spoke, there was a light tapping at the office door. The mayor's secretary stuck her head in and said there was an important call. The mayor swore quietly under his breath and asked her who was on the line.

"Lenny Green."

"That bastard has some nerve calling here!" the mayor bellowed. "Tell him someone will call him back as soon as the meeting is done."

"He says it's urgent."

"Well, what exactly did he say?"

"He said, 'I need to talk to the goddamn Chinaman.'" The secretary did a fair imitation of Green's Brooklyn accent.

Munson muttered, "Damn, Chinese tongs here too."

The men around the table snickered. One of them stood up and said, "If you can get by without me, Mister Mayor, I'll take the call in Sammy's office."

"Go ahead, Tommy. I think we can manage here."

"Clifford Thoms here."

"You're the Chinaman, right?"

"People do call me that. Am I speaking with Mr. Green?"

"Yeah. You work for Tony Cornero, right?"

"No, I am a deputy district attorney for Los Angeles County. We are conducting an investigation into Mr. Cornero's gambling operations. All of us at the DA's office, from DA Fitts on down, take a dim view of—"

"Right, right. I got it, you and Fitts are gonna put Tony the Hat in prison. Okay, before you do that I want you to help me find my daughter, Dorothy. She's been gone three days with no calls. Her car is still in the garage, and she ain't out at the beach house. She ain't in San Diego with her friends, and my men already checked out the Hotel Del Coronado. People last saw her on the *Rex*. I swear to God, if Tony hurts my little girl, I'm gonna kill him and burn down his goddamn ships, and I don't care what Benny Siegel says!"

"Have you reported this to the police or FBI?"

"No, I haven't reported it," Green said, his voice thick with disgust. "My men can't find her. What do you think, the cops are gonna do better? I ask around. People say you're a fixer. So fix this, or there's gonna be a goddamn war."

Cliff heard a click and then the dial tone. Slowly he set the telephone receiver back in its cradle. He returned to the conference room and caught the last twenty minutes of Munson's presentation. When the meeting broke up, he begged off going to have drinks with the other deputy DAs. He needed to return to his office. His secretary, Mary, was scheduled to work that day until 5:00 p.m., and he wanted to finish up a few matters left over from Friday while she was still there.

Mary's voice buzzed through the intercom. "A. J. Barnes is on the line. Are you here for him?"

"Yes. Hold my other calls." Cliff picked up the telephone. "A. J., this is unexpected. You're working Saturdays now too? So how are you?"

"Fine, Cliff. How's Lucille?"

"She's good, thank you. I suppose you're calling about the appeal. I don't have any news for you; we're still waiting for the Supreme Court. I expect to hear something this coming week."

"It's not that, Cliff. There's a more pressing matter. It's somewhat delicate. The head of the counting room on the *Rex*, Daniel Roberts, was found murdered this morning. The Santa Monica police alerted Tony's business office. We hadn't realized anything was amiss. Roberts finished his shift on Friday, and he doesn't usually work on the weekends. The Santa Monica PD has assigned the investigation to Randolph Williams and Luis Gomez. Williams is competent, but Gomez is something of a go-getter. Tony wants to know who killed Roberts, but if it was someone in the business, naturally we don't want the matter going to trial. Tony would prefer that we handle the matter in-house, as it were. Ben Siegel is aware of the situation and is leaving it to Tony to resolve. Our contacts in the Santa

Monica PD can manage Williams well enough, but this Gomez fellow is something of a loose cannon. We want you to keep an eye on the investigation and keep Gomez in line."

"A. J., I'll do what I can, but I have my hands full with the special investigation of the Canyon Killer, and with Fitts, and with Tony's case coming up this week before the court. Plus, there is another matter that just came up. I was going to call you to discuss it. It concerns Lenny Green." Thoms explained about Green's missing daughter.

"We didn't grab her if that's what you're worried about. Listen, Cliff, she is a wild child. You know she had a baby when she was eighteen or so. The kid must be five or six by now. She won't say who the father is—that takes some guts if your father is Lefty Green. Do what you can to find her; we don't want any hard feelings between Tony and Lenny.

"I'm sorry to dump all this on you at once, but the priority is to keep the *Rex* in business, which means you have to keep managing Fitts, and now you have to keep a lid on the Roberts investigation. A murder connected with the *Rex* is just the excuse Fitts and that bastard Warren need to shut down the *Rex* and the other gambling ships."

"I understand, and I'll do what I can. When things cool down, Lucille and I would love to have you and your wife over for dinner."

"That sounds good. It's been too long since the last time. Keep on top of these things, Cliff. Good-bye."

At noon on Sunday, Zoe left her home near Ocean Park and climbed into her Cadillac. It wasn't shiny new, but she truly enjoyed driving her Caddie. Cliff and Lucille lived in Pasadena, northwest of Ocean Park on the other side of Los Angeles. She knew it was going to be at least an hour-long trip. Driving along Olympic, she tried to get her thoughts in order. How much should she reveal to Mr. Thoms about herself and her talent, and more importantly, could he help her?

Once past Los Angeles, she traveled north on Mission Boulevard, which turned into Huntington Drive near the city of Alhambra. Alhambra was an upper-middle-class bedroom community, close to Los Angeles but apart from it. The houses and yards were well kept, and even in these Depression times, the town appeared prosperous. Zoe continued on Huntington—named for Henry E. Huntington who financed the red streetcars that traveled throughout Southern California—to San Marino, an upper-class city. Turning onto Sierra Madre Boulevard, Zoe found herself in a quiet, settled section of Pasadena. Cliff lived on El Nido with his wife and her father, Jesse Ross.

Cliff and Lucille sat facing each other in their living room in matching forest-green wing-backed chairs, anticipating Zoe's arrival. The room was large, and the shelves were filled mostly with law books. In addition, a twenty-eight-volume set of small, leather-bound books containing the Old and New Testaments was prominently displayed. The titles of the volumes were embossed on the spine in gold lettering. On a lamp table stood a wedding picture of Cliff and Lucille from six years ago with both looking younger and very happy. As they waited for Zoe, Lucille was smoking a cigarette and sipping a martini; Cliff was thinking about the coming interview. He was not drinking.

Lucille was concerned for her friend, and she wanted her husband to comprehend the importance of Zoe's psychic ability. Anxiously she continued trying to convince Cliff of Zoe's talent. "I know she can read minds, but she won't admit it to you." Increasingly animated, Lucille went on, "I heard her tell my friend Iris not to go to the Palladium on Tuesday, and there was a terrible accident on Hollywood Boulevard. Iris could have been in it."

Cliff listened to his wife but said nothing.

"Zoe drinks bourbon and seven. Do we have that set out?"

"We have bourbon. We may have 7-Up in the icebox."

"Be a dear and check. I'll wait for Zoe."

A minute after Cliff left the room, the doorbell rang, and Lucille let Zoe in. The ladies embraced and air-kissed. Zoe was petite, not quite five feet tall, with a slender build and light complexion. Despite her diminutive size, her appearance was calculated to draw attention. She wore her flaxen blonde hair fashioned into carefully coiffed curls. Her simple dark dress set off a double string of iridescent pearls and brightly colored costume jewelry bracelets.

As Zoe followed Lucille into the living room, she noted the wedding picture on the table and marveled at another framed picture on the fireplace mantel, this one of Lucille in a long, sheer, white satin dress and a headdress of peacock feathers from when she was in the Ziegfeld Follies theatrical revue. Zoe stepped closer to the lamp table. "What a wonderful picture. You look beautiful—and so happy!"

"Thank you. It was the happiest day of my life. My father wanted us to have a big church wedding, but I was almost thirty-five. I didn't want a big wedding and elaborate gown; that's for a starry-eyed twenty-year-old. I wanted an intimate wedding and small reception with close friends and family. Well, at least the wedding was small. We had it at a friend's house, just a few friends and relatives. You see"—Lucille gestured toward the photo—"I wore a white linen suit, with white high-heeled pumps and a cream-colored hat with a lacy veil. Cliffy wore a new business suit. Look at his smile; he was so handsome. But the reception with just a few friends turned into a large party at a rented hall—that was my father's doing. He loves a big party. He was so proud. We had a band, champagne, hors d'oeuvres. He invited everyone Cliffy and I knew. It was quite a hodgepodge of guests—some lawyer friends of Cliffy's, some gals from the Follies, other friends of mine, and the California relatives."

"It sounds delightful."

"It was." Lucille paused to look toward the hallway and then continued in a low voice, "For the most part. As I was circulating among the guests, I heard snatches of their conversations. People were curious about us. How did we meet? Who were Cliffy's parents? Would a mixed marriage last? Some ugly speculation. Some knew Cliff by his horrid nickname, the Chinaman, and most knew that I had been a Ziegfeld girl. The guests didn't know what to make of it all, but Dad was in his glory."

"Really, Jesse, Lucille makes a stunning bride. That Thoms fellow certainly made a catch for himself." The reception guest glared across the hall at Cliff with ill-disguised contempt. The guest, the wife of Jesse's banker, was in her sixties. She was dressed in a green silk sheath that was too small for her. On her head was a matching green hat that reminded Jesse of algae.

"You know, my dear, Cliff is an up-and-comer. And he's able to support her in the manner to which she has become accustomed." Jesse gave the woman a sly wink and a smile. With some effort he didn't laugh at her hat.

"What do you know about him, besides the regular lawyer stuff? We all know he's a good lawyer, but where is he from? Is he really part Chinese?"

"I've known Cliff for several years. He doesn't like to talk about his past, but over time, I've been able to put together a few facts, and I think I've worked out most of his early life."

The woman took out a cigarette and lit it with a practiced flair. "Well, I'm listening."

"Okay. Well, I know that Cliff's father was a colonel in the US Army ..." As Jesse spoke, a small group of people began to gather around him. He paused, let his new audience settle in, and began again. "Cliff's father was a colonel in the US Army. In 1890 he was stationed in Hawaii, monitoring the military situation in China where the European nations were carving out spheres of influence. For four years Colonel Harry Thoms lived in a Hawaiian paradise where he was part of the upper crust of ranchers and plantation owners by virtue of his status as an officer and a gentleman."

"I didn't know we were going to get a history lesson," one listener muttered.

Jesse continued, "While stationed in the Hawaiian Islands, in spite of the low pay, Cliff's father managed to save enough to invest in sugar and pineapple plantations. While he was far from rich, his investment income allowed him to participate in the life of the upper class—the entertaining, the polo pony, that sort of thing. Eventually Harry met a stunning and charming Chinese woman at a reception at the American Embassy. She was a friend of the Soong family who owned extensive properties in New Jersey. The woman, Harriet—I don't know her Chinese name—and Cliff's father were soon married. After their marriage, the colonel was reassigned to ... well, a fort not too far from New York City where Harry and his family had lived for generations." Jesse stopped the narrative and looked at each member of his growing group. Each pair of eyes was on him; his audience was hungry for more.

"Did the Thoms family accept the Chinese bride?" someone asked.

"To say the Thoms family was delighted to welcome a Chinese woman into the family would be an overstatement," Jesse stated. "They came to accept her because within two years she was pregnant with their grandchild. Cliff was born in February 1896 in New York City. His early years as a Eurasian boy in an English family were not pleasant. His peers mocked him and sang childish, hurtful songs, like 'Ching, chong, Chinaman, sitting on a rail, where is your tail?' Rather than being demoralized though, Cliff was determined to excel in a way that compelled their respect. By his own hard work and intelligence he did that." Jesse again paused to look over his audience. "That much of his life I'm sure about. One other thing I'm sure about: he has certainly earned my respect. Now I must go. My daughter is beckoning me to come and dance with her. It is her wedding, after all."

Cliff returned to the living room dressed in weekend slacks and a plaid shirt. In his left hand was a bottle of 7-Up. Lucille made the introductions. As they shook hands, Zoe was encouraged by the awareness that, even in casual dress on a quiet Sunday summer afternoon, Cliff projected a sense of presence possessed by the rich and powerful.

"I'm very happy to meet you." Cliff's smile was warm and genuine.

"The pleasure is all mine." Zoe smiled in return. "I hope we can come to an agreement after you hear my predicament. I know you take a few private clients; I'd like to be one of them."

"Would you like a drink, or would you like to go into my home office where we can discuss your case in private?" he asked.

"Perhaps you could mix me a drink before we go to your office. I'll have bourbon and— well, I guess you know—7-Up." She was wearing a number of bracelets that made a musical sound when she picked up her drink.

Once in his office, Cliff motioned Zoe to sit in an overstuffed chair and tried to put her at ease. "Please give me a brief summary of your problem, and tell me why you need the assistance of a lawyer. Remember, everything said here is confidential. It's important that you be completely candid with me if I am to represent you."

"I understand. I'm sure that Lucille has told you most of this before. It seems that I have two problems. First, yesterday two detectives came to visit me in my office in Santa Monica and asked me a number of questions regarding the murder of Daniel Roberts. As you may know, my husband, Clarence, works in the counting room on the *Rex*. Also, my son, Richard, is a croupier on the *Rex*. I am concerned that my son and my husband may be under some suspicion. The second problem is, of course, my profession. I am a business consultant. However, I determine answers to business questions by casting horoscopes based on astrological tenets. Those detectives accused me of fortune-telling and then asked for money to remain silent. If I didn't pay, they said they would report me to the fraud squad."

Cliff looked up from taking notes. "I would like you to

clarify something. It sounds as if you are an astrologer, but my wife tells me that you have some sort of psychic talent that allows you to predict the future. So which is it, astrologer or psychic?"

"When you phrase it that way, I'd have to say that I am a psychic who uses astrology to help me focus my psychic abilities."

Cliff pursed his lips and reflected on this response. He lit a cigar as he framed his next question. "Lucille also tells me that your predictions are unfailingly accurate and that you can read minds. Are these claims true?" His tone was sharper, more skeptical.

"Lucille flatters me. I, myself, make no such claims. Yes, up to a certain point, I have the ability to see the future, but no, I cannot read minds. I can, however, read people. It's clear to me that you don't share your wife's convictions and you think astrology is bunk, but you are open to the possibility that people can have psychic ability. In fact"—Zoe paused, surprised by a sudden realization—"your parents took you to a Chinese fortune-teller who predicted a career in law for you."

"Yes, but how ..." Cliff took a long draw on his cigar and considered this strange woman. "What can you tell me about Daniel Roberts?"

"I have no special knowledge of him. I know he worked for the mob in Oakland or San Francisco and was sent to prison. While in the pen he made a connection with a confederate of Mr. Cornero. When Daniel was released from prison, Cornero hired him. Nothing else."

"Why do you think the detectives threatened you?"

"They saw the horoscope on my desk and homed in on my perceived weakness. It wasn't the first time they have blackmailed people. It's like a game for them. Like finding money in the street."

Cliff laughed. "They took a shot at scaring you, but it backfired since all they succeeded in doing was sending you to me."

"That's just about it." Zoe seemed resigned.

"Well, if you want to hire me"—Cliff paused to relight his cigar—"my retainer is one hundred dollars." He took a puff of his cigar and watched for her reaction. Cliff's usual retainer for an ordinary businessman was twenty-five dollars. One hundred dollars was three weeks' earnings for the average worker; it was an amount intended to scare away a crackpot fortune-teller.

"That's quite a retainer. Did you know there is an economic depression going on?"

"It doesn't seem to be affecting you too much," he said with a mischievous grin.

"I don't have that much money now, but I can get it. I'll call you when I've made some arrangements." She gathered her purse with her bracelets jingling and got up to leave. She set her drink on a coaster and, together, she and Cliff walked out of the office. Lucille was in her wing-back chair flipping through a magazine. An empty martini glass was on the table between the matching chairs, and an Old Gold cigarette was smoldering in an ashtray. Zoe waved at her, shook Cliff's hand, and left.

Zoe drove straight to her office in Santa Monica. Sitting at her desk with the blue Pacific behind her, she stared at an ad in the Los Angeles Mirror for the gambling ship SS *Rex*. "Play to your heart's content in an atmosphere of unbridled luxury! Round trip from the Santa Monica pier twenty-five cents."

Is this a sign? she wondered. She picked up the phone and dialed Cliff Thoms's home number. "Mr. Thoms, I have a proposition for you. How would you like to take me out to dinner on the *Rex*? It would give you an opportunity to see the ship as a casual customer—a gambler, at that. You could have a chance to test my talent and win your retainer."

"All right, Mrs. Woolfolk. The 'admiral' claims his take is three hundred thousand dollars a month. I don't see how that is possible, however luxurious the casino."

Later that evening, two large, muscular men in expensive but ill-fitting suits lifted Zoe from a launch and onto the deck of the gently rolling ship. Zoe, escorted by Cliff, walked into the main casino. The room was surprisingly large, noisy with nervous talk, and filled with cigarette smoke. The couple walked past crowded blackjack tables and long rows of slot machines and headed toward a roulette table. Richard was nowhere in sight; it was his dinner break. Zoe did not know the croupier on duty. She watched the action on the table for a few minutes while waiting for Richard to return. Cliff went to buy some chips. He came back with ten ten-dollar chips. That was more than he was willing to risk, but buying only twenty dollars in chips was not appropriate for a man in his position. He pocketed eight chips and held the other two. When he returned, Zoe tugged at the sleeve of his coat and whispered into his ear, "Red."

Cliff plunked down the twenty dollars on red, displaying more confidence than he felt. He watched the croupier send the ball around the wheel. He looked over at Zoe and watched her expression. She watched the ball impassively. She was resigned to fate. The croupier watched the ball bounce from number slot to number slot until it came to rest. He called out, "Thirty-six red." The color bet paid one to one; the croupier stacked two ten-dollar chips on Cliff's bet. Cliff scooped up the money and looked to Zoe for further instructions.

"Nothing." Zoe closed her eyes and cleared her mind. The croupier had begun the next play. By the time the next number was called out, Zoe had whispered to Cliff, "Some number in the thirties."

Cliff placed the two ten-dollar chips he had won on the third set of numbers, twenty-five through thirty-six. He looked over at Zoe.

"Trust me," she said softly. "Double the bet."

Reluctantly he added the other two ten-dollar chips to his bet. The croupier flung the ball around the wheel. Cliff used his "show" handkerchief to dab sweat from his upper lip. The white ball bounced from number to number and came to rest at thirty-two. The bet paid two to one. Cliff had won another eighty dollars.

Zoe again tugged at his sleeve and said, "That's all for now. Let's move away from the table." Standing back against the wall, Zoe said, "You won twenty dollars and another eighty dollars. There is your hundred-dollar retainer. Winning money this way is bad karma, and I'm not doing it again, but you had to see. I was beginning to think you suspected I was a fraud."

Zoe had arranged to stop by Cliff's office the next day, Monday, in the late afternoon to sign a retainer agreement.

"Mrs. Woolfolk, would you mind if—"

"Call me Zoe, please. We don't need to be so formal if you're going to be my attorney."

"You're right. Why don't you call me Cliff."

"You have other nicknames, don't you?" Zoe said teasingly.

"Yes, I suppose I do. But then you would know that, wouldn't you? Lucille calls me 'Cliffy,' the fellows here at work call me 'Tommy,' and some people around town have been known to call me 'the Chinaman.' I was about to ask you whether you would mind if I brought you along on a visit to another client. Have you heard of Leonard Green?"

"Leonard Green? Oh, Lefty Green. Of course, but I only know what I've read in the papers. He's some sort of gangster, isn't he?"

"Yes. He's from New York. He grew up in Brooklyn and was a member of Benjamin Siegel's gang when they were kids. He came out here to LA in the late twenties before the Crash and has been running rackets ever since. He's been careful to insulate himself, so we have not had an opportunity to successfully prosecute him. He's asked me to help him ..."

"You're going to help him?" Zoe asked incredulously.

"Of course. Maybe you've heard the old Italian saying, keep your friends close and your enemies closer. I'd like to stay very close to Mr. Green."

Zoe and Cliff left downtown in his Hudson. They traveled on Sunset Boulevard all the way to Westwood, where UCLA was under construction. On this part of Sunset, there were many large mansions with manicured lawns and expensive cars cluttering impressive driveways. They turned right on Kentner and started up the canyon.

There was no tactful way to approach it, Cliff realized as he drove. He just had to ask the question: "Does your ability have any limits?"

"Of course. You need to understand that the gift I have is

like a radio in a thunderstorm." Zoe looked straight ahead as she spoke. She had anticipated the question; it was no great insight—everyone asked sooner or later. "I just receive and not always clearly. The signal comes and goes. Sometimes, with small things, like when we were on the *Rex*, I can focus my mind and receive a clear bit of information. But if you asked me about the La Sierra racetrack, I probably couldn't tell you what horse was going to win in the third race." *Although,* Zoe thought to herself, *I would tell my clients not to invest in the racetrack because rival gangsters will burn it down in two years.*

"Do you have clearer knowledge of what will happen to your family members?"

"No. In fact I have less knowledge about my family. I knew, or suspected, that my father had died when he was thousands of miles away, and I knew that the letter informing us of his death was on its way, but usually my knowledge of family members is more clouded than with strangers."

"How about me? Can you tell me about ... my death?"

Zoe closed her eyes and concentrated, but concentrated on nothing. An image flashed in her mind. In the picture, a gray-haired Cliff lay in a hospital bed in a large open ward with a dozen other beds each occupied by an old, dying man. Cliff was alone, confused, and scared. On the table beside his bed was the same wedding picture, now faded, that Zoe saw in Cliff's home. Cliff was waiting for his wife to visit. Living apart from her, living in a hospital surrounded by death, had emptied his life of joy. Zoe opened her eyes, looked up at Cliff, and smiled wanly. "You'll live to a ripe, old age."

As an experienced attorney, Cliff knew an evasion when he heard one. He also remembered the old courtroom adage: don't ask a question to which you don't know the answer. He realized with Zoe the old saying had a new corollary: don't ask a question to which you don't *want* to know the answer.

CHAPTER 4

Lenny Green lived in the Hollywood Hills in Kentner Canyon. Kentner was one of the exclusive canyons with a circuitous drive up in the hills. The Green house was situated on a large plateau on the top of a hill with a view that encompassed both the San Fernando Valley and downtown Los Angeles. He chose this place because there was only one way into the canyon and one way out. He had security that could see both the entrance and the exit.

"I notice that the gates were open when we arrived, and I haven't seen any guards," Zoe said. "They must be unobtrusive, but I feel them somewhere close."

"We've been watched since before we drove onto the property. They were expecting me, so there should be no trouble."

Zoe and Cliff parked, walked up the flagstone steps, and crossed a wide veranda. A walkway leading to a tall, wooden double door was lined with large terra-cotta pots overflowing with flowers. The house was a two-story Spanish style with a red tiled roof. The property was enormous. Zoe estimated that each floor of this house was four times the size of her beach house. Everything was in correct proportion but huge. When the downstairs maid answered the door and let them enter, they were able to see into the living room where there was a large fireplace with a marble mantle and an exquisite landscape painting. The name *Monet* popped into Zoe's head.

"Living up here in the foothills, with all this security, the folks here are virtually invulnerable," Cliff stated.

"Not quite," Zoe said, looking out an enormous arched window to the ridge top across the canyon.

"How are they vulnerable?"

"Fire."

The maid directed them upstairs and told them that Carlota would help them. Cliff and Zoe noticed several men in suits watching warily as the couple ascended the stairs. The upstairs maid met them at the top of the stairs. Carlota was a small, thin, dark-skinned woman in her sixties. Cliff recognized her as a mestiza, a mixture of European Spanish and American Indian. She led them to Dorothy's bedroom. Zoe went in and began her inspection while Cliff stood in the doorway and tried to take it all in: the spaciousness of the room, the richness of the wallpaper, the high fashion of the furniture with its chromium trim, the thickness of the wool rug atop sponge padding. He turned to the maid and asked, "Where's the closet?"

Carlota pointed to a doorway.

Zoe had made a quick circuit of the bedroom. She looked but touched nothing. She followed Cliff through the doorway and into a closet the size of her bedroom at home. There were dozens of shoes on racks with a few more pairs scattered on the floor of the closet. Parts of the closet had double rods; the top held blouses in a range of colors and materials, styles and cuts, but all displayed the exquisite workmanship of expensive dressmakers. The single-rod portion of the closet was filled with dresses and women's suits. Again Zoe touched nothing.

Handling Dorothy's possessions would only fill her with a flood of images and feelings that would overwhelm her analytical mind. Zoe scanned the contents of the closet a second time. She was looking for something, but she wasn't sure what. Then it hit her. She turned to the upstairs maid and asked, "Where are Dorothy's sundresses and bathing suits? And I don't see any suitcases. Where are those stored?"

"Suitcases are in the storage room," Carlota said in Spanish-accented English, while looking down at her shoes and twisting her body slightly.

"We should check the storage room to see if any suitcases are missing," Cliff said.

Zoe continued examining the maid. "There's no need. We'll find that two bags are missing. This maid helped Dorothy pack. Isn't that right, dear."

Carlota's head jerked up, and she glared at Zoe. "*Bruja*," she muttered under her breath.

Cliff looked at Zoe and then back to Carlota. "Woman, where was Dorothy going?"

"Miss Dorothy meet friends in San Diego."

"Green told me that Dorothy's car is still here and that his people have already checked the Hotel Del Coronado. Dorothy likes to stay there when she's in San Diego. There must be a score of other hotels and motels where she could be staying. She could've driven with someone or ..." Cliff paused to consider the possibilities—train, plane, ship? "She could have borrowed a car and driven down herself. The San Diego police could find her in a few hours if they could free up the manpower for an all-out search."

Zoe shook her head. "Mexico. She flew to Mexico. Some man, a lover. They're flying back tonight."

Carlota's eyes opened wide. She stepped back out of the

bedroom into the hall. Her bony hand quickly made the sign of the cross. "*Bruja*." She choked on the word.

Cliff grabbed Zoe by the shoulders, brought his face close to hers, and whispered, "That's not much to go on. Which airport and when?"

Zoe just stared back.

Cliff was beginning to understand. A radio in a thunderstorm. So she doesn't know exactly when or exactly where. But the maid did. "Woman, after we tell Mr. Green what you've done, maybe he'll have his boys teach you a lesson, or maybe he'll only fire you," Cliff paused to let the image of a beating sink in. "But," he continued in a more conciliatory tone, "now we have a chance to help each other. So, tell us, which airport and when are they coming in?"

Zoe watched Carlota's face. She saw fear but also something else: determination. "Dear," Zoe said sweetly as she reached out her hand to Carlota's. Carlota abruptly drew her hand back and looked at Zoe with loathing. "Dear," Zoe began again, "it's better for Dorothy if Mr. Thoms brings her home. Your *patrón* needs to feel that the men are in charge."

"Sí." Carlota nodded briefly as she made a decision. "Miss Dorothy return tonight, eleven, to Clover Field."

Zoe smiled. Clover Field was the old name for Santa Monica Airport. She knew she had been right, but it was always good to have confirmation. "Thank you, dear. You've been very helpful. Your name is Carlota, correct?"

"Yes."

"We will remember that and be sure to ask for you if we have more questions. I can have my housekeeper call. She speaks Spanish and will say she is your friend, Maria, if that will make it any easier for you."

"Yes, is better."

On impulse Zoe fished out a business card from her black satin clutch purse and handed it to Carlota. "Here, dear, just in case you need to contact me."

Hesitantly, Carlota took the card and glanced at it. As Cliff and Zoe descended the staircase, Carlota rushed to her small bedroom, which adjoined Dorothy's, and threw the card in the trash. Had she done the right thing telling these strangers where to find Miss Dorothy? The hateful *bruja* was right: better to have the man escort Miss Dorothy home. Reluctantly Carlota, her disgust outweighed by her parsimonious refusal to waste resources, retrieved Zoe's business card from the trash can and tossed it in a bureau drawer.

As Cliff and Zoe descended the flagstone steps heading to Cliff's car, he asked, "What's a *bruja*?"

"It's Spanish for 'witch'."

"And *patrón*?"

"Boss or employer."

"Oh, of course." After a few more steps, Cliff asked, "How did you know the threat wasn't going to make her talk?"

"I could see she'd rather take a beating than give up her ... I was going to say daughter. She'd never do anything to hurt Dorothy."

Cliff nodded. "You know, it's funny. We've had this house under surveillance on and off for months, but you recruited a spy in ten minutes."

They drove the winding road down the hill toward Cliff's office in silence. Zoe looked up at the ridges of the hills silhouetted against a luminescent red sunset and had a vision unmoored in time. Years from now, after the wars, both the

European war everyone saw coming and another war in a frozen place, she visualized a road running along the crest of these scrub-covered hills. On either side of the road were homes of the newly rich. A fire raced up the walls of the canyon and swept away the homes on the crest. The fire burned through the night, illuminating the sky, and left two lines of chimneys on either side of the road surrounded by smoldering debris in the morning. Ash drifted down like gray snowflakes and settled on the city below. Zoe closed her eyes and willed the vision away.

Once they were on level ground, Cliff relaxed a little. "I thought about what you said, about the limitations of your ... ability. When you searched Dorothy's room, you were really searching. And the airport. You didn't know which one, did you?"

How would she respond? Educated by bitter experience, Zoe clung to her three intangible assets: mystery, trust, and information. Mystery was a lure to her rich clients who sought answers from a frightening future and the irredeemable past. And trust was so hard to earn and even harder to give, so fragile and easily shattered. But the greatest of these three was information. It was a lesson she had taught her sons since they were first in long pants—"Never tell someone everything you know because then they'll know everything they know and everything you know." She could lie, but then she risked losing Cliff's trust; it was best to tell him the truth if not the whole truth. "The more I know about a situation, the clearer my, ah, gift is. Dorothy's makeup was gone, so I knew she expected to meet men, or at least a man. When I noticed that her sundresses were also gone, I concluded that she had gone somewhere sunny."

Cliff sighed and said, "There's no mystery. Her father was concerned that Dorothy might have been kidnapped, but any competent detective could have looked at her room and drawn the same conclusion as you did."

"No, you don't understand. From all the evidence, a competent detective would draw the same conclusion that you did, that Dorothy drove to San Diego to meet a man. I saw the same evidence and *knew* that she was traveling with a man and her two matching bags. It wasn't a deduction or an educated guess; it's like remembering a fact you know to be true. The only part I guessed was the maid had helped Dorothy pack her bag. After the maid lied about Dorothy going to San Diego, I ..." Zoe paused, reluctant to go on.

"What? You *knew*," Cliff mockingly repeated her inflection, "that Dorothy went to Mexico and was flying back with a man?"

"Yes, something like that." This was something that she would hold back, her vision of Dorothy sitting beside her lover, the man in shadow, in a cramped, noisy plane, flying north at night from Mexico. How could Cliff begin to understand that Zoe not only saw them but could also feel the couple's fatigue and satisfied lust?

Zoe and Cliff returned to his office. Zoe would continue with her consultations and report any contact between the Santa Monica detectives and her or members of her family. In the meantime, Cliff would see to it that the two Santa Monica detectives would be brought to heel.

Cliff left his office at 10:00 p.m. He wanted to leave early enough to arrive at the airport before Dorothy's plane landed, even if it was ahead of schedule. He didn't know what to expect or how to approach Dorothy. They were strangers to each other, but he assumed that he would know her when he saw her. He also wanted to meet her mysterious lover, the man Zoe couldn't see.

Cliff arrived at the airport with twenty-five minutes to spare. He listened to announcements about incoming and departing flights and learned that Falcon Flight 121, the only flight from Mexico scheduled to land at eleven, was expected to be on time. Green's men had already made inquiries about Dorothy and had been told that she was not a passenger, so it stood to reason that she was traveling under an assumed name. A porter pointed to the Falcon Airlines office; it was a small room in the corner of the terminal. Falcon's fleet consisted of a single thirdhand Ford Trimotor. Cliff strode up to the counter in front of the Falcon office and slapped down his district attorney badge. "I'm investigating a murder," he told the awed clerk. "A material witness flew to Mexico, probably on Thursday, and is scheduled to return tonight. The passenger is a woman, approximately twenty-four, with two suitcases. She is traveling under a false name. I need you to confirm her name, her departure date, and whether she is on flight one twenty-one."

The clerk fumbled through a sheaf of papers glancing up every now and then at the badge on the counter. After four minutes, he was able to confirm that a Carlota Gonzalez had flown out on Thursday with two bags and was returning that night.

Cliff thanked the clerk and walked to the cafe. The plane wasn't due for another fifteen minutes, so Cliff settled into a seat and watched through the window that overlooked the tarmac. As he sat and nursed a cup of tea, he realized how tired he was and how much he regretted not being home with Lucille. Although they had been married for six years, they still felt like newlyweds. It was unlike his first marriage to Marion in which they struggled to get along after the first year. His parents didn't actually disapprove of his marriage to Marion, but they had advised him to wait until he was established in his law practice. They were also uncomfortable with the fact that she was two years older than Cliff. He didn't tell his parents until years later that Marion was actually three years older. He married in 1918 at the age of twenty-two. For his parents he shaved a year off of Marion's age, making her twenty-four instead of twenty-five. For his in-laws—and on the marriage license—he added two years to his own age, making him twenty-four.

At almost exactly eleven o'clock the lumbering Ford Trimotor landed and taxied to the tarmac. A set of steps was wheeled out to the plane, and passengers descended with luggage in hand. Some passengers headed directly for the parking lot while the rest walked slowly to the terminal. Cliff walked over to watch the returning passengers enter the terminal and looked for a well-dressed woman in her early twenties. There was only one, and he approached her.

"Miss Green?"

Dorothy quickly studied this unknown man—medium height, medium build, nice suit, intelligent eyes, polite but not deferential. "Yes?"

"My name is Clifford Thoms. I'm an attorney. Your father asked me to be on the lookout for you. He was concerned for your safety. If you'll allow me, I'll drive you back to your house."

"Of course, but how did you know—?"

"Not to be immodest, but your father asked me to look for you because he knows I'm resourceful. I'm also discreet so, to the best of my ability, your travel plans will be our little secret. Let me take your bags. Are we waiting for any traveling companion?"

"No, I traveled alone."

"Of course you did. Shall we go?" Cliff took her suitcases, one in his left hand with the other resting on top of it, and offered her his right arm.

Dorothy smiled and took his arm. "You are a strange one, I'm sure, Mr. ...?"

"Thoms. But maybe you should call me Tommy." Cliff studied Dorothy as they walked through the terminal to his car. She was tall, as tall as he was, and her skin was a bronze color that came with time spent lounging in the Mexican sun and volleying on a tennis court. She wore off-white linen pants and a matching coat, with a pastel-pink silk blouse. She was beautiful in a girl-next-door way, not a classical beauty like Lucille. But then, how many women were?

"Tommy, I like that. Please call me Dorothy. Do you work with my dad's attorney, Mr. Willows?"

"No, but I've known Robbie for years. We've had several cases together."

"Codefendants?"

"No, actually I'm a deputy district attorney. I was prosecuting, and he was defending."

"Tommy, Tommy, Tommy, you are full of surprises. Has anyone ever told you that you are as mysterious as the East? How did my father ever find you?"

"To tell you the truth, he called, said something about killing my client and burning down his business, and then asked me to find you."

"Sounds like my father. You're not going to ask me a bunch of embarrassing questions now, are you?" Dorothy asked with a sly smile.

"No, as much as I'd like to, no. I'm taking you straight home and dropping you off, and then I'm going home to my wife."

"Lucky woman."

CHAPTER 5

Tuesday, June 6

L ou and Randy sat at their desks deciding what to do next. Sunday and Monday had been largely wasted trying to track down associates, friends, and enemies that Roberts may have made in prison and while working on the *Rex*. Once again Frankie J. at San Quentin was invaluable. The records showed that Roberts was not involved in any fights and had not been disciplined. He had no known enemies and, it seemed, few friends. The guards remembered, however, that one older prisoner had taken Roberts under his wing, and that man was a long-time associate of Tony Cornero. Since leaving prison, the only friends that the detectives could confirm were Roberts's coworkers on the *Rex*. He seemed to get along with the older Woolfolk and the young man he was training, the one who had left for the weekend. He would also spend some time with the younger Woolfolk; they had been seen having drinks together. But no enemies, no steady girlfriends, no jealous husbands.

The detectives realized that a killer with a personal motive was unlikely. They were back to the business angle. "We don't know who killed Roberts, when exactly, where, or why he was killed," Randy said, reciting the well-rehearsed facts. "We know he worked on the *Rex*, which is anchored in the bay, and that his body was dumped in the bay. We know he was a good bookkeeper and he was convicted of embezzlement. We know that he worked for Tony Cornero, who is backed up financially by Ben Siegel and God knows what mobsters out of New York. We know, well, that's all we know. Okay, we suspect that Roberts was skimming while in charge of the counting room on the *Rex*. That would bring down Bugsy's torpedoes on him. And we suspect that other New York mobsters want to muscle in on the gambling ships along with mobsters from Chicago and local boys like Lefty Green. And then there's the car that one questionable witness saw, driven by someone, maybe a woman, maybe not, that no one saw. So what does that give us?"

"A lot of motive, but means and opportunity? So the guy wasn't killed on the *Rex*. We have witnesses, besides the accountant, who rode in the water taxi with him when he returned to shore. The accountant says Roberts got in a foreign car with a dame and drove north. It bothers me that he's the only one who saw that, but we gotta follow up on it. Even if it's true that Roberts went off with some dame, she probably didn't kill him. So he gets laid, if he's lucky, and then what? The real problem is where could he get killed that three gunshots wouldn't raise an alarm? And, if he was killed in town, then someone had to carry his body from where he was shot to a boat, load it on the boat, and take it out to sea. Someone had to dump the body and clean the boat. Randy, we're talking at least two men. One of them has a .38 and is not squeamish about putting two rounds in some guy's head while standing over him. We were already pretty sure that this murder was not done by some old enemy or jealous husband, but this, this is the work of a professional. It's too cold and precise to be some hothead with a gun."

"Lou, maybe we're missing something. Drugs, hookers, bookies ..." Randy trailed off.

"No, they would want to collect, so they want him alive. It's something to do with the counting room. It has to be the money. We gotta talk to the accountant again, the deaf guy. He knows something. He tried to steer us wrong by pointing us to Roberts's enemies from the joint. Roberts didn't have any. And I need to call the *Rex* again to see if"—Lou consulted his notes—"Ricardo ever made it back."

"We should go back and, ah, have another talk with the fortune-teller with the Cadillac. You know, about the widows- and-orphans fund."

"Yeah, but later. That's a hell of a family they got there. The dad's slaving for some gangsters, the mom's a smooth grifter conning rich folks out their money, and the son's a rummy. Christ, did you smell him? And in the middle of the afternoon! How could a young man with a family not be more responsible?"

The phone rang. Randy didn't move. Lou answered it on the third ring. The switchboard gal said a county deputy DA was on the line asking for him or Randy. He said he'd take it; she put the call through.

"This is Clifford Thoms. I'm a deputy DA with LA County. To whom am I speaking?"

"I'm Detective Gomez. How can I help you, Counselor?"

"I believe that your investigation into the Roberts murder may overlap with my department's investigation into activities on the *Rex*. As you no doubt know, the DA is anxious to shut down what he considers to be illegal gambling ships. There is a second matter. I maintain a small private practice, and in that capacity I represent Mrs. Woolfolk. I gather that your interview with her ended on an unpleasant note." Cliff paused briefly, waiting for a denial or explanation. Gomez said nothing. Cliff continued. "I would prefer to discuss these matters in private. Perhaps we could meet and talk in an informal setting."

"My partner and I find eating a steak dinner at the Miramar Hotel restaurant conducive to informal conversation," Lou said with a wink to Randy.

"Fine. Seven o'clock tonight."

Mary appeared in the doorway of Cliff's office. "A. J. Barnes is on the line for you. Do you want to take it?"

"Yes. Put it through and hold my other calls. Mary, close the door; this may take a few minutes."

"Don't forget your two o'clock, and I added your seven o'clock meeting to your calendar."

Cliff waited until Mary had shut the door before picking up the receiver. "A. J., I didn't expect to hear from you so soon. The Supreme Court decision is due out tomorrow."

"Yeah, I heard. That's not what I'm calling about. What have you heard on the Daniel Roberts investigation?"

"Nothing yet. I have a meeting with Gomez and Williams tonight, however."

"Okay, well, that's a start. We need to know if the police have uncovered any threat to the *Rex*, and we also need them to stay out of inquiries into the ownership and finances of the *Rex*. Get back to me as soon as you can."

"If you want, I can call you tonight and let you know how the meeting went."

"Yes, call me at home. Get the investigation under control. Money or muscle, whatever you need."

Richie Woolfolk was born Richard Issac in Monet, Missouri, on August 18, 1909. At the time his mother was a housewife and his father, Ted, was an engineer on a passenger train that ran from Oklahoma City to Los Angeles twice a week. Richie lived in Monet with his mother and her mother, Mama Lou— two God-fearing women—in a small house in a small town. He longed to escape this smothering household in a one-horse town. As a young boy, Richie liked to fanaticize about traveling across the United States in a locomotive with his father, encountering adventures of daring-do far from the watchful eyes of his mother and grandmother.

Robert Lee Issac, his baby brother, was born in 1914 in Oklahoma City when Richard was five years old. The birth and delivery of Bobby was long and difficult. As a result, the midwife was forced to pull Bobby out of the birth canal, breaking both of his arms. As soon as Zoe was able to travel after the birth, she and Mamma Lou decided that Zoe should go to Los Angeles on a railroad pass with Richie and Bobby, even though the newborn still had both arms in casts. There they would stay with Ted. Once together in California, Zoe expected to have more money and more help with the boys. The trip on the train was tedious and difficult for Zoe but exciting for Richie.

When the three of them arrived at Central Station, she was surprised to see Herman, the brakeman who worked with her husband. "Where's Ted? He was supposed to meet us here."

"He's tied up at the roundhouse." Herman looked down at the ground, avoiding eye contact, the toe of his shoe circling a design on the mosaic floor.

"You may as well tell me, Herman. I can feel something's not right."

"Well, ah, I'm supposed to take you to a bungalow Ted rented for you," Herman said haltingly. "It's not too far from the beach; it's nice."

"No, take me to the house!" Zoe demanded. "I have the address. I need to settle in and rest with these two boys. It's been a hard ride."

"Now, Zoe, don't be getting all upset," Herman said. "I can't take you to that house. I just can't."

Zoe saw the desperation in his expression. Gently she took his forearm and, nodding slowly, said, "Of course you can, Herman. Ted will understand. He'll be glad to see us."

Herman drove along Washington Boulevard and turned right onto Rimpau, one of the many quiet, residential streets in that part of the city. They pulled up in front of the house. From the car Zoe could see into the house. Lights were on. There was a family there. Ted was sitting in a large overstuffed chair, petting a dog. In that instant, everything came into focus. All of the unaccounted-for irregularities of the past six years became clear. The extra underwear, the new coffee cup, a spool of pink ribbon tucked away in his luggage—now she understood. Ted had two households, one in Oklahoma City and one in Los Angeles. Zoe looked at Herman. All of the color drained from her face. She couldn't breathe. If not for the boys, she might have fainted. Some small part of her died in that instant of realization.

"I tried to tell ya," Herman mumbled.

"Take us to a hotel. I don't want anything from him ever again. I'll call my mother to come out and help us. We'll get along."

Zoe, the boys, and Mama Lou built a new life in Los Angeles.

With Zoe working in the millinery department at I. Magnin in Pasadena to support the family, Richard became more than a big brother to Bobby; he helped raise him. He went with him to the beach and taught him to swim, taught him how to get along with his mother and grandmother, and taught him to tell little jokes and be amusing in company. They were the best of friends.

In 1921, Zoe married Clarence Woolfolk. Clarence did not tell his mother, Eliza, about the marriage for some time. Zoe was unacceptable to Eliza's Victorian sensibilities in so many ways: she worked outside the home, she was divorced, she drove a car, and, worst of all, she was trying to turn her psychic parlor tricks into a business.

To make things less complicated, Clarence adopted the boys. They became Richard and Robert Woolfolk, but they still remembered their birth father. In their minds, their father became a hero in the life they wished for. In reality, he had little to do with their upbringing or support.

The detectives drove to the home of Clarence Woolfolk just south of Ocean Park. The frantic barking of Clarence's German shepherd stopped abruptly, and a young man opened the front door. Through the screen door they could see that he was in his midtwenties and tall, over six feet tall. He had an athletic build and a long face with a prominent nose.

"May I help you?"

"I'm Detective Gomez, and this is Detective Williams. We're investigating the death of Daniel Roberts. We're here to see Clarence Woolfolk. Is he here?"

"Yes, wait here." The young man closed the door. The

detectives heard the man walk off and in a few seconds heard him shout, "Dad, the cops are here again."

Lou and Randy stood on the porch and waited in silence. They had agreed that for this interview they would be polite and conciliatory. Clarence was not a suspect, and Lou thought that there was more information Clarence could provide. They heard the approach of heavy footsteps and saw the door suddenly jerk open. Clarence stood in the open doorway in baggy pants and an undershirt. He looked both detectives over and growled, "You bastards again. Going to try to shake me down too? You know, my wife hired a lawyer. He'll set you straight. Now get the hell off my property!"

"Dad, let them ask their questions," the young man implored loudly.

"I don't know what your wife told you, but I can assure you all we're trying to do is catch Daniel Roberts's killer. If you'd rather that Danny's death go unpunished, then we'll leave now," Lou said with all the sincerity he could muster, "but if you want to help us, let us come in."

Clarence reluctantly opened the screen door and the detectives came in. They took their seats on the couch in the parlor, again sinking nearly to the floor.

Clarence sat lightly at the edge of his overstuffed chair. "Ah, this is my son, Robert. He's visiting."

Lou looked over to Robert standing behind his father. The young man's features—his light brown hair, blue eyes, and glowing tan—bore no family resemblance to his father's brown eyes; long, narrow face; and dark brown hair shot with streaks of gray. Most striking was the difference in presentation: Robert was powerfully built; Clarence was slender and unimposing, the lean muscles of his barnstorming days lost to years behind a desk. Lou was reminded of something Richard had said:

Clarence was the boys' stepfather. Still looking at Robert, Lou asked, "Will you be in town long?"

"Oh, I live about five blocks from here. Mom and Dad are renting me their old house. I was just leaving. I start work at ten." Robert touched Clarence on the shoulder to get his attention and said, "Dad, if you need anything from the store, make a list and I'll try to pick it up after work."

Clarence nodded his head and watched his son leave.

"Seems like a nice kid," Lou said.

"Yeah, he's my good boy," Clarence agreed. "Look, I don't know what else I can tell you." Clarence eased further back into his chair.

"I had something else in mind. Could you draw the car that you saw Roberts get into? Even a rough sketch would help."

"Yeah, yeah, I can do that." Clarence got up from his chair and retrieved a blank piece of paper and a pencil. He quickly sketched the outline of a car. The drawing resembled three teardrops lying horizontally, all facing the same way. The body of the car was a large teardrop shape with a long hood projecting from the blunt end. A smaller teardrop overlapped the body on the left, and a second, elongated teardrop covered a portion of the hood on the right end. Clarence finished this sketch by drawing in the bottom portion of the wheels in the smaller teardrops. "Isn't that beautiful?" he murmured.

"When we talked to Richard, he said that Danny claimed the car could go one hundred ten miles per hour. Is that right?" Lou asked.

"No, Danny said it could go one hundred twenty miles per hour. Can you imagine that?" Clarence said, smiling for the first time. "Where would you even find a road where you could let that car unwind? That's some car!"

"Thanks," Lou said, "that's all we need for now. If you think of anything else, give us a call."

As they walked to their car, Randy took this sketch from Lou's hand, examined it briefly, and asked, "What do we do with this?"

"We take it to my brother-in-law's garage. He's a car fanatic; he'll know what this thing is."

"That," Johnny said, looking at Woolfolk's sketch, "is probably a Bugatti Fifty-Seven. I can't tell from this sketch what model."

"It's supposed to be able to go one hundred twenty miles per hour," Lou said.

"Oh, then it's the supercharged model, the Fifty-Seven SC."

"Where do you buy a car like this?"

"Not many places—Beverly Hills, downtown, maybe Santa Monica. No one's going to stock that model; that's a special-order job only. Let me get you some dealers' names." As Johnny was writing the names down, he asked casually, "How's Lola?"

"She's fine."

"Is that niece of mine going to give us a new baby anytime soon?"

"God, I hope not. Her husband still hasn't found a job."

"Things are tough all over," Johnny said and handed Lou a list of three car dealers.

The detectives returned to the station and began making phone calls. Lou confirmed that Ricardo had returned from his long weekend trip and gone to work on the *Rex* on his usual shift,

12:30 a.m. to 9:00 a.m. The paymaster confided to Lou that Ricardo was sent home early because he was so distraught by the news of Roberts's death.

Calls to the three car dealers yielded some promising leads. The Santa Monica dealer had not sold any Bugatti 57SCs, but the Beverly Hills dealer had sold two and the Los Angeles dealer had sold one. The dealers refused to reveal the names of the car buyers over the telephone. Lou and Randy agreed that they would split up—one going to the Beverly Hills dealer and the other to the Los Angeles dealer—so they could make their seven o'clock dinner date. Randy volunteered to go to the LA dealer, leaving Lou with the task of chasing down the other two owners.

Lou arrived at the dealership in Beverly Hills and spoke to the lead salesman on the showroom floor. The salesman was in his midthirties and wore a well-cut suit that hung elegantly on his broad shoulders and over his slender frame. Lou suspected the suit was silk, or at least a silk-wool blend. The man's light brown hair was combed straight back. Lou thought that the man's silver cufflinks clashed with the yellow gold of his pinkie ring, but the diamonds set in the ring were tastefully done—large enough to throw off light but not so large as to look ostentatious.

"Our customers insist on their privacy. Many are in the movie industry. You can't imagine how many people we get in every week asking for information about our customers," the salesman explained. "Many movie fans have come in with badges. It's an old trick. Oh, when I first started here, I was taken in a number of times. I'm not saying you're not a policeman, but one can't be too careful. You understand, of course."

"Do you have an office?"

"Of course."

"Let's go to your office and you can call the station to confirm who I am," Lou suggested, taking the man's elbow.

The salesman shook off Lou's hand but led him down a short hallway toward his office. Before they reached the office door, Lou grabbed the man's right arm, spun him around, and shoved his back against the wall. The loud, hollow thud caused people in the showroom to look toward the hallway, but no one walked over to inquire.

"Listen, you little faggot," Lou hissed. "When I walk in here and show you my buzzer, that means you answer my questions. If I have to come back here to get what I need, I'm going to break your jaw, and your boyfriends will go unsatisfied."

The salesman looked down at Lou. His lips trembled and it seemed that he might cry. "I'm not a fag," he said weakly.

Lou slapped him across the cheek. "I'm not with vice; I don't care whose dick you suck. Get me the information now, or when I come back, I'll be mad and won't be able to control myself."

The salesman led Lou to the business office where he whispered something to the bookkeeper. The bookkeeper's eyes opened wide. She quickly glanced at Lou and then back at the salesman. "But Mr. Diller said ..." the bookkeeper stuttered.

"Diller's not here. Just give him the information," the salesman instructed. When the bookkeeper hesitated, the salesman threw a worried glance at Lou and pleaded, "Please."

The bookkeeper confirmed that two Bugatti 57SCs were sold, one to George Raft and another to David O. Selznick. Selznick's Bugatti was bright blue. The salesman assured Lou that, even in poor light, the car's blue color would be unmistakable. George Raft's Bugatti was dark blue. Lou knew that George Raft was a friend of Bugsy Siegel and was rumored to have invested in the *Rex*. Reluctantly, after additional pleading by the salesman, the bookkeeper gave Lou George Raft's home address. Lou drove straight there.

Raft's estate in Beverly Hills was surrounded by a wrought iron fence backed up by six-foot hedges. Outside the gate, but still on Raft's property, stood two men, both in their early forties, in loosely fitted suits. The generous cut of the suits could not hide the bulge of their guns carried in shoulder holsters. Lou guessed that they were veterans who were packing Colt 1911s, the handgun favored by American soldiers in the Great War, the same .45-caliber handgun that Lou carried.

Lou pulled up to the gate. One guard came to his window; the other stood in front of the car. The one in front had his right hand under his coat at waist level. Lou realized that the guard had already pulled his gun but was keeping it out of sight. The guard at his window signaled for Lou to roll down the window.

"No visitors."

"I'm a cop. I'm going to reach for my badge. It's in my inside left-hand pocket." Lou slowly lifted his coat open with his left hand and reached into the inner pocket with his right. He pulled his badge out slowly and handed it to the guard by his window. Lou put both hands on the steering wheel and looked up at the guard in front of the car. The guard in front had his gun pointed at Lou's face. "Can you tell your partner to put his iron down? He's making me nervous."

"Jeff, don't point at the nice copper."

"Dave?" Jeff held the gun steadily pointed at Lou. A bead of sweat rolled down Lou's cheek, but he kept his hands high on the wheel where Jeff could see them.

"Just do it," Dave barked. Jeff lowered his gun a few inches. Dave examined Lou's badge. "Okay, so you're a detective from Santa Monica. So what? Ya got a warrant?"

"No."

"Then blow. If you want to talk to Mr. Raft, make an appointment with his attorney, Mr. Barnes. He's in the book." Dave tossed the badge through the window and onto Lou's lap.

Lou backed up into the street and took one more look at Dave and Jeff. Behind them, driving up to the gate from the inside, was a dark blue sports car with beautiful lines and the steering wheel on the right side. It looked like it could go one hundred twenty miles per hour.

Lou drove a half block north and waited. He watched in the rearview mirror as Jeff and Dave opened up the gate and the Bugatti pulled up. The driver of the Bugatti spoke briefly with Dave and then turned south. By the time Lou had made a U-turn, the Bugatti was at the end of the block and rapidly pulling out of sight. Lou drove back to the station.

When Lou arrived at the station, Randy was already there. Randy told Lou that the Bugatti sold by the downtown dealership had been delivered to an elderly couple in San Gabriel. Randy had driven out to see the car and its owners. The couple had adopted two boys who were now in their twenties. The old man invited Randy to sit with him on the porch while the old woman brought them lemonade. The man insisted that Randy call him "Colonel." He had fought in the Spanish-American War and was stationed in the Philippines during the Moro Rebellion when he was a captain. He returned stateside and stayed in the peacetime army. He complained that he was a captain for nearly twenty years. It was only as the army started to build in preparation for the Great War that he was promoted to colonel. Finally, the colonel pulled out pictures of his two boys standing with their snow-white

Bugatti that they obviously loved. "I should've asked about the color of the car within the first five minutes," Randy lamented. "Still, the lemonade was good, fresh squeezed from their own lemons."

Lou told Randy about getting information at the dealership in Beverly Hills, going to Raft's house, and chasing the Bugatti. "I doubt we can get a warrant for Raft's house or the car. But the car is there, and Raft probably has a piece of the *Rex*," Lou said. "We need to find the woman who was the bait, and we need to know if a couple of Bugsy's goons were working Friday night."

"Swell. Nothing to it. Guess we can take the rest of the week off." Randy was leaning back in his desk chair smoking a cigarette. He let the ash fall on the floor.

Lou glared at him. *Randy can't say no to a veteran.* Lou knew he'd never be fully accepted by some men because he had never been in the army, had never seen combat. He would never be a member of their secret club with its code words and secret handshakes and ribbons and medals and where did you do your basic training? It wasn't his fault that he had been too young for the Spanish-American War and too old for the Great War, but that didn't matter. It was just one more way he was an outsider.

The Miramar Hotel was located at the northeast corner of Ocean and Wilshire Boulevards on a bluff overlooking the Santa Monica Bay. It started as a private residence of former Senator John Jones, one of the founders of Santa Monica, and was converted to a hotel in 1921. At the center of its courtyard was a huge Moreton Bay fig tree planted by Jones's wife in 1889. The hotel was expanded over the years but had always catered to a wealthy clientele. It housed a restaurant where diners could get a club sandwich for lunch or a New York steak for dinner while sitting in booths in a dimly lit room of subdued elegance.

Cliff was waiting for the men in the entry of the restaurant when Lou and Randy arrived at seven. The table was ready, and they slid into their seats in the booth. Each ordered a steak and a highball. The men made small talk before their steaks arrived and then ate dinner mostly in silence. After the steaks had been tucked away, a second round of drinks arrived, and the men began to sip their drinks and smoke.

"As I told Detective Gomez on the phone, DA Fitts is developing a case against the gambling ships and specifically against Tony Cornero and the *Rex*. We believe that your murder investigation of the Roberts matter may have some bearing on our investigation. I would appreciate it if you would keep us informed on the progress of your investigation."

Lou and Randy glanced at each other. "You know, Counselor, we are not in the habit of giving progress reports to DAs from other jurisdictions," Lou said.

"Of course not, and normally I would not ask; however, I'm sure that your department would like to assist the county in getting rid of the public nuisance of the gambling ships. I could speak to your city DA and work out some cooperation agreement."

"Listen, Counselor, we don't report to you unless our captain orders us to," Randy said, stabbing his cigarette at Cliff.

"I understand, gentlemen, and I appreciate your adherence to departmental protocol. There is, unfortunately, also the matter of Mrs. Woolfolk. As you know, she is a business consultant who utilizes unique techniques to prepare business forecasts ..."

"Come on, Counselor, we know she's a goddamn gypsy fortune-teller, and you're both lucky we didn't haul her ass down to the station on a fraud charge," Lou said, raising his voice.

"Detective, let's not take this matter in a direction that we will both regret. My client suggests that, well, let me be blunt as well. You tried to shake her down. At first I refused to believe it, but then I made some inquiries with friends in Santa Monica. I was disturbed to learn that your own department investigated some of the citizens' complaints against you two. This is not the first time that you have suggested to citizens that they contribute to the widows-and-orphans fund. I doubt that it's a coincidence that you asked for cash that you would contribute in the name of the citizens, but I'm not here to make accusations. I was hoping that we could reach an understanding that, given Mrs. Woolfolk's importance to DA Fitts's investigation, she would not be asked to contribute to what I am sure is a worthy fund."

"I'll tell you what, Counselor, you goddamn ..." Lou said, flushing in anger.

Randy reached out, grabbed hold of Lou's coat sleeve, and said, "Lou, settle down."

In a few seconds Lou composed himself and began again. "Well, Counselor, we did some investigating too. It seems you have a nickname, the Chinaman. We know all about the LA County DA's office. All the DAs seem to be in someone's pocket. Your boss, Fitts, has been known to make murder cases against rich men disappear. I don't imagine that comes cheap. And you, you're supposed to be owned by Tony Cornero. Does your boss know that? I mean, how can he trust you to put Cornero out of business?"

"Detective, you're treading on thin ice. These accusations are actionable. You know full well that Fitts was acquitted three years ago on the bribery charges. I, myself, have never had any formal complaints lodged against me, nor have any criminal complaints or lawsuits been brought against me. If you continue in this vein, I will seek to have administrative actions brought against you."

"Don't get tough with me, you goddamn, half-breed shyster. Yeah, I know you did a little boxing. I propose that we go out to the parking lot, and I'll give you a goddamn boxing lesson you won't forget," Lou said, pushing Randy's hand away.

"Thank you for the invitation, Detective Gomez. Perhaps some other time. It's getting late, and I need to get home to my wife. We can discuss this matter further tomorrow—if you're available." Cliff slid along the seat and out of the booth. He looked at the check and put down cash for payment and a tip. He looked briefly at both men, turned, and walked away.

"Lou, what were you thinking? That guy has connections all over town. He can make trouble for us. I'm going to go home now. If you're smart, you'll do the same."

Lou usually left the office in the early evening when the traffic began to dissipate and drove to his home in East Los Angeles, but lately he'd call his wife, tell her he was working a special assignment, and would head south toward San Pedro. San Pedro, the major seaport for the city of Los Angeles, was annexed to the city in 1909 and was connected to the city by a long, narrow corridor that extended along Western Avenue. The drive from Santa Monica to the port took about forty-five minutes, just enough time to relax from the difficult days he had been having since the Roberts murder.

He used his key to open the back door of the bungalow. Maria was on the couch listening to the radio and laughing at a

Jack Benny program. She heard the back door open and knew it was Lou. He came over to her and put his arms around her. He kissed her passionately and said, "It's been almost three days."

"It's about time you showed up. There have been some creepy types driving up and down the street and hanging around here. I don't like it!"

"What does the car look like?"

"I don't know. Some kind of bus."

"Have you seen the car before?"

"No."

"How many people in the car?"

"Two in the front and I think there was some kid or little guy in the back."

"Maybe it was some family from out of town looking for an address."

"Yeah, maybe, but I think it was two men in the front seat. It didn't look like a husband and wife. What's going on, anyway?"

"Some buster got himself shot and dumped into the bay. He had some juice, so people from downtown got interested," Lou answered.

"What's that got to do with us?"

"I got into a beef with a hotshot lawyer from the county DA's office. Guy thinks he can tell me how to run my case. Some tough guy. I got ten years on him, but I can still whip that chink's ass," Lou went on. "If he already knows where you live, they can figure out what we do here. He can't blackmail me. I know his dirty laundry. He has no leverage. Those guys can screw off."

Maria got up from the couch and let her housecoat fall open. Lou looked down at her bare breasts and flat stomach. She wound herself around Lou with her arms around his shoulders and rubbed herself against his body, so her intent was clear.

When he responded by holding her face between his hands and nibbling around her mouth and eyes, she reached down and grabbed hold of his erection with just the practiced amount of strength.

"Let's go to bed! It's been three days, and when I don't see you, well, Daddy don't get no sugar at home."

Lou stepped into the alley behind Maria's bungalow at 10:00 p.m. Waiting for him was a slender man, about five foot six inches tall, with broad shoulders and black hair combed straight back. He wore tan slacks and a dark blue, long-sleeved, button-up shirt. His clothes had been expensive when they were purchased but were now worn and slightly out of fashion.

"What do you want?" Lou asked warily.

"I have a message for you," the man said with a smile.

Lou regretted leaving his gun in his car. He studied the man's waistline but did not detect the bulge of a gun. Lou stepped closer but kept his eyes on the man's hands in case he had a knife. The man's left hand flashed upward and struck Lou on the cheekbone. Lou's head snapped back, and he retreated a step. Lou went into a boxing stance with his hands up, guarding his head. The man's jab flicked between Lou's fists, crushed his nose, and snapped his head back again. In all his years of brawling on the streets of East Los Angeles and in the bars of San Pedro, Lou had never fought anyone with such hand speed and punching power. Lou threw a jab that the man easily slipped before landing a right hook to Lou's ribs. Lou winced in pain and dropped his guard for an instant. In that instant the man struck Lou's head with a flurry of punches. Lou covered up and protected this head with his forearms. The man responded with right and left hooks to Lou's ribs. Lou dropped his elbows to protect his ribs, bent at the waist, and tucked his chin down. The man squatted slightly and used his legs to drive an uppercut to Lou's chin. The punch lifted Lou onto his toes. He fell backward onto the trash-strewn alley and blacked out for a moment. When he came to, the man was wiping blood off his hands with a handkerchief and smiling broadly.

"I'm supposed to tell you that you just got a boxing lesson," the man said before turning and walking away. A moment later Lou heard a car roar off.

He sat up and took stock. His nose was definitely broken, and some ribs were most likely cracked. Both of his eyes would be black by tomorrow. But there was something familiar about the man as he stood there smiling. Then Lou remembered. He was the same young man with the same smile who was standing over his opponent sprawled out on the canvas in the middle of a noisy, smoky auditorium. Lou had seen the man fight at the Olympic Auditorium back in '35 or '36. The Fresno Kid or the Stockton Kid, something like that. He had been a contender but had gotten into trouble with drugs and lost his boxing license. Even in a depression, Lou thought bitterly, men with his skills were always in demand.

Lou struggled to his feet and stumbled to Maria's back door. He knocked weakly and waited for her to open it. Maria helped Lou to a chair in the kitchen. She held a kitchen towel to his bleeding nose and watched in horror as Lou's eyes swelled shut. "Spend the night; you can't drive home. You can't even see."

"Call Randy. Tell him to pick me up. We can get the car tomorrow. Randy can take me to Doc Morrison's."

Randy arrived in forty-five minutes. Maria had chipped some ice off the ice block, filled a bag with ice chips, and put the bag on Lou's eyes and nose. The swelling had started to recede.

"Christ, Lou. You look terrible. What happened?"

"I got jumped. I ... got jumped by three guys. It was dark in the alley. I can't describe them. They ran round the corner, and I didn't see the car."

"Well, did they say anything? Did you have a chance to pull your gun on them?"

"No, they were on top of me too fast. I just covered up as best I could."

Randy called Dr. Morrison and arranged to meet him at his office. Randy drove Lou to the doctor's office in Santa Monica. As they drove, Lou held the ice bag on his eyes with one hand and the kitchen towel under his nose with the other hand. Randy chain-smoked the whole way, lighting a fresh cigarette with the smoldering butt of the previous one. They rode in silence until they were within a block of the doctor's office.

"Saint Michael no help this time, huh?"

"I didn't get a chance to pray." Lou's voice was partially muffled by the kitchen towel. "You should give it a try."

"What? Getting the crap knocked out of me?"

"No, prayer."

"The last time I thought about praying, a Kraut bayoneted me."

"But he didn't kill you."

"Yeah, maybe he didn't."

When they arrived at Dr. Morrison's office, the doctor painstakingly examined Lou's eyes, nose, and mouth for injuries. He set Lou's broken nose and taped it into place. He took a history, trying to elicit as much detail as possible from Lou about the beating. He examined Lou's torso and noted bruising on both sides of the rib cage. Lou declined an X-ray, but both he and the doctor were sure that Lou had fractured ribs on both sides. Lou repeated the same story that he told

Randy, that he had been jumped by three men in the dark alley and was beaten before he had a chance to respond. Lou showed the doctor his hands. The knuckles were unmarked; Lou had not landed a punch. After some prodding by the doctor, Lou admitted that he had briefly lost consciousness.

"Did it aggravate your back or your shoulder?"

"My shoulder's okay, but my back, ah, it's acting up a little."

"Let me write you off for a few days. Randy can get by without you."

"We're in the middle of a case; I can't take time off now."

"Is the victim the guy off the pier?"

"Yeah. He worked on the *Rex*."

"Hell, just one mobster killing another. Take some time off."

Lou sat on the examining table, looked down, and slowly shook his head back and forth. "Nah. The guy wasn't a mobster; he was an accountant. His parents are local. Ah, Christ, the mom was crying in my hallway." Lou looked up and into the doctor's eyes. "Besides, the killer is a pro. I'd really like to catch him."

"Suit yourself. I don't want you driving. You may have a mild concussion. Give it two or three days." Dr. Morrison reluctantly wrote out a release with some restrictions. He was working on his report when Randy and Lou left. Randy dropped off Lou at home. It was after midnight. Luckily Lou's wife was asleep.

CHAPTER 6

When Lou finally woke up the next morning, he rolled over on his side and gingerly felt the swollen flesh around his eyes. As the sleep slipped from his body, he could feel the black-and-blue places all over his torso. His nose ached, and his nostrils were rimmed with crusted blood. He sat up on the bed and swung his feet to the floor. Purposefully he reached over to the bedside table, pulled an Old Gold cigarette from the pack, and watched the smoke he exhaled rise in curls over his head. Lou knew that Delores, his wife, would be in the kitchen preparing a pot of beans and making tortillas. Just then, the bedroom door opened and she walked in. Despite her round figure, which filled out the cotton housedress she wore, she moved quickly with a nervous energy she could barely contain. Lou looked up and smiled as the morning sunlight set off the red highlights in Delores's brunette hair.

"Hi," she said. "I thought I heard you moving around in here." Then she saw his face. "My God! What happened to you? Did you get into another fight?"

"It was pretty much one-sided. Three guys caught me in an alley. They won. Randy is going to be doing most of the driving for the next couple of days."

"If you didn't take on the extra duties, you wouldn't get into these fights," she lamented.

"If I didn't take on the extra duties, you and the kids wouldn't be living in a nice house, and you wouldn't have a car. We've got six mouths to feed, and I'm the only one working. Lupe can't work with the new baby to take care of, and that worthless husband of hers couldn't keep a job even if he could find one. I know Paco has been looking ... maybe you could ask your brother again if they need more help at the garage." Lou loved his son, Francisco, but he couldn't help feeling disappointed. Francisco had dropped out of high school and now ran with a group of boys who were in and out of jail. Luckily, Francisco had no felony convictions, but with his criminal record, he was ineligible for government jobs.

"I'll ask again, but people don't keep their cars up the way they used to."

"How about some bacon and eggs to go along with the beans and tortillas? I might be beaten up, but I'm hungry for some good home cooking. Have I told you about my case that involves a fortune-teller? She reminds me of your grandmother, Mama Quiqua. It's kind of an eerie feeling knowing two crazy women at the same time."

Delores went to the kitchen to prepare breakfast, and Lou followed his nose over to the stove. He lifted the lid of each pot, took deep sniffs of the aromas, and looked admiringly at his wife. Then he kissed her on the cheek and patted her fanny.

Their house was in East Los Angeles, where most residents were of Mexican descent. Delores had grown up in San Pedro on the older East Side. Her family was made up of fishermen, and her grandmother was a kind of *curandera*, who made predictions about the ships, the weather, and the catch. Lou was sure that Delores's grandmother knew about his affairs, but she never said anything. Still she had a way of getting under Lou's skin when she looked at him with her fish eye.

Lou and Delores were lingering over a cup of coffee at the kitchen table when Randy arrived to drive Lou to the station.

"Lou, the captain wants to see you right away," the desk sergeant said as Lou and Randy returned to the station from lunch.

"Me too?" asked Randy.

"Nah, just Lou."

Lou exchanged worried glances with his partner and hurried to the captain's office. The secretary, whom the captain shared with two lieutenants, showed Lou into the office. While she was still in the doorway, the captain told her, "Send them in."

"Captain, what's going on?"

"Shut up. Stay standing and strip to the waist." Lou had taken off his suit coat and tie and was unbuttoning his shirt when a photographer and stenographer walked into the office. "Take off your dark glasses, smart-ass, and the bandage."

Lou removed his glasses and carefully peeled the bandage off his nose. The photographer took pictures of Lou's battered face and torso. He could feel the heat of the flash bulbs as they went off. "Look, this is not necessary. I saw Doctor Morrison, and he's already documented my injuries. Besides, we're never going to catch the guys who beat me up."

"How stupid are you?" the captain asked incredulously. "First, we have statements from the three sailors who beat you up. They say that they were defending their friend whom you hit on the head with a pool cue. Yeah, it was cute to point out to the doctor that you didn't have bruised knuckles so you couldn't have been in a fight. Second, the bartender's statement puts you in the bar in San Pedro and says that you were drunk and that you attacked the fourth sailor without provocation. He's still in the hospital if you were concerned at all. Third, this is not for your benefit. We're doing this as a favor at the request of the LA County DA's office. They're gathering evidence in the event that the sailors want to prosecute when their ship gets back into port."

"Are you suspending me?" Lou asked, stunned by the nightmare quality of his situation and the mysterious appearance of four sailors and a San Pedro bar.

"Hell, I should fire you, but you have a guardian angel in the DA's office. It seems that Deputy District Attorney Thoms has taken pity on you. He says"—the captain looked down at some notes on his desk—"that he understands that you're the sole support of your wife, son, daughter, and a niece, Maria. He'll do what he can to keep you out of jail, but he wants you and Williams to lay off some dame named Woolfolk who's a material witness in a major investigation. Yeah, and stay away from her family unless you have rock-solid evidence against them in the Roberts murder. And Lou," the captain added as he waved the detective away, "for Christ's sake, keep out of San Pedro for a few months 'til this thing cools off."

Lou walked back to the squad room. A dozen pairs of eyes were on him. Randy was at his desk leaning back in his chair, smoking a cigarette, and waiting for Lou. "What did the captain say?"

"Not here. I'll tell you on the road."

"The guys are saying that the county is working up a case about the beating you took. Did you learn anything?"

"Yeah, I learned not to fuck with the Chinaman, and the Woolfolk broad is off limits."

Randy studied his friend with concern. "Lou, you look like hell. Why don't you go home and get some rest?"

"I've got a better idea. Let's drive over to Raft's house. We'll stake out the place. Maybe we'll get lucky, but even if we don't, today's a good day to sit around. Delores had to tie my shoes this morning. I couldn't bend over."

The detectives drove to Beverly Hills. They parked down the street from the Raft mansion and waited. A little after noon Dave and Jeff, on guard duty outside the gate, stood up from their folding chairs and talked with someone inside the gate through the open ironwork. A few seconds later the gate opened and the Bugatti rolled out. It drove toward Randy and Lou. Randy shook his partner by the shoulder to wake him up. Lou and Randy watched as the car went by. The driver was a young woman. Randy started the car and quickly executed a U-turn. They nearly lost the Bugatti on the residential streets but fell in behind it when the brunette at the wheel turned west onto Wilshire Boulevard. Randy was being careful to keep several car lengths between them and the sports car. They had a little trouble keeping the Bugatti in sight on city streets in lunchtime traffic. The woman was headed to the coast. If she turned north or south on Pacific Coast Highway, she could easily outrun them.

"Get ahead of her. Get to the Miramar. There is a phone

booth in the restaurant. I'll call the station and have cruisers posted north and south on PCH," Lou said.

"You're assuming a lot. How do we know she won't turn the second we pass her?"

"Once she hits a clear stretch of road we're going to lose her. We gotta do something to stay on her tail. Play the odds. She went north on PCH once before; maybe she'll do it again. Maybe she'll lead us to where Danny boy was killed. If she——"

"Maybe, maybe, if. Listen to yourself, Lou!" Randy shot his partner a glance. "You got it all figured out, but we don't have a scrap of evidence. We don't know if she's involved. Hell, we don't even know who she is."

"Just get ahead of her and we'll get some backup. Play the odds; what else can we do?"

Randy grunted and crossed into the oncoming traffic, leapfrogging ahead of a knot of traffic. They sped to the Miramar Hotel. Randy jumped out of the car and ran to the restaurant where they had eaten the night before. He called the station and was told that patrol cars would be positioned along PCH. He trotted back to the car. Lou was standing on the sidewalk just outside the car.

"She turned north," Lou said as they got back in the car.

Randy ran around the car to the driver's side. "So what do you think? Does she keep going north up Ocean or does she drive down the incline to PCH?"

"PCH. She's going to lead us to something; I don't know what, but it will bust this case wide open."

Randy ran the sedan full out whenever traffic allowed. After a few minutes, they caught sight of the Bugatti near Topanga

Beach. They could just barely keep up when the road was filled with curves, but each time there was a straight stretch, the Bugatti would pull away. They lost the sports car past Topanga but caught up again going through Malibu just in time to see the Bugatti turn off on Malibu Road.

"What did you say yesterday? Two guys, one with a .38. If she pulls into a driveway, we're gonna wait for some help before we go in, right?" Randy sounded out of breath.

Lou sat in silence. They couldn't expect backup from Santa Monica officers this far outside the city. This was LA County; the only police force out here was the sheriff's department. During Prohibition, Lou recalled angrily, he and a few others from his office had come to a beach not far from here to intercept a load of smuggled Canadian whiskey that was being brought ashore from a ship. He and his partners watched as rowboats made several trips, bringing in cases of whiskey each time. They watched as the whiskey was loaded into a truck. They watched as guards armed with shotguns and rifles took their places on the running boards of the truck. And, just as the police hiding in the shrubs alongside the road were ready to spring their ambush, their captain told them to stand down. In the moonlight the police could see that the rum runners' truck was an LA County sheriff's paddy wagon and the guards were in their sheriff's uniforms. "No, we don't wait. We're on our own. You ..." Lou stopped talking when he saw the Bugatti turn down a private, unpaved driveway.

Randy followed in the sports car's dust cloud. "So what's your ingenious plan, Lou?"

"Yeah, I'm thinking. You grab the shotgun out of the trunk and take cover behind the car. I'll go to the door and ... hell, I don't know. Just don't shoot me."

The dust cloud was so thick that Randy nearly rear-ended

the Bugatti when it slowed to take a sharp turn. Randy stopped the car, and he and Lou watched the young woman park the sports car and rush into a beach bungalow perched on a rise overlooking the coastline. Randy parked the sedan parallel to the front of the house. Quietly he and Lou exited the car. Randy retrieved the shotgun from the trunk and knelt behind the car with the engine block between him and the front door.

Lou drew his .45 and, once Randy was in position, walked up to the front door. He knocked and waited. He could hear a woman's voice coming from behind the door, but he couldn't understand what she was saying. "Telegram! Sorry, but you'll have to sign for it." The door opened two inches, wide enough for Lou to see the young woman clutching her dress. Lou put his shoulder to the door and pushed the woman aside. He went through the doorway and yelled, "Put your hands up! This is a raid. No one move." The woman raised her arms and dropped her dress. She stood before Lou in bra and panties with a white slip around one ankle. Lou saw a flicker of movement to his left and swung his gun around, pointing it at the head of a man. He too had both arms raised high in the air. He wore nothing but a pair of black socks and a slowly deflating erection. Lou yelled, "Is there anyone else here?"

"No, no one. I swear." The man's voice was hoarse. The woman said nothing. She was trembling.

Randy came to the door. He swung the shotgun from the man to the woman and back again. "Where's the other guy?"

"There is no one else." The man's voice sounded almost normal.

"I'll look," Lou said as he circled around the man and began to go from room to room. He came back two minutes later. "No one." Lou surveyed the scene. "Lady, throw lover boy your dress so he can cover up. Both of you, sit on the couch. Keep your hands where I can see them. Okay, buddy, what's your name?"

"A. J. Barnes."

"Barnes? Wasn't that some lawyer?" Randy asked no one in particular.

"That's right. I am a lawyer, and I want to see some identification right now."

"And, Miss, what is your name?" Lou did not even bother to look at Barnes.

"Helen. Helen Williams."

"A relative of yours, Randy?"

"Nah."

"Helen, where were you last Friday night about nine o'clock?" Lou maintained eye contact with the woman. She had wet herself a little, and he wanted to spare her some embarrassment.

"A. J. and me drove up to ..."

"Shut up," Barnes barked. "We don't have to tell him anything."

"Here," Lou said to Randy, "hold this." Lou handed his pistol to Randy, walked over to Barnes, and punched him in the face. Blood splattered on Barnes's bare chest. "Don't talk to Helen that way. Do you understand me?" Barnes pinched his nostrils and nodded. Lou addressed Helen, "Please go on."

For the first time since Lou came through the door, Helen smiled, if only weakly. "A. J. and me drove up to Santa Barbara and stayed at a hotel. We came back on Sunday."

"This is important. When did you leave for Santa Barbara?" Lou asked calmly. There was no need to rush. She would tell him anything he wanted to know.

"We left about six and had a late dinner on the wharf. It

was nice. A. J. can be nice ... when he wants to be," Helen said, looking over at Barnes.

"Did you take the Bugatti?"

"Yeah. A. J. drove. Don't tell George. I told him I was visiting my mother."

"So George doesn't know about you and A. J.?"

"Oh God, no! You know what George would do to him?" Helen laughed nervously.

"Oh, I can imagine. I've met Dave and Jeff. That's part of their job, isn't it? Straightening out people who cross George?"

"Yeah." Helen giggled.

"Did Dave and Jeff straighten out Daniel Roberts?"

Helen looked puzzled. "Who?"

Barnes sat upright. "Say, are you implying that George had anything to do with that?"

"Well, did he?"

"No, certainly not! We didn't even hear about it until Saturday."

"Are you sure that Cornero didn't ask George to take care of a problem for him?"

"Absolutely not!"

"Ah, A. J.," Randy began, "maybe you can explain why you were told about Danny's death in the first place. Is it because George and Bugsy have a piece of the *Rex*?"

"It's a matter of record that I have represented Anthony Cornero, George Raft, and Benjamin Siegel. I am not at liberty to discuss my clients' legal matters, but suffice it to say that Mr. Cornero takes the health and safety of his employees very seriously. Oh," Barnes said, nodding. "Randy Williams. That would make you"—Barnes pointed to Lou—"Luis Gomez. Battering an officer of the court. Well, Detective Gomez, I think your days on the force are over."

"Think so, asshole?" Lou growled, clenching his fists.

"Lou, don't," Randy pleaded.

Lou looked over at Randy and suddenly relaxed and smiled. "How 'bout this," Lou said. "How about if I take you in to the station dressed in your socks. Your clothes on the floor over there—they're evidence. They go in a box along with Helen's dress. Sorry, Helen. Randy, call the papers. Tell them to each have a reporter and photographer at the station in twenty-five minutes. We have a big story for them. How does that sound, A. J.? Think George will be happy to see pictures of you and Helen in the papers? Hey, Randy, what do you think Dave and Jeff will do when they find out about Barnes and little A. J. giving it to Helen?"

"I don't know, Lou. I bet they don't like lawyers much to begin with." Randy smiled broadly and stared down at Barnes.

"You've made your point, Detectives. And what, exactly, would you be arresting us for? What has Helen done? No crime. And me? What? *Attempted* adultery? What do you hope to gain?"

"We want the truth," Lou said flatly, bitterly. "Daniel Roberts was picked up by someone, maybe a woman, driving a dark-colored Bugatti 57SC last Friday night a little after nine o'clock. He was driven up PCH. He was shot and carried by two men to a boat. His body was dumped under the Santa Monica pier." Lou looked down on Barnes, angered by his cavalier attitude and frustrated by the case. The car was the key, he thought. Find the car; find the killer. But the pieces still had to fit together. Lou began again, thinking out loud, trying to force the pieces into place. "Who has a motive? Daniel counted cash on the *Rex*. Daniel was an embezzler. Raft owns a piece of the *Rex*. If someone is stealing from him, he has a motive to kill. Opportunity? Well, Roberts got killed, so opportunity is—what do you lawyers say?—moot. And means. Raft has the means. He has the only dark Bugatti 57SC in town, he has Helen to lure Roberts in, and he has Jeff and Dave to kill Roberts and dump the body." Lou nodded; the pieces fit together, but Helen's face showed incomprehension not guilt, and Barnes was sporting a knowing smile. What had he missed, Lou wondered, but he pushed on. "You ask what crime? Try murder. That makes you a material witness and Helen an accessory before the fact."

"Nice theory, but Helen and I were in Santa Barbara with the Bugatti at nine o'clock—people at the hotel and the restaurant will confirm it—and besides, you're wrong about the Bugatti." Barnes dabbed at his nose with Helen's dress. He looked at the resulting red stain and then returned his eyes to Lou. "Lenny Green's little whore of a daughter keeps her Bugatti, same model, same color, at a beach house not half a mile from here."

PART 2

CHAPTER 7

Azusa, California
January 18, 1939

Barbara Scott climbed the stairs to the Azusa Police Department. She had driven out from Arcadia along Foothill Boulevard, the famed Route 66 that ran east to west on the southern edge of the San Gabriel Mountains. The range stretched sixty-eight miles from Soledad Canyon, northwest of Los Angeles, to the Cajon Pass, north of the city of San Bernardino, sixty miles east of Los Angeles. Despite being winter, it was warm and the sky was clear. The only indication of the season was snow on Mount San Antonio, commonly known as Mount Baldy. At just over ten thousand feet, Mount Baldy was the highest peak in the San Gabriel range.

Barbara was tired, but she forced herself to keep going. Here it was Wednesday, and she hadn't slept through the night since Sunday. Her little sister, Mary Scott, was missing.

Mary, a recent graduate from Santa Barbara State College, had attended a charity fund-raiser at Santa Anita racetrack and then dinner at the Brown Derby. She was with ten members of her sorority who all went together. That was four days ago. It was the last time she had been seen by anyone.

The desk sergeant looked at the young lady who entered the police department office. She was obviously distressed. She wasn't rich, but she was doing better than most. The woman wore a blue dress that matched her eyes and a wide-brimmed straw hat. "What can I do for you, ma'am?" he asked.

"I want to report a missing person."

"How long has she been missing?"

"Since January fourteenth. It's been four days and no one has heard from her or seen her," Barbara said, almost in tears. "She just disappeared."

The desk officer gave her a quizzical look and said, "Well, Miss, why haven't you reported this before now?"

"I have been to the police departments in Arcadia, Monrovia, Sierra Madre, and now Azusa. After I leave here, I'm going to the Hollywood station. She has to be somewhere! I even called our aunt in Chicago. She's not there either. What can you do to help me find her?" She did her best to sound tough, but she could feel her lower lip quiver.

"I can take your information, but as hard as it is to accept, in most cases a young woman leaves because she wants to or she's gone off with a man. Give her a few more days. I bet she'll call you from Reno or some such place and let you know she's married," he replied. "How are you so sure of the date you think she disappeared?"

"She didn't come home from the excursion to the Santa Anita racetrack on January fourteenth," Barbara answered. "At first we thought Mary went home with one of her sorority sisters, and we weren't too worried until later when we still didn't hear from her."

"You say she went to the racetrack at Santa Anita with

her sorority sisters? Was it a sorority party?" asked the desk sergeant. He smiled, trying to alleviate her distress.

"No, it was a fund-raiser for the local children's charity. Times are tough for some children. Work for parents is scarce. We are in a depression." She glared at the desk sergeant, incensed at the implication he was making about a sorority party.

"Sorry, miss. I didn't mean to imply anything. Do you know what happened next?" he said. He tried not to smile as he enjoyed the thought that little sister was getting something big sister hadn't had.

"Yes, they all went to the Brown Derby in Arcadia, right near the track. I talked to the girls. The only thing they all mentioned was that a man about thirty years old was hanging around them and making them nervous. He was flashing money, telling everyone he had made it big at the track. He paid for a round of drinks for the girls. It couldn't have been very expensive; most of them were drinking Pepsi," Barbara answered.

"Could the girls describe this guy?" asked the sergeant.

"Well, yeah. He was medium height, medium build, with dark hair and dark eyes. The girls said he was ordinary except for the way he looked at them," she explained. "They said he gave them the heebie-jeebies."

"Here, fill out this report, and I will make sure the other municipalities get the information. If anything comes up, I will contact you," he said. He handed her the report form and a fountain pen.

Although Barbara Scott wasn't satisfied with this trip to yet another police department, she knew that there was little else she could do now. She returned to her car and headed west on Foothill toward the Hollywood substation. Maybe they'd be able to help her there; maybe they'd know something.

Ramon had left the university after only a year. Army thugs had broken up the peaceful protest against government corruption that Ramon had joined on campus. He had a rifle pointed at his head. The soldier holding the rifle was his age but had cold eyes, and he was ready to pull the trigger. Ramon was arrested, roughed up a little by the military police, held for a few hours, interrogated, and then released. The officer who had interrogated him had made a point to not only get his address but also a description of the house. Ramon borrowed money that night and left El Salvador the next day.

It had taken a few months, but he managed to get a job as a high school custodian through his uncle who had been working for the Los Angeles Unified School District for six years. Ramon was well liked by the faculty, the administrators, and other staff members. Although not always punctual, he worked hard, was intelligent, and made a point to constantly improve his English. It also helped that he was handsome and had, as many secretaries noted, "bedroom eyes."

On weekends Ramon frequently borrowed his uncle's truck and drove into the mountains north of town with a date to hike and enjoy the sun, the fresh air, the exercise, and the view, which stretched from Santa Catalina Island in the west, across the Los Angeles basin, to the vineyards of Cucamonga in the east. In addition to admiring the view, they would engage in heavy petting or even sex if his date was willing. Ramon knew many good trails in the mountains and even more secluded spots where he and his date could be alone yet see anyone approaching in plenty of time to put their clothes back on.

On Saturday, March 18, Ramon took a new girl up into the mountains and, after a strenuous hike, took her to a favorite spot beneath a lone oak tree. He hadn't been there since late fall—the ground was usually too wet for comfort in the winter—but the location was reliably private. When he and his date arrived, they were disturbed by the number of flies and the odor of rotten meat. The sound of the flies led Ramon to some nearby bushes where he spotted the carcass of an animal. It was large. He couldn't see fur; it appeared to be mostly skeleton. What flesh was left was crawling with maggots. Still, something was wrong. He had seen many carcasses on the roadside in these mountains, mostly roadkill, but he couldn't recognize what kind of animal this was. Though disgusted by the smell and the maggots, he approached it and lifted the branches of the bush that partially concealed it. The woman's body was naked. She had been blonde—some hair was still attached to her skull. Ramon was fascinated and repulsed at the same time. A woman's body had been reduced to a heap of bones and flesh, no longer a person, merely a meal for animals and maggots.

Within an hour, Ramon had led sheriff's deputies back to the spot. A search of the area turned up bits of clothing that matched the outfit Mary Scott was last seen wearing. Barbara Scott's persistence had paid off; the sheriff's office was well aware that Mary Scott was missing, that Mary Scott wouldn't run off, and that Mary Scott wasn't that kind of girl. Big sister was right after all. The deputies let their sergeant call Barbara to break the news.

Hollywood,
Monday, March 27, 1939

"We want to file a missing-person report," the man said. He was a little over six feet tall and slender, and his face was drawn and pasty. He was mostly bald; what little hair he had on the sides of his head was graying. His wife, who was short and pudgy, wore a pink-and-white dress. The curls in her hair were limp. She also looked tired. Although she had tried to cover it up with makeup, the thick coating of lightener under each eye did not fully hide the dark circles.

The desk officer at the Hollywood substation had seen this scene before. It was common for young ladies to come out to California, to Hollywood, and try their luck in the movies. Sometimes they told their parents they were going, and sometimes they left without a word. The officer passed them the necessary paperwork, and the couple began filling in the blanks.

"Is this your first trip to Los Angeles?" the officer asked.

"Oh, no. We've lived in town for fifteen years," the wife, Ellie Morgan, explained. "Anna wouldn't have run away, not without telling us. That hoodlum husband of hers is somehow behind this."

"Yeah? Who's her husband?" the officer asked, suddenly interested.

"Pietro Mara. The greaseball goes by 'Peter,'" Ellie's husband, Hank Morgan, said bitterly.

"Yeah? That wouldn't be Pete 'the Snake' Mara, would it? One of Jack Dranga's men?" the officer asked as he reached for a notepad.

"Four years now he's worked for that bastard, and we still don't know what he does. I tell him to get an honest job, but does he listen? No. He likes playing the tough guy. He likes making easy money. Well," the father said, his voice rising, "I hope that rat bastard gets what's coming to him."

The couple's daughter had been missing since Friday. For the first two days, their son-in-law Pete was also gone, and the couple assumed that their daughter and son-in-law had taken an unexpected trip. On the third day, the couple was contacted by the county hospital where Pete was being held for observation. The couple assumed that Anna and Pete had been in a traffic accident, so they rushed to the hospital to check on Anna. Only Pete was there, and he didn't know where his wife was.

Pete told his in-laws that he had been held incommunicado from Friday night until Sunday at the Harbor station. The police had worked him over from time to time, but he had told them nothing. On the third day, he had blacked out and woke up in the hospital. His body was covered with bruises; he had two black eyes. His doctor wanted to keep Pete for another day or so to see if he had symptoms of a concussion. He had several bloody bruises on the back of his head, the sort of bruises made by saps. When Pete heard that Anna was missing, he got dressed, discharged himself from the hospital, and pleaded with his in-laws to give him a day to find his wife.

The Morgans gave their son-in-law the one day he asked for, but when they had not heard from him by ten o'clock the next morning, they drove down to the Hollywood substation and filed their report. The desk officer, knowing the mob connection, turned the matter over to his supervisor, the duty officer, Sergeant James. James immediately dispatched a car and had Pete picked up for an interview. While waiting for Pete to be brought in, the sergeant made a call to the Harbor station and verified that Pete had been held, unofficially, and interrogated. On Friday night Pete had prevented vice officers from entering the back room of a pool hall long enough for the bookies to destroy their betting records. In the process Pete had knocked around a couple of the undercover officers who had arrived before the uniformed boys showed up. Pete claimed that nothing illegal was going on and he didn't know that the undercover officers were cops. The DA declined to prosecute, but the officers at the station wanted some payback. The station records showed that Pete was cut loose the same night he was taken in, but the desk officer at the Harbor station confided that Pete had been their guest for the weekend.

Sergeant James called the Morgans into his office. He sat behind his spartan, government-issued wooden desk, and the couple sat opposite him in sturdy wooden chairs. James quickly scanned the missing-person report. "Your daughter is twenty-five years old and blonde?"

Mrs. Morgan nodded weakly; Mr. Morgan stared straight ahead.

The sergeant looked up at the latest addition to the bulletin board on the wall behind the Morgans. It was a notice that the body of a twenty-two-year-old blonde woman had been found in a canyon above Altadena. Nausea and dread swept through him. Slowly he reached for a pack of cigarettes on his desk and shook one out. He lifted the cigarette to his mouth and lit it, his mind racing. "Could I get some clothes from your daughter? People sometimes go for a hike in the foothills and get turned around. A good set of hunting dogs will find them even if the scent is a few days old."

"Of course. If you think it will help," Ellie said.

"Hiking? She might go to the park, but she would never go hiking. And where would you start looking? Malibu? Hollywood? Azusa? Hell, you could keep going all the way out to Cucamonga! You don't expect to find her alive. She's alive. Why don't you sweat some of Dragna's goons? That's who has my Anna." Hank was leaning forward with both palms on the desk, looking directly into the sergeant's eyes.

"Why would they grab your daughter?" the sergeant asked.

"It's obvious: to shut Pete up."

"But when did he learn that his wife was missing?"

"Well," Hank struggled with the question. Why would it matter when Pete learned? "Someone told him when he was in jail."

"There's no evidence that he was contacted by anyone from the outside the whole three days he was in jail. He didn't talk because he hates cops. From what you've told me, it sounds like he didn't know Anna was gone until you told him in the hospital. The blackmail angle doesn't pan out. Besides"—the sergeant leaned back in his chair and made an effort not to look at the coroner's notice again—"Dragna's boys are in and out of jail all the time, and they all keep their mouths shut."

"I'll bring you some of her clothes. Do what you can to find her. We just want her home," Ellie said with resignation.

After the Morgans left to retrieve some of Anna's clothes, the desk officer stuck his head in James's office. "She could have run off. If we give it a few days, she could turn up."

"It's the Scott girl all over again. If she was alive, she would have called her momma."

"Okay, so maybe she's dead. But Mr. Morgan is right. Where do we start looking? There are miles and miles of foothills."

"Let's get hold of that Mexican kid who found the Scott girl."

"Salvadorian. He's a kid from El Salvador."

"Yeah. Okay. Salvadorian. Let's talk to him. He can give us some place to start."

Sergeant James called the Los Angeles County Sheriff's office in Altadena to get the telephone number of the school where Ramon worked. James called the school and held the line while the principal's secretary got Ramon on the phone.

"This is Sergeant James with the LAPD Hollywood substation. We are looking for a missing woman, twenty-five, blonde. We think ... maybe ..."

"You think she's dead and want to know where to look for the body."

"Yeah."

"There are about seven or eight places. One good place is near Arroyo Seco and another north of—"

"Wait. What was special about the place where you found the Scott girl?"

"It's a good summer place. Good view. Nice shade. A little close to a road, but you can see cars coming so you can ..." Ramon paused, wondering how to explain the situation to a policeman. "Well, we are men here. You have time to put your pants back on."

"When you say 'nice shade,' does that mean there's a tree there?"

"Yes, a tree. I don't know the English word, *un roble.*"

"Robe-lay? Hold on," James said. He held the receiver against his chest and yelled from his chair, "Maria, honey, what's 'robe-lay' mean in Spanish?"

Maria appeared in James's doorway and folded her arms under her breasts. She watched as he unconsciously licked the corner of his mouth. "It's a tree."

"Yeah, but what kind?"

"Oh, an oak."

"Thanks, honey."

Maria stretched her arms above her head, arched her back, and inhaled deeply. "Anytime."

James watched Maria walk away for a second and then returned the receiver to his ear. "Robe-lay is an oak."

"Yes, oak. That is the name of the tree and of the wood?"

"Yeah. Okay, so is there another place like that, like where you found the Scott girl? Near a road, with a tree, where you can see cars coming from a long way off?"

"Yes. Yes, a good one. It is north of Arcadia. You go north on Santa Anita Road, through Sierra Madre. The street changes names, but it takes you into the mountains. It's hard to explain."

"Can you show us?"

"Now? I'm working."

"I'll square it with your boss."

It took James a couple of hours to assemble his team. There were four deputy sheriffs in one car; James, Ramon, and another officer from the Hollywood substation in a second car; and a paddy wagon with three search dogs and their handler. Ramon led them to a spot. It was as he described it: a lone oak tree near a dirt road, with privacy and a view of approaching cars. A woman could scream her lungs out and no one would hear, no one but her killer.

The vehicles parked on the road, and everyone hiked over to the tree. The dogs' handler gave them the scent, and immediately the dogs found a place that interested them under a horizontal branch of the oak. The grass under the branch was trampled and slick with rust-colored slime.

"Our boy likes to work in the shade," James observed.

"Think we'll need shovels?" one of the deputies asked.

"Doubt it. Too much work to bury her," James said. He was distracted, watching the dogs noisily descend a grass-covered slope. "Hey, Ramon!"

"Yes sir?"

"You found the Scott girl under a bush, right?"

"Yes." Ramon watched as the dogs rushed down the slope toward a clump of bushes.

The dogs excitedly yelped and circled the bushes at the edge of a natural terrace. "I think the dogs have something," their handler shouted up to the knot of people standing in the shade of the oak.

James started down the slope. "You coming, Ramon?"

"No. I stay here. I don't want to see."

"Don't blame you."

"Did animals do that to her?" one deputy asked.

"Some of it," James responded. He examined the body carefully. James had studied the report on the Scott murder he had received from the sheriff's office. The sheriff's department had a crime lab and could handle the complex cases. The crime lab's report went out to sheriffs' offices and police departments of cities along the San Gabriel mountains, everywhere Barbara Scott had filed a missing-person report. The report allowed offices to close their files on Mary Scott, who was lost, then found, and returned to her family. The report noted, "Vertical scoring of the bones." James saw the reason. Whoever took Anna had made a series of vertical cuts down to the bone on her arms, legs, and torso. He had managed to miss the veins and arteries. No, not managed—he had deliberately missed the veins and arteries so she wouldn't bleed out too quickly.

"There will be more. Our boy enjoys his work," James said, thinking out loud. He knew there was a monster among men in Los Angeles; there would be more bodies before the search was over. "Photograph everything and let's try to find her clothes," James shouted to the deputies. He'd have to radio for more help, get the coroner out there, and transport the body to the sheriff's crime lab. He'd also have to call Anna's parents. The mom knew; she just wanted her baby back. The dad? He knew too, but he wouldn't accept it. James had seen this before. Some parents couldn't accept their child's death, not until they saw the broken body and the chest not moving or touched the cold flesh. Only then could they admit that their child wouldn't be coming home.

Inglewood, California
Friday, May 19, 1939

"Ladies in the Science Club may sign up for an adventure in horseback riding to explore the flora and fauna of the Baldwin Hills and continue with equestrian training. Only sixteen spaces are available." Sister Mary Ellen, the biology teacher at Saint Mary's Academy in Inglewood, read the daily bulletin. She smiled and absentmindedly fingered her crucifix as she read the good news aloud. There was immediate stirring and excitement as the girls digested the information. Sister Mary Ellen could hear the normal noises in the classroom: books closing, a pencil dropping on the floor, someone erasing. Each girl was dressed in a white blouse and blue skirt. They were turning around in their seats, talking, and nodding their heads in agreement.

One of the girls raised her hand and asked, "Are we going to be able to ride the horses belonging to the stable at Hollywood Park? Last time the trainer gave us free lessons. And it's not very far away."

"No, not this time. We want to explore the Baldwin Hills, especially near the oil wells. The Science Club is concerned with the plants and animals that live around the wells," Sister Mary Ellen explained. She was delighted at the enthusiasm generated by the announcement. "There are many miles of trails, with cutoffs, drop-offs, and cul-de-sacs," she went on, now excited herself. "Mother Superior is always concerned about the safety of you girls and has made an arrangement with Red Riding Academy. The stable will not only supply the horses but will also provide a guide."

"Sister Mary Ellen, is it true that La Ballona Creek starts in the Baldwin Hills and flows all the way to Santa Monica Bay?" asked Jane. "My mother always calls it Baloney Creek and says it's named after a whale." She was short and blonde and always asking questions.

"Yes, Jane. Your mother is right. *La ballona* means 'the whale' in Spanish. And yes, the headwaters are in the Baldwin Hills. This is going to be an exciting adventure."

On the following Wednesday, the morning sun shone down on the girls from Saint Mary's Academy as they descended from the yellow school bus. Some of the girls were laughing and joking about Baby Snooks on the radio. The older girls were too sophisticated to listen to *The Baby Snooks Show* and said they would rather talk about Errol Flynn and Tyrone Power. They wanted to ride like Flynn did. All were anticipating the horseback ride. They strolled up to the stables where the wranglers were waiting for them. It was a short walk, and there was the smell of stables in the air. The odor of hay and horse manure filled their nostrils. Two Australian shepherd dogs also greeted them, barking in a friendly manner.

Guy, the head wrangler, instructed the students on how to saddle a horse and told them the names of each piece of equestrian equipment. Then he helped the girls into their saddles, adjusted the stirrups, and showed them how to hold the reins. The guide was careful to explain safety precautions: stay together, don't follow too close, and keep on the trails. The horses were gentle and well trained. Guy, who also served as the trail guide, was as concerned for the horses as he was for the girls. He explained that the dogs were along for protection and companionship. The warm air foretold a much warmer afternoon. The students were restless and eager to get started, but they were well-behaved Catholics who understood obedience.

As they climbed the incline along the trail, they saw miles of rolling green and yellow hills stretching before them. The smell of fresh grass and wildflowers surrounded them. Occasionally a large oak tree loomed on the top of a rise, appearing to have been in that same place for centuries. The girls watched for animals; it was part of their school assignment. They spotted rabbits, coyotes, hawks, squirrels, and two deer. The dogs helped them find the animals by barking and chasing squirrels and other creatures.

For lunch Guy led them to a shaded area where the grass was green and there was a small creek that eventually found La Ballona. It was pleasant. The horses were hobbled so they could eat as well as the girls. Then, from a distance, the dogs began to bark. It was a long howl, different from the friendly barking around people. "It sounds like the dogs found something," Guy mumbled.

Sister Mary Ellen, still in her habit, said, "This is an interesting place. In 1932 the first-ever Olympic Village was built right here in the Baldwin Hills, very close to this exact spot." She opened her arms and gestured at the vast amount of empty land. "The village was only for men," she added. Several of the girls asked why. "Well, you have to remember that 1932 was the worst of the Depression and the city had trouble affording the village at all. There were nearly thirteen hundred male athletes and fewer than one hundred thirty women. Still," the nun added softly, "it hardly seems fair." Sister Mary Ellen began to get annoyed by the dogs' continued howling. "The village covered three hundred thirty acres and had an amphitheater and all kinds of special buildings for the games."

"What about the women? Where did they stay?" asked Bonnie, one of the seniors and an accomplished athlete.

"The women athletes lived in Chapman Park Hotel on Wilshire Boulevard."

Jane said, "Sister, how do you know so much about the Olympic Village?"

"It was only seven years ago. I'm surprised that you don't remember more about it."

A tall girl with a ponytail asked, "Can we go see if there are any buildings remaining from the Olympics? And find out what the dogs are barking at?"

"I don't see why not, if our guide is in agreement. Let's go do some exploring," answered Sister Mary Ellen.

"Always stay with a buddy; don't go off alone," said Guy. "Let's saddle up!"

He led the way toward the derelict Olympic Village. He had been there before and knew there were still some buildings standing, although they were not in good condition. He pointed out where the post office had been and gave instructions and suggestions about where to go.

When the group came to the tumbled-down building where the dogs were barking, several of the young ladies ventured in. The painted surfaces of the building were faded and peeling. The door hung partially off the hinges, and the girls could see animal tracks in the dust that covered the floor of the dilapidated remains. They cautiously followed the smell that emanated from the interior. The barking dogs beckoned them to continue.

Patches of the ceiling had fallen down, allowing the girls to see sunlight through holes in the roof. They moved farther into the building, careful to step around the crumbling plaster and broken lath. They followed the sound of the barking dogs through the debris-strewn hallways until they came to a room bright with sunlight. Most of the middle portion of the ceiling had fallen in, exposing some ceiling joists. The fallen lath with its attached plaster had been heaped in the far corner. The first girls in the room were startled and then frightened by what they saw. Slowly they backed out of the room. A rust-colored liquid, long since dried, had been poured in the center of the floor and splattered on the walls.

"Is it paint?" one pale girl asked.

"Maybe it's blood," another speculated in a thin voice.

Guy, who had been raised on a farm, pushed his way past the knot of girls in the doorway and walked into the room. He called the excited dogs over to him and passed them back to be held by girls in the hall. He examined the ceiling joist in the center of the room and studied the dark red spray on the walls. "Ah, hell, some farmer butchered his hogs here. See where he hung them from the joist?" Guy pointed to a groove in the middle joist. "Damn fool. Not his property. A big hog would've broken this joist. He could take them to a slaughterhouse ..."

As Guy spoke, the girls came into the room in twos and threes. They were mesmerized by the dried blood that had pooled on the floor, sprayed on the walls, and splattered on what was left of the ceiling. Soon girls filled the room and were poking through the debris on the floor.

"Hey, what's that?"

"Looks like a diamond ring!"

"I saw it first!"

The girl closest to the ring reached into a pile of debris and came up with it. Immediately she began to scream. The ring still circled a severed finger. Other girls in the room began to scream even before they saw the finger. The rest of the class came running and ran into the rush of girls trying to escape the room. One of the girls lost her lunch.

Guy, who had served in the infantry during the Great War, remained strangely calm. "There's too much blood for one body. Do you see those drag marks on the floor? Bodies have been dragged out of here. They wouldn't have carried them far. They'll be buried somewhere close."

In a monotone Sister Mary Ellen asked, "How will we notify the authorities?"

"We'll have to send the other wrangler and one of the girls down to the stable," Guy answered.

The girls, realizing what they had stumbled across, prayed for the victims who had died here. Sister Mary Ellen settled the young ladies down and then divided them into groups and assigned areas to search.

They found the first body about twenty minutes later. It had been pulled from its shallow grave by animals. The decomposing body was that of a young woman. The girls found the shredded and bloody remains of her clothes buried beside her. From what they could tell by her clothes, she had been dressed to go out on a date. The body had wounds with ragged edges where the animals had chewed, but here and there on desiccated flesh and exposed bone, it also appeared that the body had been sliced with a knife. As the enormity of the damage done to the young woman entered the girls' psyches, one young student began to shake violently. Another girl turned away from the hideous sight and sobbed out more prayers for the victim.

By the time Los Angeles County sheriff's deputies arrived, the girls had discovered another "grave" that they had marked with a cross. The second body was also of a young woman. She was missing a finger. The deputies combed the area but did not discover additional victims. After a thorough search of the killing room, a forensics team did, however, find a knife, dull and bloody, in the corner under the ceiling debris.

The bodies were transported to the LA County Coroner's Office for an autopsy and identification.

CHAPTER 8

Los Angeles, California
Friday, May 26, 1939

"Cliff, have a seat." District Attorney Buron Fitts gestured to a chair. "I don't know if you know Dr. Yashida of the Los Angeles County Coroner's Office."

"Of course. We worked together on a case, when? A year or two ago?"

"Yes, two years ago. Difficult case. Tricky." Yashida nodded, remembering that he could not come up with enough evidence to allow Cliff to go forward with a prosecution.

"Well, good," Fitts said, eager to get down to work. "Something's come up. You remember the so-called Canyon Killer the papers were talking up a couple of months ago?"

"Sure. Two girls, cut up, left in the hills under some bushes."

"Yes. Well, the new murders, the Baldwin Hills killings, they—"

"Excuse me, Buron, but the papers said those girls were shot. Different MO suggests a different killer."

"Well, yes, if they were in fact shot. We fed that fact to the papers." Fitts smiled briefly and began again. "No, they were butchered the same as the other girls."

"The same?"

"Yes. Dr. Yashida, bring Cliff up to speed."

Yashida rose from his chair and stood as if delivering a lecture. "The Canyon Killer case—newspapers love alliteration. On Saturday, March 18, a pair of hikers in the mountains north of Altadena came across the decomposing body of a young woman. Animals had been at it, so, under normal circumstances, it would have taken a long time to identify. However, the victim's sister had been reporting her missing for two months to all the police departments along the foothills and had been returning to the stations weekly. Really made a pest of herself. Can't blame her. When the body turned up, the first thing my office did was to match the teeth of the decedent to the dental records of the Scott woman. Identity verified.

"On Monday, March 27, the Morgan family reported their daughter, Anna Mara, missing. Same physical description as the Scott girl: white, medium build, blonde, above average height. The sergeant put two and two together and looked for the body in the same sort of place the Scott girl was found. Got lucky. He found her the same day in the mountains north of Sierra Madre. This body was almost fresh. We saw the damage. Eviscerated, probably raped, cut to ribbons. Looked like she was suspended from a tree branch and, well, I don't want to speculate. An investigator from my office returned to the scene of the first killing. He found marks on a tree branch there as well. He, the killer, hangs them up to work on them. Damned brazen, but not the worst I've seen.

"On Friday, May 19, a week ago, the Baldwin Hills girls are found. Here is where we have an interesting development. It's two months later and twenty or more miles away, yet the knife marks on these bodies were the same as those on the bodies we found in the canyons. Instead of hanging them from branches, the bodies were suspended from a ceiling joist, but it's the same, *unique* technique. The murderer makes his victims suffer. The knife work is unmistakable. We have a modern-day Jack the Ripper. He's not going to stop."

Fitts watched Yashida take his seat and then turned to his assistant prosecutor. "Cliff, I've decided to form a special squad—county detectives, city detectives, whoever you need—to apprehend the murderer. The bodies were found in unincorporated parts of the county, but almost surely the victims were kidnapped in incorporated towns. We have to have all police departments and the sheriff's office working together on this. If news of the connection between the Canyon murders and the Baldwin Hills murders gets out, there will be panic. Keep the papers out of this and wrap it up quickly."

"Do we know who the Baldwin Hills victims are?"

"My investigators tried to match the bodies with missing-person reports, but nothing fits. Maybe they aren't local girls," Dr. Yashida said with a shrug.

Cliff and Fitts agreed to label the case the Scott-Mara investigation, omitting any reference to the Baldwin Hills victims. The team drawn from police departments across the county would be known simply as the "Scott squad." Cliff was determined to get the investigation up to speed as quickly as possible, so when he left the meeting with Fitts and Yashida, he drove directly to the Arcadia Police Department to see if he could get a copy of the department's report on the Mara killing. He already had the sheriff's department's report on the

Scott murder and a description or artist's sketch of the man the sorority girls described. Officers had gone to the Brown Derby to interview the waitress and the bartender. The reports stated that the bartender and waitress both said that the possible suspect had been there at least three or four times. He always came in from the racetrack, showed off his winnings, bragged about his ability to pick the winning horses, and tried to pick up tall blonde ladies. Statements from the sorority sisters agreed that the suspect was somewhere between five foot six and five foot eight inches tall, around thirty years old with a medium build, dark hair, and dark eyes. He was a flashy dresser and often wore a loud green-checked coat. They also all agreed that he made everyone uneasy, even when he was trying to pick up the women.

Cliff returned to his office and began to assemble his staff for the Scott squad. He left messages at various sheriff's offices soliciting detectives for temporary reassignment. On Monday, May 29, he would assemble his team, set up offices, borrow some clerks, brief everyone, and assign tasks ... so much to do. Starting Monday they'd look for their needle in a haystack. If it was the same guy for both sets of murders, he would have moved on from Santa Anita to Hollywood Park. That made sense. Santa Anita ran from the day after Christmas until late April; Hollywood Park ran from late April until sometime in July. Cliff felt overwhelmed. He knew he'd need at least three teams: one to reinterview the witnesses who saw the guy at the Brown Derby, a second team to interview people at Hollywood Park and all the local watering holes, and a third team to review missing-person reports and known criminal offenders with similar MOs. On Monday they'd have a description and the artist's sketch to show around. Someone would know the guy or something about him. Cliff looked up. Only his office was illuminated; everyone else was gone. He dropped copies of the reports from the Arcadia PD into his briefcase and went home.

Ray Sanchez and Bill Wright, the two detectives assigned to the second team of the Scott squad, took a day and a half to interview people at Hollywood Park. They asked the staff at the track if any of them remembered a man, about thirty, medium height, with dark hair and a wad of money. They showed the artist's sketch to anyone who would look. No one knew the fellow. Most people said the same thing: the description fit a thousand men but no one in particular. On the second day, the detectives moved on to the local restaurants and bars. The answers were always the same: no one recognized the man with young, tall blondes. They came and went. Did the officers know the women's names? People might remember the names. The detectives went to dozens of bars and restaurants but didn't turn up anything substantial. After ten days, team two had made no progress. Team one fared no better. They reinterviewed the sorority girls, as well as the waiters, waitresses, bartenders, and coat-check girls at the Brown Derby. No new information turned up. Cliff didn't even ask team three for a report; the detectives' desks were stacked high with missing-person reports and more were stacked on a library cart pushed against a back wall.

Wednesday, June 7, 1939

Mary poked her head into Cliff's office. "Fitts needs you in his office right now. I guess the Supreme Court finally did something."

Cliff picked up the catalog case in which he kept the files on People vs. Stralla and carried the heavy case over to Buron Fitts's office. Stralla was Anthony Cornero Stralla, aka Tony the Hat. Fitts, with encouragement from Attorney General Earl Warren, had been trying to close down the *Rex* and Cornero's other gambling ship for over a year. Fitts had won at the trial level, but Cornero had won his appeal at the appellate court, and both sides had been waiting for the California Supreme Court to make a final decision.

"Sit down, Tommy. The Supreme Court, in another display of wisdom, is giving both sides more time to file rebuttal briefs, and then it's giving itself ninety days to issue a decision. It looks like it will be another four months before this thing is resolved. I can't spare you to work on the rebuttal brief; I need you to wrap up the Canyon Killer investigation. I'm turning the rebuttal brief over to Van Cott, J. J. Sullivan, and Tom O'Brien.

"So how is the investigation going?" Fitts asked, seemingly without interest. He sat behind his desk busily massaging his bad knee, the one that had been shot in the war. Cliff wondered whether Fitts would have to go in for another surgery. He couldn't help but admire Fitts despite the case-fixing allegations. They lived in dangerous times, and it was only two years before that Fitts had been wounded in an attempt on his life.

"I have the squad working every day looking for leads and reinterviewing witnesses. There's not much to go on, but we'll keep at it. A little luck wouldn't hurt though."

As Cliff stood up to leave, Fitts said, "Leave the briefcase.

I'll see that O'Brien gets it. Oh, one more thing. Warren is supposed to call. The scuttlebutt is he's not going to wait for the court's decision; he'll try to shut down the gambling ships on a nuisance theory."

"Well, let me know what the plan is. I'd like to be able to contribute." Cliff turned and walked out of the office. Fitts was still massaging his bad knee.

Cliff worked in his office all afternoon. The Scott-Mara investigation was going nowhere and now the Stralla matter was being pulled from him. Fitts was right to give the Stralla matter to the appellate boys, but it still stung a little, and the frustration with the Scott-Mara thing was beginning to eat at him. Mary's appearance at his door interrupted Cliff's mental drift.

"Tommy, there's a Marion Taylor on the line for you. She says it's a personal call. Do you want to take it?"

"Yes, and hold any other calls that come in. Ah, could you close the door, please?" He picked up the receiver, heard clicks on the line, and then heard Marion's voice.

"Your secretary has no idea who I am, does she? Am I your little secret?"

"I don't pour out my life to everyone. She's my secretary; we have a professional relationship."

"You should tell her that. She has a crush on you, you know. A wife can always tell."

"Lucille told me the same thing. So how are you feeling?"

"The doctors tell me that I'm in remission. I feel better. Thank you for getting me in to see Dr. McCarthy. Even my regular oncologist was impressed. That was thoughtful of you, Tommy, but this is something even you can't fix."

"One does what one can."

"Well, I just wanted to call and say thank you. If you'd like to do something for me, why don't you take me out for dinner for my birthday? You and Lucille, of course. It's only four months away.

"It's funny. I've started planning my life around milestones. My next birthday, Christmas—hell, even New Year's. Will I be here for the next one? Sorry. Maudlin, I know.

"How's your mother? I miss the old gal. Do you still keep her under wraps? Chinese nobility and all that?"

"She's fine, soldiering on. I'll let her know that you asked about her. October twenty-fourth, right? Sure, I'd love to take you out. Maybe we'll leave Lucille at home; it'll just be the two of us. You know, if there's anything I can do for you, you just have to ask."

"I know. Thank you, Tommy. October, don't forget. I'll see you then."

"Take care. Good-bye."

At nearly five o'clock, Mary reappeared at the office doorway. "Mr. Thoms, there is a Dorothy Green on the line for you. Shall I take a message, or does she also require your special attention?"

"Mary." He had forgotten how possessive she could be. "I'll take the call."

"No need to ask; I'll close the door."

Cliff's phone clicked several times, and then he heard music in the background. "Dorothy, this is a surprise." The happiness in his voice was unintended. He hadn't realized how much he had been thinking about her. He attempted a more professional demeanor. "What can I do for you?"

"Tommy," Dorothy said brightly, "ah, may I still call you Tommy?"

"Yes, of course."

"Those girls, the ones found dead in the Baldwin Hills, I think I know who they are. I thought I should talk to the police, but my father, well, he never voluntarily talks to the police, and he said that I shouldn't. But this is just so terrible." The strain was audible in her voice. "Perhaps we can get together, and I can tell you what I know. It would have to be private; I wouldn't want it to get back to my father that I met with a deputy DA. We could meet at my friend's apartment in Hollywood. She's away for the evening. Maybe tonight at seven?"

"I understand why you would want to be discreet, but I'm uncomfortable with us being alone at an apartment. I, too, have to worry about people talking."

"Sure. Maybe I'm setting you up. Hidden microphones, hidden cameras, slip you a Mickey, take some embarrassing photographs. Yeah, that's all we mobster molls do. I hope this phone call wasn't too inconvenient. I'll just wait until a couple more girls are dead, and then I'll call back." Dorothy's voice was bitter. She sounded hurt.

"Martyrdom doesn't suit you," Cliff said dryly, checking his anger. "You can worry about appearances, but I can't. Is that it? So let's try it again." *First principle*, Cliff thought. *What's the goal?* "I want your information. I agree that we need to be discreet, but I'm not going to meet you at your friend's apartment. So where are you now?"

"I'm at my dad's club on Wilshire in Santa Monica. The drinks are watered down, but they're free, to me at least."

"We can meet at a client's office near you. The furnishings

are comfortable, and people in the building don't take notice of who comes and goes." Cliff gave her the address, and they agreed to meet at seven o'clock. As soon as they hung up, Cliff called Zoe and asked if he could use her office that evening for a private meeting. She consented and said she would arrange to have the landlord open her office at ten minutes to seven and lock it back up after the meeting was over.

Cliff arrived first. He went through the unlocked door and into the dark office. His attention was drawn to the only source of light in the room: the bar along the rear wall of the office. It was a three-foot-wide, six-foot-tall cabinet in bleached wood with a lower compartment for storage and an upper compartment with shelves to store and display bottles and glasses. The upper compartment had a fold-down, stainless steel shelf for mixing and serving drinks, which Zoe had left open. A small, bare bulb illuminated the compartment, making the red Chinese interior shine like lacquer. The bright red of the interior against the muted white of the exterior was striking. Cliff walked over to the desk at the far end of the room, set his briefcase down, and turned on the desk lamp. He looked without interest at an unfinished astrological chart on the desk; then he went around the room and turned on the lamps on the tables. When the office was fully illuminated, he studied the room for the first time. The furniture was comfortable without being too casual or too formal. The materials were good quality; their designs were modern and sophisticated. There were no traces of the dark, heavy, ornate Victorian style that some people in their fifties still embraced. One particular table lamp caught his attention. Its base was about two feet tall and made of white ceramic strips in an open weave design. The cylindrical shade was made of pleated white satin. The effect was of understated elegance. *Zoe*, Cliff thought, *may be an odd bird, but she does have style.*

Cliff heard a soft knock on the office door. He crossed the room and opened the door about a foot. Dorothy stood in the hallway. Cliff quickly looked beyond her to confirm that she was alone. He saw no one, so he opened the door wide and stepped back. He followed Dorothy with his eyes as she walked by. She was dressed in a bias-cut, ankle-length halter dress that hugged her full, round breasts like a second skin. The gold silk lamé fabric complemented her smooth bronze skin. The effect was stunning. Cliff continued to watch in silence as Dorothy walked over to the couch and sat down. She looked over at Cliff and cocked her head and then crossed her legs as she smiled seductively. Cliff felt his face flush but managed to ask with a steady voice, "Can I get you something?"

"Oh, there's a bar here? Sure, an imperial, if you have the maraschino liqueur and bitters. Otherwise, a martini."

"I'll see what there is." Cliff walked over to the open bar and found gin, vermouth, and a bottle of maraschino cherries. "I don't see any bitters," he said, kneeling on one knee and searching through the lower compartment.

"A martini would be lovely."

Cliff mixed the cocktail and poured himself a finger of bourbon. He turned around with a drink in each hand and froze. Dorothy had untied the halter strap; the top of her dress lay in her lap. Her bare breasts were beautiful. Their ivory color contrasted with the bronze of her shoulders. Cliff's eyes flicked up to Dorothy's face. She was looking at him as if gauging his reaction. "We can't do this," Cliff said hoarsely. "I came here to talk."

"Tommy." Her voice was a plaintive murmur. "Don't you want me?"

"I'm married. I have responsibilities. Fix your dress." Cliff watched as Dorothy pulled up her dress and tied the halter strap. Then he walked over and handed her the martini. "Did you really know those dead girls, or do you just find broken-down old lawyers irresistible?"

"Only the married ones." Was that anger, sorrow, disappointment, or embarrassment in her eyes? Cliff couldn't read her at all. "I'm sorry. I shouldn't joke. Yes, I knew those girls. We would meet at the track and then go to bars afterward. The first time wasn't planned. We were all between boyfriends. We each showed up at Santa Anita without a chaperone. We stuck out like sore thumbs. Young women alone and unescorted at a racetrack. But then we ran into each other and just started palling around together. When the season ended at Santa Anita, we started meeting at Hollywood Park. After the races, we would go out together to the local bars. Naturally, men would try to pick us up."

"And?"

"Well, you know the joke. Sometimes you go out, go home, and go to bed. Sometimes you go out, go to bed, and then go home." Cliff detected a slight blush to Dorothy's cheeks. "A girl's not young forever. Got to have a little fun."

"But then your friends disappeared."

"It wasn't like that. Sometimes we'd meet; sometimes we wouldn't. Sometimes one of us would leave with a guy; most times we wouldn't. After a while Helen just stopped showing up. She didn't have a phone, so we couldn't call her. Virginia and I figured that she found a man who was taking care of her and we'd hear from her sooner or later. Then Virginia stopped showing up. Well, you don't think some crazy bastard has killed them both and dumped their bodies in the hills. You think maybe they found someone handsome and rich. Maybe the next time I hear from them is when they send me a wedding invitation. I don't know what I thought. Hell, if I always thought things through, would I have a five-year-old? But there was this one guy—six foot tall, blond—who scared me. He made like he was some rich boy. Always flashing money, saying how he won big at the track."

Dorothy considered her drink. She took a sip and then another. Cliff waited, letting the silence build its own pressure. "He was a mobster. I can smell them a mile away. From New York, but not Brooklyn like my dad or"—Dorothy gave a quick, small smile—"like you. Yeah, I can still hear it in your voice even though you try to hide it. No, this guy—he called himself Vincent—hell, he didn't even know how to spell Vincent. He carried a gun in a shoulder holster. I'm pretty sure he had a knife too."

Dorothy stopped again. Cliff sensed there was more, something that she wanted to add but didn't. She finished her drink in one gulp. "He couldn't get the rich-boy act right. He'd look at you the wrong way. Cold. Not like he wanted sex. More like he wanted to"—Dorothy paused and stared at her empty glass—"like he wanted to hurt you. It was creepy." Dorothy looked at Cliff with an earnestness she'd never displayed before.

They spent the next twenty minutes nailing down dates and times. Cliff had Dorothy tell him everything she knew or had observed about the two girls and the blond man, no matter how insignificant. He took notes on a legal pad. The details were a jumble. Maybe the detectives assigned to the case could make something out of them. When they were done,

Dorothy raised her arms above her head, took a deep breath, and stretched. Cliff wondered whether the halter top would hold. Maybe, he hoped, it wouldn't, but he suppressed those thoughts. "It's getting late. I have to go."

"Home to your wife?"

"Yes, home to my wife."

"One of these days I'll have to meet this lady. I picture her looking like a movie star. Am I going to be disappointed, Tommy? Is she five feet tall, two hundred pounds, with a light mustache?"

"No, no, she really does look like a movie star. And more. She has grace, charm, and intelligence. I'm a lucky man."

"You're not going to tell her about the dress thing, are you? I don't want to get you in trouble."

"I think I'll leave that part out. She'll wonder where you got that dress, and I don't think I can afford it on my salary."

CHAPTER 9

Richard walked out on the deck of the *Rex*. He was glad to get out of the din and glare of the casino, happy to have a break from dealing. It was Wednesday night, and his week was half over. He looked toward the mainland and the lights of Santa Monica. Moonlight illuminated the beach and the bluffs. He took out a cigarette, cupped it in his hands, and tried to light a match. A breeze from the east blew just hard enough to make the flame dance and die. On his second try, he succeeded in lighting his cigarette and inhaled deeply. Leaning over the rail at the stern of the gently rocking ship, he saw an approaching water taxi rising and falling on the ocean swells. From his vantage point on the fantail, Richard could see the excitement written on the faces of the taxi passengers as they drew close. There was jubilance in the air; the players were ready for fun. His break almost over, Richard flicked his glowing cigarette butt into the ocean and took one last look at the luminous white bluffs before returning to finish his stint at the blackjack table. Just as he was turning around, his stepfather joined him on the deck.

"Marie called to say that she and her sister are going to Los

Angeles tonight to a lecture by Manly P. Hall," Clarence said. "She left the kids with Bobby and Margie."

Richard acknowledged the information with a nod. "What's the topic?"

"Hall's going to discuss his book, *The Secret Teachings of All Ages*."

"Sounds like a barn burner."

"Yeah, that's what I thought." Clarence reached out and cradled Richard's elbow. "Ah, your mother is going to be there with some clients."

"Oh. Well, maybe they won't run into each other. How is it possible," Richard began with a shake of his head, "that they both like Manly P. Hall and are interested in the occult but are so different in so many ways?"

"I don't know, but Mama Lou is at the house, and your mother gave her an earful of Marie's many faults. To hear her tell it, you married a witch who gets messages from songs on the radio."

"She does, actually," Richard admitted, "but Marie doesn't see that as much different from Mom getting messages from her horoscopes. In fact, she says she knew to vote for Roosevelt in thirty-two from the messages she got from popular songs."

"Oh, Lord, spare us," Clarence said wearily.

"Zoe, dear, you really look dandy in that black silk dress. Silk is so slimming." Mama Lou was truly proud of her daughter. She was proud of her looks and her ambition. Her eyes lit up with pleasure as she watched her daughter dress for some engagement. "Where are you going tonight?"

"I'm going to take the Caddy and pick up some important

clients. We're going downtown to the Wiltern Theater to hear Manly P. Hall." Zoe was excited to be going to such a stimulating event and to be able to bring along her clients. She loved to dress the part of a celebrity. Her hair was blonde, and when she dressed in black, she was a stunning woman.

"Do you think Marie would go to the same lecture?" Mama Lou asked, suddenly alarmed.

"I hardly think so. The tickets are two dollars. And Richard has the car. What do you think of this small hat with a net veil? Is it too much?" Zoe asked. She turned gracefully like a model showing off her beautiful clothes.

"No, it's perfect. Now if that daughter-in-law of yours shows up, don't go anywhere near her. She'll spoil everything. She has so little style; it's as if style was left out of her basic makeup." Mama Lou frowned imagining the encounter.

"You know what's strange about her?" Zoe offered. "She was raised partly by her rich grandparents. She lived on an orange ranch in Whittier and had all of the newest amenities. But she doesn't care anything about wealth or riches; she just wants to have a good time. Never did see the beat of that woman." Zoe averted her face as if repulsed by a foul odor. She lovingly put on a string of pearls and attached a pair of pearl-and-diamond earrings. Again she gazed into the mirror and did another model stance.

"I wouldn't put anything past Marie. If she wants to go, she'll find a way. You and she are the same in that regard. You both go after the things you want." Mama Lou gave a little grunt. She was happy to stay home and read the Bible. She could quote from any book of the Bible and give chapter and verse. "What is he going to talk about tonight, besides mysticism?"

"The subject tonight is astrotheology. I'm eager to hear what Hall has to say. He may give me some insights into my work.

There aren't many practitioners of astrology. It takes so much knowledge to set up a horoscope. I revel in the challenge. I love to be able to say, 'Your moon is in the seventh house, and Uranus is on the cusp.'" Zoe pronounced the planet's name "yur-a-nus." She took one last look at herself in the mirror. As she took on the mantle of a seer, she drew herself up to her full height, threw back her shoulders, and prepared herself for her audience. She kissed her mother on the cheek and strode out the door and down the alley to her car.

Zoe drove to the Santa Monica home of Warren and Margaret McClaine. Both were little known to the public, but Warren was a successful financier who had produced a string of acclaimed films. His wife, under a stage name, was a movie star from the silent era. Zoe felt privileged to have them as clients. As she drove them to the lecture, they chatted about the scholarly pursuits of religion, mythology, mysticism, and the occult they expected to be exposed to this night.

They drove east on Wilshire Boulevard past the La Brea Tar Pits and continued on to Western. The Wiltern Theater was on the corner of Wilshire and Western. All three of them watched as they approached the enormous building, its tower looming over the intersection. The theater, an Art Deco landmark, seated over two thousand patrons. Zoe entered an adjacent lot where a valet drove the Caddy off to be parked.

As they approached the entrance to the theater, Margaret asked, "Zoe, who is that strange young lady getting off the streetcar and waving at you? She seems to know you."

Zoe took on a red hue when she saw Marie and Angela, Marie's younger sister, descend from the Red Car. Marie was dressed in a pair of slacks and a blue cotton blouse. Zoe was mortified. Angela, in a resounding voice, said, "Hi, Zoe, cast any horoscopes today? Hey, is fortune-telling still against the law in California?" Marie smiled at the McClaines and strolled toward the theater. She could see the anger rising in her mother-in-law's face. Zoe's blue eyes narrowed, and she pursed her lips.

Zoe, ignoring the younger sister, faced Marie and cooed, "How charming. I see you dressed up for the occasion." She then gave a shake of her head and strutted off like a movie star.

They all entered the magnificent foyer of the theater. The lights and decor were exquisite. The entire interior was magnificently appointed. It was a perfect setting for an adventure in the occult, mysticism, and the influence of the stars. As Marie took her seat in the balcony with her sister, she considered her actions. *Negative energy feeds destructive karma.* Where had she read that? She couldn't remember, but she knew the truth of it. She decided that for the sake of her husband and her children, herself, and even Zoe, she must let go of her dislike for the woman. That decided, she engaged completely in the lecture.

Zoe sat with her guests in the loge, shining in the light. She knew that in this auditorium she was well known and respected. Still, the encounter with Marie troubled her. She resolved, for the sake of her son Richard and her grandchildren, not to be drawn down to her daughter-in-law's level but rather to be magnanimous and civil to Marie.

CHAPTER 10

Thursday, June 8, 1939

Lou arrived at the squad room early. Barnes's revelation from the night before left the detective feeling anxious and pressed for time. Lou had wanted to go directly to Dorothy's house Wednesday night and arrest her, but Randy had talked him out of it. Randy was right; they had to build the case properly. Her father could afford the best defense lawyers, who would demolish a hastily assembled case. Dorothy had to be interviewed, and whatever alibi she offered had to be investigated. The Malibu beach house had to located and searched. Ownership of the Bugatti had to be determined.

A call to the county assessor's office quickly established that the Green family owned a home in Malibu and its address. It was the logical place for the murder, but Lou needed evidence to support a search warrant. He knew that his theory about the case had several weaknesses. They were assuming that Barnes was telling the truth when he said that Dorothy owned a dark-colored Bugatti 57SC and that she kept it at her beach house. They were also assuming that there were only two such Bugattis.

Lou formulated his plan of action for the day. As soon as Randy came in, they would go to the Greens' house and interview Dorothy. While he waited for Randy, Lou would start drafting the application for a search warrant, even if the application had to be vague in certain respects. A friendly judge might overlook a few flaws considering this was a murder case and the house was a vacation home, not a full-time residence. Lou would have a secretary call the local Bugatti dealer and double-check whether any dark-colored Bugatti 57SC had been sold recently. Finally, Lou would review his notes from Tuesday. They still hadn't caught up with Ricardo Stralla from the *Rex*. He'd have a secretary call and find out if tender Ricardo ever recovered from his fainting spell on Monday.

When Randy arrived, Lou filled him in on the plan for the day and allowed him to finish a cup of coffee. Together they drove to the Green residence. There was a delay at the gate while the guard received permission to let them pass. Once at the house, they were met at the front door by Lenny Green himself. He explained in no uncertain terms that the detectives could not interview his daughter and that they must speak only with his attorney, Robert Willows. He then made some suggestions about their family relations and ordered them off his property. As he was walking back to the car, Lou was tempted to explain to Green that neither he nor Randy could have sex with their mothers since both had passed on, but he assumed Green's point was rhetorical.

Once back at the station, Lou finished the search warrant application. Randy said he had had a difficult night, hadn't eaten breakfast, and was going to take an early lunch. Lou was eager to obtain the search warrant and wanted to hand carry the application to a judge before the court broke for lunch. They agreed to meet back at the office after Randy returned from lunch and go together to search the Malibu house.

Lou fully expected the judge to issue a search warrant for the house. The application was reasonably complete. It included a confirmation from the county assessor that the Green family owned a Malibu house; a confidential informant's statement that Dorothy Green had access to one of very few dark-colored Bugatti 57SCs in LA and that she kept the vehicle at the Malibu house; and finally, witnesses' statements that Roberts was picked up in a dark-colored Bugatti and was later found dead in the Santa Monica Bay. The judge, however, saw things quite differently. He raised issues of jurisdiction and legal sufficiency based on the lack of disclosure as to the background of the witnesses and their reliability. The judge specifically requested that the confidential informant be identified and that Lou produce his testimony in the form of an affidavit signed under penalty of perjury. Lou knew that A. J. Barnes wanted to keep his name out of this matter and would never voluntarily produce an affidavit. As Lou left the courthouse, he began to wonder if the judge was in some gangster's pocket. If so, he would have to act quickly to look around the Malibu house before Lenny Green got wind of the search warrant application and cleared away any evidence.

Lou stopped at a market and used a phone booth to call his office. Randy wasn't back from lunch. This was a pattern from the old days when Randy was on the sauce. Lou couldn't wait and drove directly to the Malibu home. The house was off a dirt road that followed along a finger of land thrust into the Pacific Ocean. As Lou bounced along the road, he could see the house at the tip of the finger. While still one hundred yards away, he pulled his car into a small clearing in the chaparral. Lou approached the house on foot, looking and listening for signs of occupation. As he drew near, he saw that the house was built on a bluff overlooking a cove. The house, which looked to be one story from the road, had a second level reaching down toward the water that gave access to the sea. It was a home built for smuggling. During prohibition a motor launch could bring in cases of whiskey to be off-loaded directly into the home. With the right kind of bribes, a man such as Lefty Green could build himself a profitable business.

Lou picked his way down the bluff until he was below the second level. Climbing over supporting braces that held up the part of the house that extended over the water, he made his way under the house and found an access door. The door, which was unlocked, swung up and into the house. Lou was able to scramble through the trap door and into the house's lower floor. Once inside, Lou allowed his eyes to adjust to the darkness. The bottom level hung over the water six feet or so and extended for some distance into the hillside where it ended in shadow. From what little light came through the trap door, Lou could see along the wall to his left a wooden staircase to the top floor. He climbed the staircase and found a light switch at the top. After turning on the lights, he examined the room. It was eighteen feet long by about fifteen feet wide. The floor over the water was wood, but the portion of the room cut into the hillside had a concrete floor. Near the center of the concrete floor was a large, rust-brown stain. Stretching out from the stain were brown streaks leading to the trap door. Lou knew that the sound of three gunshots would be lost in the crashing of the waves. It would have been simple to lure Daniel Roberts to this place, shoot him, drag his body to the trap door, and then lower it into a waiting powerboat. The *how* was easy; now Lou wanted to understand the *why*.

He descended the steps and squatted beside the brown stain. He was studying the spots where it appeared two bullets had impacted the concrete when he heard a car drive up and four car doors slam shut. A few seconds later Lou heard the front door open and three sets of footsteps walking on the floor above him. Quietly he made his way up the steps and listened at the door to the top floor. Through the trap door he heard rocks tumbling down the bluff and splashing into the sea.

After an instant of indecision, Lou prepared to move, silently mouthing the words, "Saint Michael the Archangel, defend us in battle; be our protection ... be our protection." Then he stepped through the door and flashed his badge at the three men at the far end of the living room. Two of the men sat at the built-in bar while a third stood behind the bar with a bottle in his hand. Lou recognized one of the seated men as Lefty Green. "I'm conducting a search of this house. If you men interfere, you'll be subject to arrest."

"Shut up, copper," Lefty said as if he were talking to an incompetent employee. "You don't got a warrant. You got nothing." Lefty slapped the shoulder of the man seated beside him and said, "Buddy, work him over."

Buddy stood up and put his glass down on the bar. He was big, heavyset, and a good six inches taller than Lou. The bodyguard's face was flushed, and his nose had that swollen, red-veined look of a habitual drinker. Lou looked him up and down. It was no use running back down the stairs and trying to get out the trap door. There was a man waiting for him on the bluff. Buddy was big, but he looked unsteady on his feet as he walked over to Lou. If Buddy was even a little drunk, Lou knew he had a chance. He watched the thug's hands but didn't see a weapon. Buddy balled his right hand up into a fist and drew his arm back. Lou thought, *Haymaker.* The looping punch came at medium speed toward the detective's head. Lou did a bob and weave under the punch and stepped to his left. Buddy had lunged forward with the punch, and the men's bodies were almost touching. Lou reached up with both arms; his right hand hooked behind Buddy's neck and his left hand grabbed a handful of coat. He pulled the bigger man toward him and drove his right knee under Buddy's rib cage and into his kidney. Buddy let out a guttural sound, pulled away, and turned to his left. Lou hopped back on his right foot and, with his left leg, kicked out the big man's right leg. Buddy fell backward to the floor in a heap. Lou thrust his right heel into the side of the fallen man's head for good measure. Buddy was down and dazed but not out. Lou pulled his .45 out of its holster before Lefty and his bodyguard could recover from their surprise. The men stood with their drinks in their hands and looked at Lou without a trace of fear. He kept his eyes on them as he slowly backed out through the front door.

Once outside, Lou turned and ran, keeping low. He squinted against the bright sunlight, felt sweat run down his ribs, and heard the crunch of gravel beneath his feet. Lou was a little surprised to hear no gunshots or sounds of anyone following him. Rounding a bend in the road, he glanced over his shoulder to see if Buddy or the other bodyguards were in pursuit. Before passing behind a clump of bushes, he caught a glimpse of the third bodyguard, who had climbed up the bluff and was bent over with his hands on his knees, catching his breath and looking red-faced at Lou.

Driving back to the station, Lou decided not to tell Randy about the search of the house. Green had a stable of attorneys who could make trouble for Lou over the illegal search. If Randy wasn't informed about the search, he could honestly swear he didn't know and might be spared the worst of any consequences. As he drove, Lou was nagged by the thought that the situation wasn't right. They let him go too easily. Why didn't they kill him since he had just found evidence of their complicity in a murder? They were drinking at the bar and didn't pull their guns—it was like they didn't care about what he had found. Why was there evidence to find in the first place? Lenny Green was known to use murder only as a last resort; surely he'd clean up after himself if he had someone killed. Maybe Green didn't know about the murder at his house. Did Dorothy act alone? Did someone else use the house to commit the murder and throw suspicion onto Green? Lou knew how easily he got in; anyone in reasonably good shape could have gotten in through the trap door and then unlocked the front door. *Okay, someone else could be behind the murder, but then how do you explain the Bugatti?* Sitting in traffic, Lou reconsidered. *Maybe Green is behind the murder and is just sloppy. Maybe he is a murderer but a good father. He could have used a disposable woman as bait and sent his daughter away to Mexico to keep her from being involved. Claiming Dorothy was kidnapped would get the Chinaman involved, and that would only strengthen the daughter's alibi.* Pulling into the parking lot at the station, Lou was despondent. New evidence is supposed to help narrow down the possibilities; however, not only didn't the new evidence help, but Green's men were also busy eradicating every trace of the shooting. Green was right, Lou realized: he had nothing.

Cliff spent most of the afternoon reviewing his interview notes and taking out all references to information that could be traced back to Dorothy. She was now a confidential informant, and he didn't want to jeopardize her safety. When he was done, he turned his revised notes over to Bill Wright and Ray Sanchez, the detectives of team two. Armed with the names and descriptions of Helen, Virginia, and Vincent, they made fast progress. At a restaurant called the Red Onion on Manchester Avenue, just north of the Hollywood Park racetrack, one of the waitresses remembered that Vincent came into the restaurant a couple of times and was odd enough to stand out.

"What was unusual about him?" Detective Wright asked.

The waitress said, "There was just something about him. He looked like he was mad at the world. A trouble maker."

"Height, build, age, hair color—whatever you can remember," Detective Sanchez said while taking notes.

"He was kind of tall, maybe six feet. Early or middle thirties. Medium build. And his hair—it was blond, might have been a wig. Maybe he was bald. His hair didn't quite fit his face."

"Why didn't you tell us any of this last week when we were in here?"

"You were asking about a different guy, weren't you? Am I supposed to tell you about every wacko who comes in? That drawing you showed me last time, well, it looked like some dago. Naw, this Vincent was white, maybe with a tan. He sounded like he was from the East Coast. Maybe Jersey or New York City. And another thing—he kept flashing money when he was paying for his drinks. He said he made a killing at the racetrack. Not that he left any for me." The waitress waved at a table to let the customers know she'd be right there.

"If he comes in here again, please call me. We want to talk to him," Wright said.

"He hasn't been in for a couple of weeks. Maybe he got tired of women telling him to get lost," the waitress said with relish. She was amused by the bully's failure and humiliation.

The detectives thanked her for her help and went to talk to the bartender.

"When we talked last week, you said it would help if we had the names of the girls who were missing," Sanchez said. He told the bartender about Helen, Virginia, and Vincent.

"Yeah, Vincent. I remember him. He was in here a couple of times. I'm pretty sure he left with that Virginia gal a couple of weeks ago. She hasn't been in since then. But I can't be sure." The bartender stopped mixing a drink and looked up at Sanchez. "Was she one of the girls who were found?"

"Yeah."

The bartender dropped his head and began to wash glasses. "There was something strange about him. He scared off some of the customers. He almost got in a fight a couple of times. If we wanted to get rid of him, I had the bouncers stand behind him. Just stand there. Didn't touch him, didn't say a word. He hated that. That would get him to leave.

"He was a blowhard," the bartender said without looking up. He continued to wash and dry the glasses. "He talked big about winning at the track and flashed money, but he didn't tip very well. 'Mr. Charm,' we called him. A couple of times he tried to pick up several girls, but they all gave him the cold shoulder. When this pretty blonde brushed him off, he got real mad. He looked like he wanted to punch somebody."

"Have you seen any of those girls back at the bar?" Sanchez asked.

"Most of the girls here are locals. They live in the neighborhood and come in regularly. But the girl who got his dander up hasn't been back. Ellen or Helen, or something. We thought she went to see relatives in Missouri," the bartender mused as he poured a shot of tequila and put a piece of lime on the side. He caught the waitress's eye to have it delivered to a table.

"Can either of you give us the names of some of the girls who Vincent might have talked to?" Sanchez asked as the waitress joined the detectives and the bartender at the bar. Both investigators wrote in little notebooks as the waitress and bartender recalled the names of some of the regulars.

"Billy, what about Sam?" the waitress asked the bartender.

"Who knows? Maybe they just went for a spin," Billy said, shrugging his shoulders.

"Who's Sam?" Sanchez asked.

"Sam is a creep who comes in sometimes. He's a dope peddler. I heard him tell Vincent that they could take a ride in his Cadillac. Billy heard it too." The waitress shot a look at the bartender.

"So does this Sam have a Cadillac, or does he sell Cadillacs?" Detective Wright asked.

"Sam drives a Ford." Billy's voice was barely above a whisper.

"Are we talking heroin or cocaine?" Wright asked.

"I don't know," Billy said angrily.

The waitress looked at Billy and shook her head. She looked at Sanchez and said, "Sam sells both, but he's his own best customer for heroin. I think Vincent likes his candy. He'd go into the john and powder his nose. He'd come out and, you know, feel like a tough guy and want to start a fight."

"Have you see Sam lately?" Sanchez asked.

Billy and the waitress looked at each other but remained silent.

"Well?" Sanchez demanded impatiently.

"Sam comes in on Fridays. About six. People cash their

work checks and come in loaded with dough and, you know, talk to Sam," the waitress volunteered.

"We never see Sam sell anything," Billy hastily added.

"No, of course not. You're busy washing glasses. Look," Sanchez addressed Billy, "we want to talk to Sam. If he's not here tomorrow, I'll figure you told him to stay away. That would be bad for you, Billy. Maybe I take you in and we have a long talk. Or maybe the state liquor people close this bar when they find out drugs are sold here." Sanchez heard Billy catch his breath at the prospect. "A law-abiding boss would just fire you. A mobbed-up boss, well, I think you know what would happen."

"He'll be here," Billy said in a small voice.

"If that Vincent guy comes in," Sanchez said, handing Billy and the waitress each a business card, "let us know. In any case, we'll be back tomorrow."

At two more bars that Dorothy suggested, the officers got the same story about Vincent flashing money, trying to pick up blondes, and making a pest of himself. As the detectives returned to Cliff's downtown office, they were aware that their interviews had verified most things Dorothy had said and had given them a new list of people to interview. More importantly, it had produced two new leads: Vincent had a drug contact who could be exploited, and he perhaps was bald and wearing a blond wig.

Wright and Sanchez found Cliff still working in his office although everyone else had left. They gave Cliff a summary of what they had heard, explained that a *Cadillac* was a one-ounce packet of cocaine or heroin, and recommended that he follow up on the New York gangster angle. Cliff made a note to contact the LAPD and LA County sheriff's intelligence divisions to learn what information they had on transplanted New York mobsters. He also told Wright and Sanchez not to wait for Friday. He instructed them to track down Sam immediately. They could contact the boys of the narcotics squad for leads.

After Wright and Sanchez left, Cliff called A. J. Barnes at home. "A. J., let me ask you something. You've dealt with the Syndicate boys from all over—New York, Chicago, Detroit— have you ever heard of a killer who strings his victims up and cuts them with a knife?"

Barnes leaned back in the chair in his den and took a couple of puffs on a cigar. "No, can't say that I have. Is this about that Canyon Killer case?"

"Yes. Fitts has put me in charge of a team, the Scott squad, to find the killer or killers. It looks like there may be two fellows working together. One, about six feet tall, and the other is average height or a little shorter. The short man has dark hair and may be Italian, and the other is possibly blond, or bald, and wears a blond wig. These men, they're ... they're sick bastards. They cut up their victims, torture them really. We think that the tall one is from back east and was a member of a gang. I'd appreciate it if you asked your contacts in New York if they've heard about a killer with the same MO."

"Of course. I'd be happy to help. Ah, Cliff," Barnes said as if struck by an idea, "is there much evidence at the crime scenes?"

"No, not really."

"So these guys could be long-time criminals and are careful about leaving evidence."

"Yes."

"There is another possibility." Barnes flicked cigar ash at a distant ashtray.

"What's that?"

"Ah, how certain are you about the heights of the suspects?"

"Well, fairly certain," Cliff said, wondering where A. J. was going.

"Could it be that the suspects are six foot two and five foot six inches?"

"I suppose it's possible."

"Have you considered the possibility that we're not dealing with regular criminals but with police officers?" Barnes listened for Cliff's reaction. "I mean, wouldn't that explain the lack of evidence at the crime scene? And how could untrained individuals evade police detection for months while leaving bodies around?"

"Did you have someone in mind, A. J.?"

"Do we know any Mutt and Jeff police duos, one of whom is a hot-blooded Latino?"

"Oh, you can't be serious! Yeah, maybe they aren't as pure as the driven snow, but it's a long way from shaking down grifters to butchering coeds and housewives. I ... I ... I can't believe it." Cliff denied the possibility even as he recalled Williams's bald head and Gomez's temper.

"Just something for you to keep in mind. The facts, as far as they are known, support this hypothesis. Of course, once they get wind of this suggestion, they will no doubt try to discredit me. In any event, I will talk with my contacts in New York and elsewhere about a ... what did you call him? ... a butcher.

"Ah, Cliff, I almost forgot. Will you be working on the rebuttal brief for the Supreme Court?"

"No, that was assigned to Van Cott, Sullivan, and O'Brien. How about you?"

"No, thank God. It's going out to our appellate attorneys. So

Warren will sit tight and wait on the court's decision?" Barnes had set down his cigar and was preparing to take notes.

"Hardly. Why wait for the courts when you can take matters into your own hands? He's bringing a nuisance action."

"I can just see the complaint now: 'dens of iniquity, families reduced to poverty, wailing and gnashing of teeth.' Self-righteous prig," Barnes said bitterly. "What's a nuisance action going to accomplish?"

"Well, if Tony fails to comply, I guess the state will have grounds to raid the ships and seize all the equipment."

"Maybe so," Barnes said as he jotted down notes. "Luckily it's not my problem anymore."

Cliff's telephone rang as soon as he hung up after talking with Barnes.

"Tommy?"

Cliff didn't recognize the voice—a young woman, not scared exactly, but rushed and breathless. "Yes?"

"Tommy, a couple of detectives from Santa Monica were here looking for me. They say I was involved in a murder. Someone named Daniel Roberts. I've never heard of the guy. My dad said you could get them to back off."

Dorothy. Why didn't she call her dad's attorney, Robbie Willows? Santa Monica detectives—Williams and Gomez? "Dorothy, who were the detectives? Did you talk to them?"

"Oh no. My dad told them to ... well, he said they would have to talk to my attorney, and then he sent them away. The short one is named Gomez. Dad says you know him. I didn't get the tall one's name."

So Lefty knows about the thing in San Pedro—just the

beating or the frame-up too? Cliff realized he was vulnerable to blackmail. "Dorothy, I don't know if I can represent you in an official capacity. Perhaps in an informal or unofficial capacity."

"Dad says ... I think he likes you, Tommy. Not as much as I like you, but he was impressed that you found me at the airport on Sunday when his own people didn't. He'd never tell you that himself. He said you might be reluctant to represent me. He wants you to know that he'd consider it a personal favor if you helped me out with the detectives. Will you?"

"Yes. I'll call them tomorrow morning. Gomez and I have an understanding. We can—"

Dorothy's laughter cut Cliff off. "That's not the way I hear it. Daddy said that you had Gomez beaten up. He said it took big brass ones to do that to a cop. He said he doesn't know what you have on Gomez but wants you to 'twist the knife.' I haven't heard Daddy laugh that hard since the *Excalibur* sank."

Cliff recalled that the *Excalibur* was a gambling ship that burned and sank two years before. Arson was suspected. Lefty had quite a sense of humor. "You can't believe everything you hear. I'll talk to Gomez tomorrow. Ah, did you get a look at the tall detective?"

"I saw him but not up close. I was upstairs with Carlota. I saw them walk up to the door and watched them leave."

"Someone said that the tall detective looks like Vincent. Is that true?"

"Oh, hell no!" Dorothy laughed. "Vincent is not as tall and is about fifteen years younger. No, two different guys. Whoever told you they look alike is all wet."

"I suspected as much."

CHAPTER 11

Friday, June 9, 1939

C liff had Mary call the Santa Monica Police Department to set up a meeting with Gomez and Williams. The call was put through to Lou.

"What the hell does the Chinaman want now? Cornero have another chore for his boy?"

"Mr. Thoms is assisting Dorothy Green—in an unofficial capacity, of course. He wanted to meet with you before you interview her. He is free this morning before lunch. Would it be convenient for you and Mr. Williams to come here at ten?" Cliff stood at Mary's desk as she held the receiver away from her ear so Cliff could listen to the reply.

"You tell that chink bastard we'll meet him at ten, but it has to be here in the squad room."

Mary's face flushed red, but Cliff merely nodded his agreement. "I'll let Mr. Thoms know that you prefer to meet at your, ah, squad room. Ten o'clock, then."

A few minutes later, Detectives Wright and Sanchez came to the office. Mary sent them straight in to Cliff.

"We got him," Wright said triumphantly, "we got the little dope-peddling bastard."

"Good, good. Tell me what happened." Cliff smiled and nodded; it was the first time he'd sensed that the squad was making progress.

Sanchez sat on the edge of one of the leather-seated chairs facing Cliff's desk while Wright stood, too restless to sit. "We tracked Sammy boy down to his cave about seven this morning. He had just settled down for the night, just him and his favorite syringe." Sanchez looked back over his shoulder and caught Wright's eye. Sanchez gave a small smile; Wright nodded in response. "He's being processed now. He's still doped up but coherent. We caught him with five Cadillacs of H and six of candy. If you had something in mind, he'll play ball with us. Tonight's his night for doing business at the Red Onion. The candy store opens at six."

"Can he contact Vincent?"

"Yeah. I, ah, had a little talk with him on the way back. He can get hold of Vinny, but not directly. He says they have a mutual friend. He won't say who. I can work on him some more," Sanchez said, glancing at the knuckles of his right hand, "but he's still feeling no pain. I might have slapped him around a little in the car, but he just smiled at me. He'll feel it in a few hours, the little shit."

"Keep him on ice. Don't put him in the general population. I don't want anyone to know we have him."

"Got ya."

When Cliff arrived at the Santa Monica Police Station, he stopped in to pay his respects to the captain. His arrival caused a stir at the station. The other officers had heard rumors—in some Cliff was the hero who went to bat for Lou; in others he was the villain who, through some devious machinations, had almost brought Lou to ruins. While Cliff was in the captain's office behind a closed door, Fred Tsheppe walked into the squad room. He stopped, looked around until he spotted Lou, and then walked up to Lou's desk.

"Detective Gomez, *¿Cómo está usted?*" Fred said, extending his hand.

Lou stood up and shook hands with Fred. "*Estoy bien.* I wanted to thank you for your help. We were able to identify the decedent."

"Good, good. Glad I was able to help. I was at the Santa Monica courthouse on a parole violation hearing and thought I would drop over to see how things are going, Detective."

"We are pretty informal around here. Why don't you call me 'Lou'?"

"Sure. And I'm 'Fred.' This must be your partner." Fred reached out his hand to Randy.

Randy slowly rose from his chair and shook Fred's hand. "Randy Williams."

"Fred Tsheppe. So I understand that you were in the army. My father was in the army and served under Teddy Roosevelt in the Spanish-American War. We still have a letter from Roosevelt thanking my mother. We're proud of our service to this country."

"No one from the old country who fought for the Kaiser?" Randy asked. His voice was cold.

"Oh no. My family has been in this country for fifty years. We lost touch with any family in Europe decades ago." Fred watched as Randy sat down again. He sensed that he hadn't

THE TRUTH WON'T HELP THEM NOW

won Randy over, but he hoped that he had stifled any hostility. "So," Fred said, turning to Lou, "any progress on the case?"

"Yeah. The victim worked on the *Rex*. His boss in the counting room was able to help us identify the car that the vic drove off in. We're tracing the car down and have a possible lead on the driver."

"The boss of the counting room ... that wouldn't be Clarence Woolfolk by any chance?"

"Yeah. How did you know?"

"He's my brother-in-law's stepfather. My brother-in-law is Rich Woolfolk. He's married to my sister, Marie."

"Yeah. We interviewed them. They have a kid."

"Actually they have two. Joanie is three and baby Caroline is four months old. Ah, yes. Rich said he was interviewed. I didn't put the two together, the Shell Q guy and Danny's death. Rich took Danny's death hard. I gather he had been drinking before you met him."

"He wasn't potted, but you could tell he had an edge." Lou tried to conceal his disgust.

"You know, Marie said something interesting about you two, you and Randy. I didn't know you two were the detectives on the case at the time."

"Yeah? It didn't seem like she was paying much attention to us. What did she say?"

"Well, you have to understand a few things. Have you spoken with Rich's mother yet?"

"We had the pleasure of making her acquaintance," Lou said, glancing over at Randy.

"In some ways Marie and Zoe are alike; both claim to have psychic powers, and they share some, ah, occult beliefs." Fred noted Lou's expression of skepticism. "I can understand why you don't believe them. I don't believe everything they say, but sometimes, sometimes, they are able to know things that they couldn't possibly know in any ordinary fashion. It pays to listen to what they have to say—taking it with a grain of salt—and keep an open mind. You might be surprised at what you could learn.

"Why don't you, and of course Randy, let me drive you over to Rich's house tonight and just listen to what Marie has to say. I think you'll find it worthwhile."

"Six o'clock?" Lou asked. "Randy, why don't you come along? Just for laughs."

"Nah, I have a date with a bottle of bourbon. I can't stand her up."

"Six o'clock is good," Fred said, smiling broadly. "I'll let Marie know I'll be bringing you by."

"Fred, stick around. Here is someone you should meet," Lou said as he watched Cliff walk up. "Well, well, Counselor, glad to see you made it. I understand that I have you to thank for keeping my job." Lou felt the bile rise up in this throat. He fought the impulse to spit.

"I do what I can. I wouldn't want to see your family hurt— your wife, your children, or," Cliff dropped his voice, "your niece."

Lou kept his eyes on Cliff even as he gestured toward Fred. "Deputy District Attorney Thoms, I'd like to introduce you to Fred Tsheppe. Fred, this is Deputy DA Thoms." Lou was aware of the tape on his nose and the pain in his ribs every time he inhaled. "Fred is a probation officer in the LA office."

"Counselor," Fred said, offering his hand to Cliff.

"Tsheppe? That's German, isn't it?" Cliff said, shaking hands.

"Yes. My family came over in the 1880s. And Thoms? I'm not familiar with the origins of that name." Fred looked intently at

Cliff's face. *Eurasian,* he thought. *Perhaps Siberian, but the accent was wrong. This man sounded like he was from New York, possibly Brooklyn.*

"It's an old English name derived from Thomas. My family, my father's family, is English. My mother, as you may have guessed, is Chinese."

"Family! Isn't it wonderful," Lou said with mock gaiety. He still hadn't taken his eyes off Cliff. "Fred has a swell family—sister Marie, brother-in-law Rich—why, he is even related by marriage to your client, Zoe Woolfolk. How is the dear woman?" Lou's voice choked with sarcasm. "Prospering, I trust."

"Yes, thank you," Cliff replied sweetly. "She is doing quite nicely now that we are able to keep the riffraff out of her office."

Fred looked back and forth between Lou and Cliff, disturbed by their exchange. "I must get back to the office. Very nice to meet you, Mr. Thoms. Lou, Randy, I hope to see you soon, maybe over a drink." Fred shook hands all around and abruptly left.

"Three sailors in a bar? That took some juice to pull off." Lou sat down and lit a cigarette.

"It was four; don't forget the one you battered. Did you read their affidavits? Quite compelling." Cliff sat down facing Lou. He glanced over at Randy and saw that, while younger than Lou, Randy looked as old or older than his partner. No one would mistake him for the thirty-year-old suspects described by the witnesses at the Brown Derby or Red Onion restaurants.

"Now I'm confused, Counselor. I knew you were dirty. I knew you were on Cornero's payroll, but here you are *unofficially* representing Dorothy Green. So who exactly are you in bed with? Tony Cornero, Lefty Green, or maybe"—Lou paused to study his cigarette—"Dorothy Green?"

"Don't push me, Gomez. I'm the only thing standing between you and the soup kitchen. Here's how it's going to be: you can interview Dorothy, but only with her attorney, Robert Willows, present. And—"

"Willows? Another mob mouthpiece. Is he as honorable as your friend, the esteemed A. J. Barnes?" Lou asked with a twisted smile.

"So you know Barnes? I see you smiling, so I assume that is a yes. Well, Barnes likes you too. He thinks you're the Canyon Killer. You might want to work on your alibi. Speaking of alibis, before you interview Dorothy, be sure to check with Falcon Airlines. Dorothy used the name of her maid, Carlota Gonzalez, to travel incognito. I think you'll find that Dorothy was in Mexico from last Thursday until Sunday. I picked her up at the airport myself."

"Detective Williams," Cliff addressed Randy while glaring at Lou, "if Detective Gomez here tries to arrest Miss Green without ironclad evidence of her guilt, you will be looking for a new partner, and Gomez will be looking for a new job or maybe a criminal defense attorney." Cliff stood up to leave.

Lou's face flushed; he didn't like being treated like a punk. As Cliff was walking away, Lou taunted him, "Some tall blonde with tits tells you a sob story and you turn into a sap." Cliff turned on his heels at the word *sap*. Lou's anger made his mind race. *Everybody lies to this guy, but he's too stupid to see it*, he thought. *And Dorothy? If she's using Thoms to run interference, maybe she is up to her ass in Roberts's murder*. Lou would set the Chinaman straight.

"Did she tell you about ..." Lou begun gleefully but then stopped himself. Thoms had to know that a Bugatti picked up Roberts on the night of his murder, but Lou guessed that

Thoms didn't know about Dorothy's Bugatti or the beach house in Malibu, or that there were only two dark Bugatti 57SCs in town. And he certainly didn't know that A. J. Barnes and Helen had driven one of those Bugattis to Santa Barbara last Friday night.

"Tell me about what?" Cliff demanded.

Like a fast-moving storm, Lou's anger abated, and a cool professional replaced the kid from the barrio with a chip on his shoulder. "We have a witness who will testify that Roberts was killed at a house in Malibu in the presence of two men and a young woman. Naturally, we'll check out Dorothy's alibi after we interview her, and we will continue our investigation of the witness's statement." Lou watched Cliff to gauge his reaction. Then, in his most disinterested bureaucratic voice, he added, "Thank you for coming in this morning."

"I want the name of the witness and a copy of the statement," Cliff said.

"Well, Counselor, I'd love to accommodate you, but you are merely Miss Green's *unofficial* representative, so you're not entitled to any discovery. I hope you understand."

Cliff turned and wordlessly walked out of the squad room.

Lou and Randy watched him walk out the door. "So, when were you going to tell me about this witness?" Randy asked.

"It's only logical. It had to be Dorothy's Bugatti that picked up Roberts. We know the Greens have a house in Malibu. It would take two guys to move the body." Lou wondered how much he should tell Randy. "If our theory of the case is correct, then some woman—maybe Dorothy, maybe someone else—picked up Roberts last Friday and took him to the Malibu house where he was killed by two men. I'd like to think there's someone who knows all four were together."

"So, no witness." Randy looked tired. His hand shook ever so slightly as he lit his cigarette.

Lou wondered if Randy was back on the sauce. Maybe he wasn't joking about a date with a bottle of bourbon. "No, no witness."

"Is there something you're not telling me?" Randy sounded hurt, distrustful.

Lou stared silently at Randy a second too long. "No. I want Thoms to think we have a witness so he'll report back to Dorothy. We'll beat the bushes and see if the quarry flushes."

Cliff knew he had a chance to trap Vincent if Sam the dope peddler would cooperate. Cocaine could be a lure, but that wasn't what Vincent most desired. The bait would have to be tall, blonde, young, and pretty. Janice in the typing pool would be an excellent choice, but he couldn't ask her to put her life on the line. There were too many unknowns. Vincent was not predictable and, if his short partner was there to assist him, the danger was more than doubled. Cliff needed to know more before he could set a trap and hope to capture his prey. His inquiries with the organized-crime squad had not developed any leads, and he had yet to hear back from A. J. Barnes. He wouldn't, couldn't, bait a trap for Vincent without knowing a little more about what to expect. He knew of cases where researchers had interviewed murderers in prison to learn how killers thought. The findings were interesting, but Cliff couldn't remember a case with a killer exactly like Vincent or his shorter friend, and it would take weeks or months to conduct his own research. The bodies would pile up in the meantime. Reluctantly he made a decision: he had his secretary call Zoe Woolfolk and invite her to lunch. He wanted her to come to his office first so they could talk.

"Zoe, you have probably heard that I'm heading up a special squad looking for a killer who is responsible for several deaths in and around Los Angeles."

"Yes. You're referring to the Canyon Killer, right?"

"Yes. We've run down several leads, but we don't have any solid suspects. I'm wondering if you could help."

"I'll do what I can, but I can't promise anything. Sometimes I get nothing, like on the Daniel Roberts murder."

"I have police reports, crime scene photos, and some physical evidence. What would help you?"

"This man, he uses a knife, right? If I could touch it, I think I could tell you something. Do you have a knife that he handled?"

"Yes, but I can't let you touch it with your bare hands. You might leave fingerprints that would confuse the jury and help the defense."

"I don't need direct contact. If I could hold the knife with your handkerchief, I think that would work."

"That would be all right. Stay here in my office. I'll bring you the knife."

Zoe waited for five minutes. She looked at law books in the bookcases that filled three of the office's walls; she examined Cliff's old, glass-topped wooden desk; and she admired the wedding picture of Cliff and Lucille in a silver frame on a shelf beside the desk. Cliff needed only to turn his head ever so slightly to see the photo while working at his desk. As usual she touched nothing. Cliff returned bearing a brown paper sack with a label on it. He set the sack on his desk and pulled the "show" handkerchief from his breast pocket. He untwisted the top of the bag and drew out the knife by the blade. Zoe came around the front of the desk and stood beside him. Slowly she reached up and took the handkerchief-covered knife in her left hand. She swept away the first image in her head— Lucille ironing and folding the handkerchief—and waited for more images. No picture came, not at first. Suddenly she was engulfed by sensations of darkness and suffocation, of struggling to be released from bindings. Then she had the sensation of slashing. The knife was slippery with blood in her hand. She saw a woman's eyes open wide with fear; she heard the moans and straining grunts muffled by a gag. Zoe became light-headed and unsteady. She dropped the knife onto the desk and held herself up with both hands clinging to the arms of Cliff's desk chair.

"Are you okay?"

"That was ... a little overwhelming."

"What can you tell me?"

"Animal."

"We know he's an animal, but what can you tell me about him?"

"Not *an* animal, 'the Animal.'"

"You mean like a nickname? Well, that's something. Can't be more than a few dozen 'Animals' in California."

"Oh, he's not from California. He's from New York, north of New York City."

"What else can you tell me?"

"He functions on a level of primitive drives. It's hard to explain. Maybe that wasn't helpful. When he's killing, all I can perceive is a rush of sensation. There is no rational thought, just a desire to destroy something beautiful. And one more thing. I don't understand it. It's like a compulsion to make parallel cuts.

Does that make any sense?" Zoe's head was still swimming. She struggled to suppress a wave of nausea. "I can tell you that he's unstable, but"—Zoe laughed dryly—"I guess you didn't need a psychic to tell you that."

"What drives a man like that? What does he want? What ... what does he feel?"

"When he's killing, he feels"—Zoe looked into Cliff's eyes as she searched for the definitive word—"*ecstatic*. You can't stop him from killing again. He'll risk anything for another chance to violate a special woman."

Cliff helped Zoe to a chair facing his desk and sat down in his desk chair. He watched Zoe, tried to read her expression. She looked shaken. Did he believe her? More to the point, did he believe *in* her? Parallel cuts. That's what she said. They kept that fact out of the newspapers.

In silence Cliff lit a cigar and took a puff. *A special woman.* He knew exactly what Vincent wanted: tall, blonde, young, pretty—and unobtainable. Dorothy. Dorothy who had rejected Vincent before, who had given him the cold shoulder and humiliated him.

But there were two of them. How did the short man fit in? Who wielded the knife? Did Vincent just procure? In any event, it would take two of them to control a struggling woman. That made sense. "Does this Animal have a partner?"

"No."

"No? Just no? How can you be so sure?" Cliff regretted asking the question as soon as it was out of his mouth.

"I tell you what I see. My knowledge isn't perfect, but I give it to you as I get it. If it doesn't match your expectations, well, I don't embellish what I get to suit your preferences."

Radio in a thunderstorm, Cliff recalled. She had her limitations like everyone else. Her insights were unique but not infallible. "Thank you. I didn't mean to sound ungrateful. You've given me a solid lead. I didn't have one before. Ah, do you still have an appetite for lunch?"

"Yes, but I believe I'll skip the steak tartare today."

CHAPTER 12

After lunch, alone in his office, Cliff put a call in to the district attorney's office in New York City. "May I speak with Mr. Munson? This is Clifford Thoms from the Los Angeles County District Attorney's Office. Yes, I'll hold."

"Mr. Thoms. I'm sorry I don't recall you specifically. I see your name on the list of guests from the seminar I gave on Saturday."

"Oh, I think you have some recollection of me. I was called away. I'm the Chinaman."

"Yes, of course. How are you? But, I guess, this isn't a social call. What can I do for you?"

"I thought that perhaps you could help me. We're tracking down a pair of killers, one or both of whom originated in New York City. We believe one of them is nicknamed 'the Animal.'"

"As you might expect, we have many animals here in New York City. Could you be more specific?"

"I've been told that he is not an animal, but *the* Animal. He favors a knife and enjoys his work. He likes to make it last from what we can tell."

"Well ..."

"One more thing: he suspends his victims from a branch, a ceiling joist, whatever."

"Hold the line." Cliff heard the phone receiver being set down and an animated conversation in the background. The conversation ended and he heard the receiver scrape across a surface. "I think ... I think I know who you're talking about. We call him Nicky the Animal. We don't know what name he's going by now, but I can tell you what we know about him."

"Please."

"We became aware of him two years ago when a sixteen-year-old boy barricaded himself in a bedroom. He had blocked the door so it couldn't be forced open and shot at the door when people tried to kick it in. Finally, we got him out when he got hungry. We lowered some food to his window from the floor above; we put dope in the food. That put him to sleep. We got him out and took him to the hospital. When he came to, he put up quite a struggle and the doctors had to restrain him. They kept him pretty doped up. After a day or so, the kid had calmed down enough so a detective could take a statement. It seems that the kid, his older brother, and a friend of the older brother thought they could make a big score. The older brother was running with a faction of the Tatalia family and knew about a plan to hijack a truck. He figured he could hijack the stolen truck and fence the goods, and the Tatalia family would take the heat. Well, the boys pulled off the hijacking. The older brother, he was twenty, and his little brother drove off with the truck and later met up with the friend. The friend, who was eighteen, had acted as a lookout but didn't know where the brothers had stashed the truck. The Tatalia family sent three of their goons to track down the boys. The goons found the boys hiding north of town in an old, abandoned house. No neighbors were around.

"Well, one of the goons decides he knows how to get the brothers to talk. He gives the third kid, who was the lookout, to Nicky and tells him to make the lookout scream. The goon figures five minutes of this and the brothers will be singing. So Nicky takes the lookout to another room and starts working on him. And yeah, that kid screams his head off. But the brothers don't talk right away. And so Nicky keeps doing what he does, and the lookout keeps screaming. After about fifteen minutes, the brothers spill their guts. But when the goons go to the other room to tell Nicky he can stop, they find that the door is locked from the inside. They can hear noises coming from the room, and they're yelling at Nicky to stop and just kill the boy. After another twenty minutes Nicky opens the door. The kid is strung up from a light fixture. He's been cut to ribbons, but he's still alive. One of the goons starts to pull his gun out to shoot the kid, but before he can, Nicky cuts the boy's throat and lets the spray of blood hit him in the face. The younger brother swears that Nicky just stood there laughing hysterically."

"Jesus." Cliff stared at his phone while trying to take in the scene. Seconds later he heard Munson clear his throat and realized that Munson had more to say. "What happened then?"

"Well, one of the goons throws the twenty-year-old down to the floor in the middle of the room and shoots him in the head. He's dead. They cut down the kid who is still hanging from the light fixture. So there's blood and bits of flesh all over the room. The goons find some gasoline, drench the room, and burn the place down. They don't kill the sixteen-year-old. They want him to let everyone know what happens to people who double-cross the Tatalia family.

"Anyway, they made their point, but no one wants to work with Nicky. The Syndicate bosses decide that the Animal has his uses, but no one wants him in town. They ship him to

Cleveland where he pretty much single-handedly ended a turf war. Once the war was over, Cleveland shipped him to Chicago. Something happened in Chicago, something strange, and nobody wants to talk about it. After that we lost track of him."

"In Chicago, any strange disappearances, I mean, of civilians? Of women?"

"Hard to say. You know, the wife gets sick of the gangster life and takes off. Some thug's girlfriend decides the big city isn't for her, and she goes back to the farm. Happens occasionally. It happened in Chicago."

"Any bodies of women ever turn up? With their flesh cut in long, vertical strips? Cut down to the bone?"

"Not that I know of. Someone's girlfriend disappeared. We heard the story secondhand. I guess there were some accusations made against Nicky. A lot of hard feelings. We heard that Nicky got shipped off. We suspected that maybe he was taken for a ride and didn't come back. What's going on in Los Angeles? Is there something we need to know here in New York?"

"So no one knows this guy's name? How about a physical description? Or does he go around with a bag over his head?" Cliff couldn't keep his frustration in check.

"Mr. Thoms, this fellow has used half a dozen names that we know about. He's never been arrested, never been fingerprinted, has no mug shots. We will give you all the cooperation we can, but I think you could do me the professional courtesy of telling me what is happening there."

"You're right. In mid-March, the body of a young woman was discovered in a mountain canyon north of Altadena. A week later another woman's body was found in another canyon a few miles away. Both women were taken from a restaurant in Arcadia. Arcadia police set up patrols and stakeouts on the roads into the foothills. Nothing. But in mid-May, the Los Angeles sheriffs were alerted to another pair of bodies ..."

"More women?"

"Yes. But this time the bodies had been dumped in the Baldwin Hills, miles from the other bodies. DA Fitts decided to set up a countywide squad to conduct the investigation. We've been able to identify the women. The suspect in the second pair of murders is six feet tall and blond, or possibly bald and wearing a blond wig, possibly a gangster from New York, and calls himself Vincent. The suspect from Arcadia is a man around thirty, five foot six inches to five foot eight inches tall, with dark hair and dark eyes, who flashes money around. We don't have a name for him, and we didn't get any solid leads for either. As you can imagine, Fitts is pressing me and I'm pressing the police—"

"Wait, how can you be sure the murders are related?"

"More than just the similar victims, there was the same type of attack—kidnapped, possibly raped, probably tortured, strung up, and butchered with a knife."

"Ah, yes, the shorter one sounds a lot like Nicky. So how do you know the tall guy was a New York gangster?"

"One of the witnesses recognized the accent and saw that he carried a piece in a shoulder holster. She's known a few gangsters in her time."

"Okay, but how did you know about the attacker's nickname and the short guy's links to New York? Surely you have a witness who knows this fellow or an informer."

"Uh"—Cliff imagined trying to explain Zoe—"a rumor from a thirdhand source that we couldn't trace back to its origin. We are grasping at straws, following any and all leads."

"Hard work makes its own luck. I think you're on to

something. Hang on, I'll transfer you to the detective sitting on Nicky's file."

"He's actually a very intriguing fellow, this Nicky. I often wonder what Freud would make of him. Do you think that the knife is a phallic substitution?"

"Sometimes a knife is just a knife," Cliff said. He was growing impatient waiting for the detective to come back on the line with the file. The detective's girlfriend was making small talk while her boyfriend had gone to track it down. Cliff had no interest in discussing Freudian analysis of a killer with a young lady who had never seen a dead body.

"Sorry to keep you waiting, Mr. Thoms. I have the intelligence file here now. Mr. Munson was right; Nicky has gone by at least half a dozen names. We have his birth name as Santos deVenza. He was born in Sicily in October 1910. The birth date is either the sixth or the eighth; both dates are in the records. He immigrated to the United States with his family in 1920. We have the immigration records. His father was a butcher so, I guess, that accounts for Nicky's love of the knife. Nicky was in and out of school. We're pretty sure that he ran with some street gangs before he joined up with the Tatalia family. That was about 1927. That's the year he started using the name Nicholas Benzer. He was a soldier for the Tatalia family for ten years, running errands at first, but then he was used as muscle to collect debts and extortion payments. It seems that in the last few years he had been growing more violent and more erratic. I guess you heard the story of what he did to the kid who was the lookout on the truck hijacking. That's where he got the nickname 'the Animal.' He uses different names when he travels. And he changed his name when he went to work in Cleveland and again when he went to Chicago." The detective read off a list of Nicky's aliases, carefully spelling them out for Cliff.

"We know he disappeared from Chicago six months ago. We picked up a rumor that he was killed by the Outfit, but we couldn't confirm it. If he is still alive, and if he left Chicago, and if he followed his usual procedures, we can assume that he used a new name for traveling and took a different name when he got to his destination. Pretty much we don't have a clue if he's alive, or where he is, or what name he's using. Sorry. For physical description, we have him as five foot six or seven inches tall, approximately one hundred sixty-five pounds, black hair, brown eyes, no known scars or tattoos, prefers using a knife, and sometimes carries a handgun, a Smith & Wesson M&P, .38 special, with a four-inch barrel."

"You don't have a picture of this fellow, but you can describe his gun?"

"Oh, one of our informants was pistol-whipped by Nicky. You might say the gun made quite an impression." The detective laughed at his own joke. "One more thing: he is known to be unusually strong. That's all we have. Good luck, Mr. Thoms; good hunting."

By midafternoon Cliff knew he had just a few hours in which to set the trap. If Sam didn't show up at the Red Onion at his usual time, a wary quarry like Vincent would know that something was wrong. Cliff first called Buron Fitts and explained his plan.

"Not much of a plan," Fitts growled. "You expect a mobster's daughter to risk her life to help catch a criminal, you expect a dope peddler to convince a street-smart criminal to show up at a restaurant, and you want to capture a dangerous killer with as few men as possible. Did I miss anything?"

"Well, we're not sure the dope peddler can reach Vincent, and Vincent might bring his even more dangerous partner with him, but you have the gist of it."

"You want to use just the men on your squad—six, right?"

"Right."

"I'd have twice that many at the restaurant and would alert the local police departments and the nearest sheriff stations to provide backup."

"The more people who know, the greater the chance that some officer on the mob's payroll will get word back to Vincent. If this plan has any chance of working, it has to be done with only the people on the squad. Besides, if there are more officers around the restaurant, it's more likely that Vincent will sense a trap."

"Yes," Fitts reluctantly conceded Cliff's points, "but I don't like having to assume cops are on the take. I suppose it happens. Hell, the outrageous crap people say about me ..."

Cliff thought about the rumors that the mob put two million dollars into Fitts's 1936 reelection campaign.

"And about you. I hear the rumors—the Chinaman, the fixer, owned by the mob. I don't believe a word of it.

"Okay, let's assume that you're right: cops on the take. Maybe you weren't around ten years ago. During Prohibition after twenty-nine, the only ones with money were the gangsters. It was so easy for officers to make money—just look the other way. That's all they had to do to get an envelope full of cash. Who could blame them? It's not like drinking was bad, not bad in itself. It's jurisprudence class all over, you know *malum in se* and *malum prohibitum*—something bad in itself versus something bad because it's prohibited. What you're suggesting, not just looking the other way but actually reporting to the mob, I don't like it. Still, once you've crossed the line"—Fitts hesitated to complete the thought—"it gets easier and easier to take the next step."

Cliff remembered Prohibition. He remembered actually admiring Tony Cornero. Cliff heard that during Prohibition Tony brought in Canadian whiskey, the good stuff, the stuff that didn't make drinkers go blind. Cliff thought of it as a public service. And when Cornero started with the gambling ships, Cliff admired that too. People wanted to gamble; the cops did it in the precinct house playing nickel-dime poker. It would be hypocritical to say it was wrong for others to gamble. Besides, Tony ran a clean game, and he ran it outside the three-mile limit where it was legal to do so. After Cliff became a deputy DA, sure he took the money. What was wrong with taking money to allow a fellow to do something that was more or less legal? Looking the other way on prostitution was more of a problem, but Cliff knew that sometimes it was the only way for women to make money to feed their families, to keep a roof over their heads, to make a living during this damn depression.

"This plan of yours probably won't work, and if you do lure this guy in, somebody might get killed."

"True, but the alternative seems to be to wait for Vincent to kill again and hope he leaves some clues. The squad has been at this for two weeks and this is the closest we've come to him. If he figures out we're hunting him, he'll leave town and kill girls in another city. He's killed four in LA County that we know of. So"—Cliff took a deep breath—"go or no go?"

"Do it," Fitts said with military decisiveness, "and, Tommy, you better pray this doesn't turn out to be a disaster. Ah, keep tomorrow open. I might have a new assignment for you, especially if you wrap up this Canyon Killer thing."

Cliff returned to his office and documented his conversation with Fitts. A possible new assignment. On a Saturday. *No use speculating—keep focused on the task at hand*, Cliff thought.

Cliff picked up the phone and started to dial the Green residence. He hung up before the call went through. A home secretary would never allow a deputy DA to talk with Dorothy. After a few seconds of thought, Cliff shouted, "Mary, how's your Spanish?"

Mary's reply came through the open office door. "*Mi padre tiene un lápiz.*"

"What did you say?"

"I'm not sure," Mary said, standing in the doorway. "I think I said, 'My father has a pencil.'"

"Find me an older woman who is a native Spanish speaker."

Five minutes later Mary produced a small, frightened Mexican woman. "Mr. Thoms, Marta here sells homemade tortillas. She also sells tamales at Christmastime."

"Marta, I'm glad you're here. I need your help. You do want to help me, don't you?"

"Jess."

"I'm going to call a number. I want you to speak in Spanish and ask for Carlota. Tell whoever answers that you are Carlota's friend, Maria. Can you do that?"

"Carlota's friend, Maria. Jess."

Cliff dialed the number and handed the phone to Marta. Soon Carlota was on the line and Marta handed the phone back to Cliff. "Hello, Carlota. This is Mr. Thoms from the district attorney's office. I came by with my bruja friend on Sunday."

"Sí."

"I need to talk to Dorothy."

"Esperése un momento."

Cliff heard the receiver being set down. Then he heard her voice: "Tommy!"

"Dorothy, did you ever hear more from Detective Gomez?"

"No, he called Robbie Willows and set up a time to interview me at Robbie's office. Thanks for getting that straightened out. I go there next Tuesday. I meet Robbie on Monday to go over my statement. Do they really have a witness? How could they? I wasn't in town last Friday night."

"It could be a bluff, or maybe they found someone who thought he saw something. It could even be a publicity seeker. I doubt that Gomez and Williams would suborn perjury. I'm sure that Robbie has already made a demand for the witness's statement. By the time you talk with him on Monday, Robbie will know what you're up against.

"There is something else; we've had a break in the case."

"Thank God."

"Did you ever see Vincent with a shorter man with dark hair? The shorter man could be Italian."

"No. No, wait. Yeah, I did see him with some guy, but I think he was Mexican. He's a dope peddler, I'm pretty sure."

"Sam?"

"Yeah, that sounds right."

"How about a mobster, shorter, Italian, also from New York?"

"No."

"What would you do to help catch the guy who killed Helen and Virginia?"

"Anything—well, almost anything."

"Would you meet up with Vincent? We'd be there to protect you."

"Ah ... when did you want to do this?"

"Tonight. It has to be tonight. We have Sam. He can call Vincent, or at least we think he can. We'll have Sam call about seven to set up a meeting at the Red Onion. We'll have two men out back, two waiting in a car out front, and two in the restaurant."

"Where will you be?"

"In another car in front but down the block. My face has been in the newspapers and someone might recognize me if I'm around the restaurant. You'll have to pretend that you're drunk and asking for Vincent. Think you can do that?"

"The drunk part, yes; maybe I won't pretend. But asking for him? I don't know."

"I wouldn't ask you to do this, but I think he'll find you irresistible."

"I wish *other* men found me irresistible," Dorothy cooed coyly.

"Just a word of advice—wear something low cut and a skirt you can run in, just in case."

"What aren't you telling me?"

"We can't be sure, but Vincent may have a partner. If he's with a shorter Italian guy, just run out the front door to the officers parked in front."

"Does the short guy have a name? How will I know him?"

"He's really not short. He's about five foot seven inches tall. He has used a lot of aliases. We know him as Nicky."

"Does Nicky have a nickname in case Vincent calls him by that?"

"Nickname? No, none that we know of. Go to your father's

club in Santa Monica. I'll have an officer in street clothes pick you up in an unmarked car at six. What will you be wearing?"

"Oh, he'll have no trouble spotting me. I'll be wearing a red silk Chinese dress with a deep V neckline and a flowing skirt. The neckline plunges past my sternum. People notice," Dorothy said dryly. "Maybe it's the rhinestone belt or maybe it's the lack of a bra."

"Your father's club, six o'clock. More people than you know are counting on you."

Cliff hung up and called down to the squad room where the detectives on the Scott squad were housed. He told Detectives Sanchez and Wright to pick up Sam and take him to an interrogation room in the city jail. He'd meet them there in twenty minutes. He reminded the detectives that they needed Sam's cooperation so they should treat him civilly.

When Cliff arrived at the jail, the desk sergeant directed him to the interrogation room where Sam was being held.

"Boss, this is Sam." Detective Sanchez gestured to the seated prisoner. Sam's hands were cuffed behind his back, and bruises were starting to appear on his face. Fresh blood trickled from his nose and dripped onto his shirt. "Sam, this is Mr. Thoms, deputy district attorney."

Cliff looked at Sam and then shot Sanchez a cold look. "Sam, I pulled your jacket. Seems that this isn't the first time you've been caught with narcotics. I'll lay it out straight for you: you can do a nickel up north for possession with intent to sell, or you can do sixty days in the county for drug paraphernalia. We want Vincent and we need your help."

"Vincent is dangerous," Sam said, looking up at Cliff. A drop of blood rolled down his upper lip and fell to his chin where it hung briefly before falling to his lap. "Maybe I like my chances better in the pen."

"Vincent doesn't have to know that you helped. Just one phone call. Get him to come to the Red Onion tonight. My men can take him in the parking lot."

"I don't know. Vinny is awfully sly. He can smell cops."

"It's up to you. I was going to suggest San Quentin, but maybe," Cliff paused and waited for a glimmer of hope to appear in Sam's eyes, "there's an open cell in Alcatraz. I hear the cold salt air is quite bracing."

"Hey, Boss, you know Sam here would be the only one in Alcatraz who's not a murderer, but hey, Sammy"—Sanchez smiled broadly at Sam—"you'll make lots of friends there. Hell, who knows, you may even get married. You'd make someone a lovely wife." The sound of Detective Wright snickering emerged from a dark corner of the interrogation room.

"Hey, not so fast." Sam glanced back over his shoulder at Wright and looked up imploringly at Cliff. "Maybe we can work something out. You don't know Vinny; he'll kill me if he ever finds out I helped you guys. How 'bout this: I'll make the phone call and get Vinny to come to the Red Onion. You guys lose the dope you got off me, and I'll get out of town for a couple of months."

"Boss, we caught this guy holding," Wright reminded Cliff.

Sanchez offered up a new suggestion. "Hey, Boss, why don't you let me beat the phone number out of him. We can use the crisscross directory to get the friend's address."

"And then what, Ray? Raid the place? Suppose Vincent's not there. Suppose Vincent is there but gets away. Suppose no one is there when we show up. Why don't we just put an announcement in the paper letting Vincent know that we're looking for him?" Cliff made a mental note of the blood staining Sanchez's shirt cuffs. "Okay, Sam, you go to the Red Onion at six and make the call by seven tonight. If Vincent shows up, we'll grab him and cut you loose with a bus ticket to—"

"San Diego," Sam suggested.

"Okay, San Diego, but the dope stays in our evidence locker for a year. If you show up in LA County during that time, we'll arrest you and prosecute you. No deals, no breaks."

"Yeah, all right, I can use the vacation. I don't want to be anywhere near that crazy bastard." A thought suddenly occurred to Sam. "Hey, what do I do between six and seven, stand there with my dick in my hand?"

Cliff masked his disgust and managed to reply in a matter-of-fact tone, "No, tell people that you're meeting your connection at eight and will have dope to sell then."

CHAPTER 13

The riskiness of the plan gnawed at Cliff, but he knew the more officers that were around, the greater the chance that Vincent would spot the trap. He did, however, alter his original plan by enlisting tall, blonde, pretty Janice from the typing pool and his secretary, Mary, to sit in the restaurant with the detectives of team three, Lewis and Lopes. He thought that two couples would be less conspicuous than two men sitting alone, nursing beers, and watching everyone around them. He assigned the two detectives from team one, Frank Wallace and Harry Clark, to sit in a car across the street in front of the restaurant, and the two detectives from team two, Sanchez and Wright, to stake out the parking lot behind the Red Onion.

The two couples took their positions at separate dining tables close to the bar by five thirty. They ordered drinks and appetizers. The plan was for them to linger over each course so they could stretch out their stay until at least eight o'clock. Wallace and Clark arrived at five forty. They parked their unmarked car in a lot across the street from the Red Onion. Five minutes later, Wright, dressed in a deliveryman's uniform, drove a panel truck into the parking lot behind the restaurant.

He parked near the rear entrance of the restaurant, got out of the truck, and raised the hood. He stood at the front of the truck and fiddled with the engine every time someone walked by. Unnoticed, Sanchez, dressed as a bum, had arrived on foot at the rear of the parking lot. He loitered around some trash cans, smoked incessantly, and muttered to himself in Spanish.

Precisely at 6:00 p.m. Cliff parked his car on the street a block away from the Red Onion and let Sam out. Cliff slid down in his seat so he could just barely see over the dashboard. He had brought his gun, a Colt Model 1908, which he'd had since he was a young attorney but felt ridiculous whenever he wore his shoulder holster. He pulled the pistol out and laid it on his lap. He preferred this semiautomatic to the .38-caliber revolvers most officers carried; it was easier to conceal and reload, and held seven rounds rather than the five or six shots of a revolver.

Dorothy was dropped off in front of the restaurant about six twenty. She silenced conversations as she made her way through the crowded restaurant in her red Chinese dress. Both men and women stopped to look at her—men with lust, women with jealousy—as she passed.

Dorothy's arrival was Sam's cue to make his call. Nervously he entered a phone booth, pulled the door closed behind him, and dialed the number.

"Is Vinny around? ... Sam. He knows me from the Red Onion ... Yeah, he knows me. Tell him we went for a spin in my Cadillac ...

"Hey, Vinny! How ya doing? I'm here at the Red Onion, and there's this broad asking about you. Tall, blonde, a real looker. Dorothy somebody. Nah, she doesn't seem mad ... Yeah, maybe a little primed. Yeah, she's asking for you ... She's alone ... A red dress. Christ, her tits are hangin' out ... Cops? Nah, haven't seen any. Twenty minutes? Okay, I'll tell her ... Yeah, I got some candy. I'll hold back a couple for you ... Yeah, see you in twenty."

Fred arrived at the Santa Monica Police Station a few minutes before six. Lou was adding notes to the book on the Roberts murder when Fred walked into the squad room.

"Have you had dinner?"

"No, but I had a big lunch. Will this take long?" Lou asked as he gathered up his hat and coat.

"No." Fred was starting to regret suggesting that they meet his sister. "I think you'll find it worthwhile," he added, not quite believing it himself.

The men walked to Fred's car, a green 1936 Oldsmobile coupe, and got in. They drove in silence. Lou seemed preoccupied, and Fred did not want to intrude on his thoughts. After a few minutes, Fred asked, "What's the story on Randy?" Fred realized that Randy was not like other war veterans that he knew. Fred appreciated the fact that the Great War was its own special hell, deeper and darker than the trauma faced by his own father in the Spanish-American War, yet Fred wondered what damage Randy had suffered that twenty years of peace had failed to heal.

As Lou considered the question, he watched the city scenes pass by: shuttered storefronts, a line of people outside a soup kitchen, a row of cars outside of a nightclub. What *was* the story on Randy? "Randy joined the Marines in April 1917, the day after we declared war on Germany. He was twenty-three years old. He'd been working in his father's shoe store for five years. He hated it. He didn't get shipped out to France until spring of 1918.

"By mid-July, his unit had been fighting on the line for over a month. The Marines were in some wooded hills. Randy said they'd been trading ground with the Germans; the Marines would attack, take the German's position, and the Germans would counterattack and take the position back. He said it wasn't like farther north where the trench lines went on for miles and the machine-gun emplacements had clear fields of fire over a no-man's-land. In mid-July they got the word from Intelligence that the Germans were massing for a counterattack. The Marines were ordered to keep up what they called harassing fire."

"Harassing fire?"

"Yeah. You have to understand that the soldiers on both sides lived like nocturnal animals. They stayed in their firing pits during the day and moved around at night to eat and fill their canteens and move the wounded back. Harassing fire was shooting at anything that moved in the trenches or behind the trenches. It made it dangerous to go behind the lines for dinner or to fill your canteen. But Randy says the Germans knew how to pay the Americans back. They would shell our lines for half an hour to let our boys know they didn't appreciate being shot at. The shelling was dangerous enough, but then sometimes the Germans would follow up with raiding parties. Those Heine bastards would sneak into our lines, kill a few, and grab one or two to take back to interrogate.

"The Marines had been keeping up harassing fire for a few days, and the Germans responded by shelling our lines. Randy was in a connecting trench about one hundred yards back in the front line. He was running a message between dugouts or something when a shell landed in soft dirt about ten yards away. The soft dirt saved his life, but the explosion threw him out of the trench and knocked him unconscious. As he came to, he was vaguely aware of a German raiding party swarming around. He stayed absolutely still, closed his eyes, and slowed down his breathing. He said he could hear them all around him whispering in German. Then he heard one of them come up and work the bolt of his rifle. Well, naturally Randy thought, 'Oh God, it's my turn,' but not that day. The German bastard thought Randy was dead. I guess the concussion from the shell made him bleed out of both ears and his nose. Not worth a bullet, but that bastard bayoneted Randy in the thigh just to make sure. Hell, Randy didn't even flinch, so the German moved on. After the raiding party passed by, Randy crawled to the nearest dugout. They were all dead inside. The Bosch had thrown in a grenade. Randy hid under one of the mangled bodies for who knows for how long until a squad of Americans came looking for survivors."

"Damn, that's enough to keep you awake at night," Fred said without looking over at Lou.

"That's what I thought when I first heard him tell the story, but ya know, it doesn't. I've spent the night with Randy on surveillance, and it doesn't keep him up. Oh, it'll wake him up. He'll doze off and wake with a start and kind of a yelp, but getting bayoneted doesn't keep him awake. It took me years to learn, as bad as it was, that wasn't the worst."

"My father used to talk about the Spanish-American War, what a Mauser bullet will do to a man," Fred said quietly.

"Yeah, quite a difference between what a handgun will do and what a rifle will do. Nah, in the Great War the main killer was artillery. Worse than the gun or the bayonet was the artillery. Randy said it would leave chunks of a man hanging from the barbed wire, men's limbs would disappear in a pink mist, shrapnel would open men up—make them look like an anatomy diagram."

"Oh God," Fred murmured.

"Still that wasn't the worst."

"There's worse?" Fred asked incredulously.

"Yeah. Randy never said it, but what was worst was"—Lou paused as he turned to face Fred—"he liked it."

"The war?"

"No, the killing. That's what keeps him up at night, knowing he could take pleasure in shooting Germans in the back as they turned and ran. Shooting surrendering prisoners who put their hands up a little too slowly. Bayoneting a man in the gut so hard that the blade gets wedged in the hip so you have to fire your rifle to free the blade. He never told his folks. He could barely tell me and only after we'd worked together for ten years. I think he's deeply ashamed."

The men drove with the windows down. There was another half hour before the sun would set. The air was only then beginning to cool after the heat of the day. To the north, the foothills were veiled in a thin haze. The hills were still green from late winter rains, but by the end of summer, they would be brown and ready to burn.

Knowing that they were approaching their destination, Lou's curiosity overcame his loathing of mysticism and superstition, the sort of beliefs he thought pulled Catholic teachings down to the level of ignorant folk religion. "Has your sister always been a fortune-teller?"

"Well, I wouldn't say she's a fortune-teller. But to answer your question, no. She was like most everyone, fun loving and a bit adventurous. About nine years ago, the four of us— my brother, Vic; our sisters, Marie and Angela; and I—were swimming off Ocean Park. We are all strong swimmers and fearless. Marie swam out far, around the pier. As she swam back, she was caught in an undertow near the shore. She was dragged under, and Vic and I swam out to help. Vic reached her first and pulled her out; we towed her to shore. She was underwater, oh, minutes; I'm not sure how long. Swimming out to her, it seemed like an eternity. We got her back on shore and revived her. She told us that she felt as if she had died and had started to ... I guess the word would be ... *ascend* to heaven. As she ascended, she was met by dead relatives and by spirits who sent her back. They said it wasn't her time. Ever since then she claims that she gets messages from these spirits—she calls them her guides—and that she can sense people's emotions."

"What do you think?" Lou had turned back to the open window.

"Do I think she's crazy? That's what you mean, isn't it?" There was an edge to Fred's voice.

Lou just shrugged and continued to look out the window.

"No, I don't think she's crazy. Like I said before, listen to what she has to tell you. Maybe there is something in there, some gem, hidden within all the dross."

Lou and Fred arrived at the little bungalow at the top of the hill in Redondo Beach. They climbed the steps to the small porch, but before they could knock, they heard Marie calling out, telling them to come in. Marie was back at her card table playing solitaire. Her children were in the bedroom. Fred could hear three-year-old Joanie's voice as she spoke to baby Caroline.

"Marie, I brought Detective Gomez along so he could hear what you have to say. Tell him what you told me."

Marie was dressed in powder-blue slacks and a blue blouse with a floral print. Her black hair was styled in fashionable waves. She was barefoot. There was a cigarette burning in an ashtray and an empty beer bottle on the table. Marie stood up and offered Lou her hand. "Hi, Detective. Please sit down."

"Where's your husband?" Lou asked as he sat down on the small loveseat.

"Oh, he's at work." Marie turned the chair at the card table to face him and sat down.

Fred returned from the kitchen with another chair. He sat down and repeated, "Tell him what you told me."

Ignoring Fred, Marie locked her eyes on Lou and asked, "How long have you known Williams?"

"Oh, we met in twenty-six"—Lou paused to recall—"so I guess thirteen years."

"Doesn't it seem like you've known him longer?" Marie asked so slowly that Lou suspected she was drunk.

"Yeah, now that you mention it, it seems like I've known him forever."

"You've known him for one thousand years," Marie said matter-of-factly. "You've fought side by side, sometimes as brothers, in one hundred battles. Hasn't there been a time when you felt as if you and Williams had been in a war together?"

"Funny you should ask." Even though he was surprised by the question, Lou knew exactly what she was asking about. "There was a time when Randy and I and about twenty other officers were on the shooting line qualifying with our handguns, and it reminded me of British soldiers taking up a firing line and shooting at natives charging them. But you know, it wasn't like me thinking about the British soldiers; it was like we *were* the British soldiers. It was the damnedest thing, like we had fought, maybe fought and died, together." Lou had never told anyone that story before, not even Randy. It seemed too crazy, too dreamlike, but it felt real at the time.

"Déjà vu," Fred muttered.

"It seemed real because it was a memory. You and Williams, you fought and died together there." Marie looked puzzled for an instant and then said, "Africa, I think. You remember the red coats, don't you?"

"Yeah, yeah, that's part of the memory. I went to the library the next day and borrowed a book on the Zulu war. It all seems so ... familiar, but I had never studied that war before." Lou didn't like where this conversation was going. He didn't believe in reincarnation and didn't want to talk to this crazy lady who not only believed in reincarnation but also thought she knew about his past lives.

"You asked for him to be your partner, didn't you?" Marie asked ever so slowly. "You knew you two belonged together. It was like finding the person you had been looking for, but you didn't even know you were looking for him." Marie looked down at her hands in her lap, palms up, fingers slightly spread. "It's too bad; his aura has been damaged." Marie looked up from her hands and into Lou's eyes. "He's not the man you expect him to be."

"Aura?" *More Eastern mysticism bullshit,* Lou thought, but still he couldn't deny that Marie had described his feeling better than he could have described it. It did feel like he had been waiting to find Randy.

"An aura in several religious traditions is a emanation of light of different colors that is thought to display a person's emotional, physical, and spiritual condition," Fred explained.

"Damaged aura. I'll have to tell Randy about that. Maybe he can take it into the shop and get it fixed." Lou stood up. "Look, I don't have time for this. I have a killer to catch." He felt that the last five minutes had been a waste of time. He was angry at the crazy lady and her mystical nonsense and with himself for listening to her. "Fred, let's get going. I need to pick up my car."

Lou got back to the station a little after seven. A small stack of messages had appeared on his desk. He flipped over the stack and began reading them in chronological order. The earliest one had been written at three o'clock but was not put on his desk until after he left around six. Silently he cursed the clerical staff. The message said that a call to the *Rex* confirmed that Ricardo Stralla had not returned to work after leaving early on Monday. He had called in to say that he was sick and needed to return home to Cucamonga. The message noted Ricardo's home phone number. The next message related a conversation with Ricardo's mother at 3:10 p.m. She said, and this was in quotes, that Ricardo was "having a crisis of faith," was seeking spiritual counseling from his priest, and couldn't come to the phone. There was a final message from Ricardo's mother saying that the sheriff's deputies were holding Ricardo at the San Secondo d'Asti Catholic Church in a place called Guasti. Her call came in at 6:50 p.m. She left the phone number for the church.

Lou first called Randy at his house. He wanted his partner with him if they needed to drive out to Guasti to pick up Ricardo. The phone rang eight times before Randy picked it up. He was drunk. From the sound of his voice, Lou decided that the call had woken him up. It was like the old days, but Lou didn't know if he had the patience to cover for his partner this time. Disgusted, Lou warned Randy that if he didn't show up at the station in the morning, Lou would not make excuses for him to the captain. Randy said something unintelligible and hung up.

Lou then called the church in Guasti and spoke to the priest, Father Luigi Conti, who passed him to the deputy sheriff handling the matter.

"We have your boy."

"Hold him until we get there."

"Oh, he's not going anywhere. We got him stretched out on a table."

"Is he sick?"

"Nope. He's plenty dead."

Lou felt his face flush but managed to ask, "Did you secure the crime scene?"

"Well, wasn't much of a scene. Father Luigi here heard some noise and found your boy dead outside the church. No witnesses, no shell casings, no tire tracks, no nothin' 'cept some bloody mush on the ground."

Lou cursed under his breath. Murder, suicide, accident? "Can you ship him to us in Santa Monica? We can perform the autopsy. I assume his death flows from our ongoing case."

"'Flows from our ongoing case.' Hell, you must be a college boy. Yeah, we'll just finish up our report and get him ready to ship. Was he a suspect or what?"

"Up until now, he was just a potential witness. As of now, yes, he is a suspect in a murder case. Oh, and, Sheriff, we'll need a copy of your homicide report." Then, as an afterthought, Lou asked, "It was a homicide, wasn't it?"

"Boy, howdy. You should see him. He's a mess. Left most of his brains where he fell. Now, Professor, ya'll have to come and get him. Our meat wagon can't leave the county."

"Okay. Keep him on ice. We'll come and get him tonight."

Where the hell is Guasti, and how the hell do we pick him up? Lou was exhausted and frustrated. The case had just started to come together yesterday when he located the scene of the murder, but this morning there was the confrontation with Thoms, and later on he had been chewed out by the captain who reminded Lou that Thoms was heading up the Scott-Mara investigation. That investigation, the captain made a point of emphasizing, had top priority, and Thoms could call on all resources in the county. The captain expected Lou to cooperate fully with Thoms and ... then it hit him. He called the LA County Sheriff substation in San Dimas, close to the border with San Bernardino County, and told the desk sergeant that he was working with Deputy DA Thoms on the Scott-Mara investigation and that Thoms had directed him to have the LA County Sheriff pick up a body in Guasti. It seems there was a memo that had circulated in the substation saying that Thoms's investigation was high priority and to give unquestioned cooperation. The meat wagon would be sent as soon as the sergeant got off the phone.

Next Lou called the coroner's office and asked the clerk to call Dr. Jenson and tell him that he'd have a new patient arriving in a couple of hours.

"Dr. Davis, what are you doing here? I thought the boss didn't have to come in at night."

"Normally I wouldn't, but Jenson has the day off. Apparently some inconsiderate detective called him in last Saturday morning for a rush autopsy. I guess this detective thinks the department has unlimited funds. We had to give Jenson comp time off."

"Yeah, that inconsiderate detective would be me. Now that you're the supervisor, they got you squeezing nickels. Figures." Lou tried to look around Davis to see the body behind him on the autopsy table. "So what do we got?"

"Ricardo Stralla, midtwenties, nice Catholic boy like yourself; cause of death: multiple gunshot wounds. Three shots from what looks like a .38."

"Three? What are you saying? Some jealous husband

unloaded six shots of a revolver and happened to hit the guy three times?"

"No, the shooter was a pro. He—"

"Wait! Don't tell me. One in the chest and two in the head."

"Oh, you've seen this movie before. Yeah, the one to the chest is on the left side about an inch from ..."

"The nipple. It went into the heart, and the two shots to the head were from close range."

"Well, if you don't need me, I might as well go home. Damn," Davis muttered after looking at his watch, "I'm missing the end of *Grand Ole Opry.*"

"I didn't figure you for listening to hillbilly music."

"Me either. I used to listen to the classical music program that came on before *Grand Ole Opry.* One night I kept listening, thinking I'd get a laugh from the rube music. Turns out I liked it, and I just kept listening."

Lou grunted an acknowledgment but continued to examine Ricardo's hands and forearms. "No defensive wounds. Yeah, any idea how long he's been dead? The San Bernardino sheriff's report doesn't even venture a guess. Do we know—"

"Hey, I'm just paid to examine the bodies. You're running the investigation. From body temperature and degree of rigor, I'd say he's been dead for three or four hours. It appears that the decedent and the killer were facing each other, and the killer is a little taller than average. The chest shot was a through and through at a slightly downward trajectory. If the sheriff's people are able to recover the bullet that went through the chest, we might be able to get something from it. The other two bullets went through the head and are too flattened to match them to a particular gun. It's been a slow week, so we can put a rush on the autopsy for this guy. Call my office at nine thirty tomorrow morning—"

"Tomorrow?"

"Lou, don't even start. They're watching my budget. Jenson's off, and I'm not supposed to be here now. I'll come in early tomorrow morning and finish up. Mr. Stralla isn't going anywhere. I'll have a preliminary report for you by nine thirty, no sooner, so don't drop in and pester me. Oh"—Davis looked up from the body—"what did the padre say?"

"What padre?"

"The priest who came in with the body, the one from Guasti. He's in the hallway. Wanted to talk to your partner, but I suppose you'll do."

"Guess I'll have to," Lou said as he stepped into the hallway.

By 7:15 p.m., Dorothy had been at the Red Onion for nearly an hour. Vincent was over half an hour late. Maybe he wouldn't show at all. She had been hoping that the police would kill him when he showed up. She wanted him dead, as dead as her friends Helen and Virginia. Although she had already had three drinks, she found it hard to relax. The possibility that she'd have to face Vincent was bad enough, but knowing that he might have a partner who Tommy thought was even more dangerous made her want to run away. Still, she would play her role—she would seem drunk and ask for Vincent. She struggled to maintain the illusion that she was there to have a good time and felt relieved when she needed to use the ladies' room. Finally, she could get away from men offering to buy her drinks and staring at her chest.

As she exited the restroom, a man gripped her arm with the strength of a vice. Dorothy felt the wetness of a wadded cloth napkin being slapped over her nose and mouth. The napkin had been soaked in something sweet-smelling—chloroform? She inhaled deeply, preparing to scream, but the ice-cold vapors made her light-headed. She tried to push her attacker's hand away, but he was too strong. Despite herself, she took another breath and almost vomited. Her attacker was behind her, dragging her toward the restaurant's rear exit. Dorothy tried to pull away, but instead she lost her balance and fell back onto her attacker's chest. He used the opportunity to grab her hand and lock up her wrist and elbow in a way that caused so much pain she was afraid her arm would break when she tried to pull away. She'd seen bouncers at her father's club use the same kind of hold to control drunks and get them to leave—a "come along" she remembered it being called. As her attacker steered Dorothy to the exit, he continued to press the napkin against her mouth and nose. After another breath, Dorothy felt her arms and legs begin to go numb. She struggled to get loose and fought to think clearly, to plan an escape, to control her fear, but her body refused to cooperate. Her stomach was roiling, and she had to pee again. She knew that the police were watching, but where were they? A picture of her daughter at the beach with her nanny, Carlota, invaded her mind. Now darkness was crowding out her thoughts, and fear swept through her like a sudden fever. The fumes were overpowering. Her head began to spin. She was losing consciousness.

Suddenly they were outside in the warm night air. Dorothy knew it was Vincent. She was aware that he was holding her up and that they were walking. With his arms around her in a loving embrace, he walked her out the back door of the Red Onion, across the parking lot, and through an alley to a 1936 blue Chevrolet sedan. Vincent maneuvered her into the front seat of the waiting car. He straightened her legs and shoved her upright into a sitting position. He bound her wrists together with a piece of cord from a clothesline. As if in a dream or a hallucination, Dorothy watched as Vincent walked around to the driver's side, took off his blond wig, and laid it carefully in the backseat. He removed his suit coat with padded shoulders. Underneath he wore a blue chambray workman's shirt. Without the longish blond wig, his hair was dark brown and cut short. Dorothy could barely keep her head up, but she managed to watch Vincent out of the corner of her eye as he opened the trunk and appeared to change shoes. When he walked up to the driver's door, he was several inches shorter. *Lifts, lifts and a wig*, thought Dorothy, *that's all it took, and now this Nicky is going to kill me.* Nicky got into the driver's seat and started driving. Dorothy closed her eyes and let the darkness take her.

PART 3

CHAPTER 14

"Is she still in the can?"

"I guess so. Do you want me to check on her?"

"Yeah."

Mary walked into the ladies' room and called out, "Dorothy?" All quiet. Mary checked under the door of each of the three stalls, but all were empty. She walked out and asked Billy, the bartender, if he had seen Dorothy. He said that he saw her go into the ladies' room but didn't see her leave. Mary stepped out the restaurant's back door and into the parking lot. The light above the door illuminated a half circle thirty feet in diameter. To her right, fifteen feet away, she saw a busboy in silhouette leaning against the wall. He was short and stocky with a dark complexion and an aquiline nose. The tip of his cigarette glowed red against a black background. She could smell the cigarette; the smoke was luminescent in the harsh light of the bulb above her head. To her left, she noticed the panel truck but didn't see Detective Wright. Mary went over and looked into the cab of the truck. It was empty. Puzzled, she started circling around the rear of the truck. Stepping into the shadow of the truck, she stumbled over Wright's foot. He lay stretched out along the length of the truck with his head resting against the right front tire. Reluctantly Mary knelt down and felt for a pulse. The detective's pulse was weak but steady. Somewhat relieved, Mary reached down to move Wright's head to make him more comfortable when she felt warm, sticky blood on her hand.

Mary stood up and yelled out to the busboy, "Hey, did you see a lady in a red dress come out this way?"

"Yeah, she was very drunk. The blond man helped her into a car."

"What kind of car?"

"Oh, I don't know. I don't know cars. It was blue. They went that way," the busboy said, pointing east.

Mary ran back into the restaurant and up to the two detectives. "Vincent grabbed Dorothy, and Wright is hurt. I don't know where Ray is."

"Go tell the boss," one of the detectives hollered above the music.

"Janice, call for an ambulance," Mary shouted as she rushed away.

Mary ran out the front door of the restaurant. She stopped at the curb and hesitated. To her left she saw Cliff in his car a block away. After a second of indecision, she ran straight across the street to the two detectives sitting in the car in the parking lot. She ran awkwardly in high heels and tried to shout but was too out of breath to yell. Each detective opened his door and stepped out of the car. Harry caught Mary and held her by her arms until she caught her breath and was able to tearfully choke out, "He's taken her; Vincent's taken her."

The detectives were trying to ask for details when Cliff drove up, got out of his car, and rushed up, asking, "What's the problem?"

Mary turned to Cliff and threw her arms around his neck. "Vincent took her. Wright is hurt, and we can't find Sanchez. A busboy said he heard a car going east, but he didn't know what kind of car it was."

"Is that all we know?"

"Yes. No. The car is blue. I'm sorry I wasn't watching her closer. She just went to the ladies' room. When she didn't come back ..."

Cliff peeled Mary's arms from around his neck. "It's okay, Mary. We'll find her." Mary noticed she left Cliff's coat label wet from her dripping nose and sheepishly took a couple of steps back. He looked off into the distance as he envisioned the main streets in the area. To the east was Crenshaw running north/south. Dorothy's kidnapper could take Crenshaw due north and then go east or west on Florence or Slauson, or continue north and be in the Baldwin Hills in a few minutes. Florence going east ended at Alameda, but Slauson went east and met up with another highway going north toward the foothills. "Harry, get on your car radio and—"

"An APB?" Harry suggested.

"I'm thinking," Cliff muttered. He realized that they didn't know the make or model of the car. He also didn't know if Dorothy was in the passenger seat, laid out in the backseat, or stuffed into the trunk. "Ah, hell, just nix the APB. See if you can contact Culver City PD, tell them it's related to the Scott-Mara murders, and have them send some officers over to the Baldwin Hills. I doubt that Vincent will go back there, but we shouldn't overlook the obvious. Next, contact the sheriff's office and have them be on the lookout for blue cars driven by blond men possibly with a blonde female passenger going up toward the foothills. Let them know that it's a possible Scott-Mara situation as well."

Cliff looked over his team one detectives, Frank Wallace and Harry Clark. Both were on loan from LAPD Burglary and both were in their fifties. Their captain wanted them out of the unit and looked for excuses to open their slots for younger detectives. Cliff studied Frank's pallid face, his hollow cheeks, and the way his old suit, now too big for him, hung off his broad shoulders. "Frank, how are you doing?"

"Okay, just a little winded, that's all," Frank replied as he walked back to the car to sit.

It was impossible not to notice Frank's weight loss and constant coughing. While the department doctor wouldn't confirm it, everyone in the office suspected lung cancer. "Frank," Cliff called out in a gentle tone, "drive the car around the back of the restaurant and supervise the search for Ray. Stay with the car and near the radio. I don't want you running off to save Dorothy on your own—no matter how attractive she finds you.

"Mary, if you and Janice want to go home now ..."

"Boss," Frank shouted out from inside his car, "a civilian spotted a man moving a woman from a blue sedan to a gray Studebaker. The witness says they're headed east on Slauson. The man is average height and has dark hair. The woman is wearing a red dress."

"Clever," Cliff said nonchalantly. "Vincent stays with the blue car while Nicky goes off in a different car. They'd have us chasing our tails all night. Okay, so Nicky and Dorothy are headed to the foothills."

"Do you still want me to contact Culver City PD?" Frank asked.

"Yeah, and send out the APB on both cars. This Nicky is wily. He'll change cars when he gets a chance, and he might double back. Frank, you and Harry find Sanchez. Tell Lewis and Lopes to follow me—north on Crenshaw, east on Slauson, and northeast where Slauson changes to Atlantic. Mary, you and Janice go home."

Mary clutched Cliff's arm. "What are you going to do?"

Cliff lifted Mary's hand from his arm and held her hand in both of his. "He has at least a two-minute lead. I can catch him if I go now," he explained. "Be a good girl and go home. I'll tell you what happens in the morning."

Cliff drove quickly and flew through intersections slowing only enough to see that the way was clear. He regretted not having a siren or a radio, and after several minutes still did not see the detectives' car behind him.

Cliff was on Atlantic Boulevard before he caught a glimpse of the gray Studebaker. The car was going only slightly faster than the speed limit but seemed to speed up as he closed the gap between them. Soon both cars were racing down the dark road. On either side of the road were shallow ditches filled with dry, yellow grass, and beyond the ditches stretched potato fields growing dark in the fading light. *If I can get ahead of him, I might be able to slow him down and the other car can catch up,* Cliff thought. *If Nicky's surrounded, he can't hold Dorothy hostage for long; one of the three of us will have a clear shot.* Cliff sped up and moved to the left, waiting for an opportunity to pass. The Studebaker sped up and began to swerve side to side in the lane. Cliff saw the driver of the gray car reach to his right, across his passenger, and do something with the door. A few seconds later Cliff could see that Nicky had rolled down the passenger window. Suddenly, the gray car crossed over the centerline and began fishtailing as its brakes locked up. Cliff hit his brakes but had to jerk the wheel to the right to avoid hitting the Studebaker. As Cliff passed Nicky's car on the right, he heard a shot. A hole appeared in the frame of his door, and the window cracked but did not shatter. Cliff jerked the wheel to the left and tried to sideswipe the Studebaker, but Nicky was already accelerating and moving to the right, trying to force Cliff off the road. The cars crashed together, Cliff steering hard to the left and the Studebaker to the right. Gradually, the lighter but more powerful Studebaker pushed Cliff's Hudson off the road. The Hudson slowed only slightly as it left the pavement and encountered the soft dirt on the shoulder of the road. In an instant, the car slid down the embankment into a dry ditch where it plowed along carried by its momentum. Cliff felt himself suspended inside the car, heard metal straining and glass shattering, and saw a bright flash in the darkness as he struck his head on the car ceiling. Then darkness and silence and stillness.

CHAPTER 15

Mary led Harry through the restaurant to the third team of detectives, Paul Lewis and Roger Lopes. Harry relayed Cliff's instructions to them. The detectives threw money on the table to cover their bill and rushed to their car in the parking lot. Mary and Janice followed on their heels.

"Hey, where ya going?" Harry asked. "The boss said you ladies were to go home."

"We're going with them. The boss can fire us if he wants," Mary said defiantly.

As the two couples left, Frank pulled up in his car. "Where are the girls going?"

"Don't ask," Harry said, shaking his head.

Frank and Harry walked over to the panel truck and found Wright lying on his back, his face turned to the side. In the light of their flashlights, they could see that Mary had pressed a wad of Kleenex against the head wound. The wound had stopped bleeding, and Wright didn't seem to have any other injuries although he remained unconscious. Harry squatted down and went through Wright's coat pockets as Frank looked on. He threw open Wright's coat, and both detectives could see that the gun was missing from his shoulder holster. Harry let his hand follow around Wright's belt until he felt the empty case where Wright's handcuffs should have been.

"Where's the damn ambulance?" Harry asked angrily. "We need to find Sanchez. I'll search the west side of the parking lot; you search the east side."

A few minutes later, Frank yelled from behind some trash cans, "Harry, I found him."

Harry hurried over, but once he got around to the other side of the trash cans, he could see that there was no rush. He dropped to one knee and pressed two fingers to Sanchez's throat. "No pulse." Harry looked over at his partner who was bent over at his waist with his hands on his knees, coughing. There were flecks of blood on Frank's lips. "Frank, maybe you should call it a night."

"No, I'm okay. I just get so ... congested." Frank pulled a handkerchief out of his back pocket and wiped his lips. He examined the bloodstains on the handkerchief in the dim light, refolded the handkerchief, and put it back in his pocket. "I'll radio for the meat wagon and the crime scene boys. It'll be good to sit down for a minute."

Lewis and Lopes were Colorado boys who came to California in the twenties. They were on loan from Hollywood vice, and both had survived the purge following the last great cleanup of the department. Their lieutenant was eager to get rid of the pair, if only for a while, because of their drinking and their reputation for carousing with prostitutes. Paul Lewis was tall and lean with sandy-blond hair. During the Great War he stayed stateside and instructed recruits to shoot. It took a few years in LA before he stopped wearing a cowboy hat, but he continued wearing cowboy boots, a trait that exposed him to ridicule by his more cosmopolitan colleagues. Roger Lopes, born Rogilio Lopez, was medium height and either slender or pudgy depending on if he had his drinking under control. As a young man before the war, he had been a successful door-to-door salesman. After he was drafted, Uncle Sam realized Lopes's skills and made him a recruiter.

The detectives and their passengers drove northeast through the hills on Atlantic on the lookout for Cliff's car. They ran their lights and siren. The drive had a surreal feel for Mary: the traffic moving aside for them, the lights, and the constant noise. The officers, Janice included, seemed like they enjoyed it; Mary knew she could never get used to it, could never experience it with anything but dread. After driving several minutes, they noticed smoke rising from the road up ahead. As they drew closer, they could see skid marks on the southbound lane that swung back and forth for a distance. Farther on they saw a car on fire in the ditch beside the road. They could see where the car had crossed onto the shoulder and slid down the embankment into the ditch. The car had bounced along the ditch and ended up lying on its side against the embankment on the far side of the ditch. They parked on the shoulder in line with the burning car. It was Cliff's car. The car body was mangled, its windows busted out and the passenger compartment fully engulfed in flame. Mary, in the backseat, began to sob. Lewis radioed for assistance. He demanded a fire truck and an ambulance immediately. Lopes got out of the car, stood at the edge of the ditch, and watched the car burn. The flames spread through the dry weeds. He was muttering, "Oh shit, oh shit." Janice sat silently next to Mary, tears running down her cheeks. Then they heard a noise, indistinct at first, but as it grew louder, they recognized it as shouting in a foreign language. Looking southward, they saw Cliff Thoms limping toward them, hatless, his suit torn and bloody. He held a handkerchief to his forehead. Blood had soaked the handkerchief and was dripping off his nose. Cliff was swearing at them in Chinese.

"I didn't know you could speak Chinese," Lewis said as Cliff walked up.

"Just the dirty words. Were you planning on standing there all night watching me burn?"

"Nah, Boss. We were leaving soon; we have an eight-thirty dinner reservation," Lewis said, checking his wristwatch. "Barbecue sounded good."

"We should at least wait for the fire truck and ambulance," Lopes said, vastly relieved. "You may need some stitches; that cut on your head looks deep."

Deputy sheriffs soon arrived. They took Cliff back to the East LA sheriff's station where a doctor met him. After the doctor cleaned and stitched his wound, Cliff refused to be taken to County-USC hospital for observation. He rode back to the Red Onion restaurant with Mary, Janice, and the detectives.

When he arrived, the ambulance attendants were loading Bill Wright. Wright was conscious but could not tell them anything about his attacker. Harry and Frank told Cliff that they were still waiting for the coroner's truck.

Cliff walked over to where Sanchez lay and illuminated his body with a flashlight. Sanchez was lying face down beside trash cans set along a stretch of dirt between two parking lots. A small amount of blood had soaked into the dirt. Cliff patted the body down and located a snub-nosed revolver that Sanchez had hidden in an ankle holster. "What do you think, Harry?"

"It looks like Vincent got Ray first and didn't take time

to search him. Then he got Bill and knew no one else was watching."

"Yeah, that's how I see it. Do you think he spotted all of us?"

"Sure. Sam called, what, six twenty-five? Vincent said he'd be here in twenty minutes. Okay, so maybe he gets here at six forty-five, cases the place for half an hour, and then makes his move. He sees us, but we don't see him. The guy is a ghost," Harry concluded, shrugging his shoulders.

Cliff didn't see the gesture; he was still looking at Ray. "We should have seen him. We were waiting for him. We knew he was coming. Now Ray is dead, and Dorothy is as good as dead." Cliff sounded despondent. "I need to call Fitts."

Better you than me, thought Harry.

In his rearview mirror, Nicky saw the Hudson disappear off the road and a second later throw up a cloud of dust as it plowed along the ditch. He pulled to the shoulder and watched the Hudson burst into flames. He stayed long enough to see that the driver did not crawl out of the burning car, and only then did he continue on his way. Nicky turned west on Valley Boulevard and headed to El Monte. He slowed once he came to the walnut orchards and pulled into several before he found what he wanted: a pickup truck with the keys left in it. He carried Dorothy to the cab of the truck and crammed her into the foot well on the passenger side. He then took his extra clothes, the blond wig, and the lifts and tossed them in the cab. Finally, he pushed the Studebaker into a ditch and threw a few branches over it. They'd find it in the morning, Nicky knew, but it wouldn't provide any clues to where he and Dorothy were headed.

He drove north on Rosemead Boulevard all the way to Route 66 and then headed west to Santa Monica. To a cop, he'd look like any other truck farmer or laborer heading into the big city. No one stopped him; no one even gave him a second look.

Harry gave Cliff a ride to his office. Cliff asked him to wait while he made the call to Fitts. It was just after nine o'clock. Reluctantly he dialed Fitts's number. The receiver was lifted on the first ring.

"Buron, sorry to call you at home, but—"

"Tommy, I heard what happened. I have been getting calls from sheriffs' offices and police departments for the last hour. How's your head?"

"It took a few stitches to close up the wound. I still have a headache. Buron, I just wanted to say how sorry I am about how things turned out. I could've had more men stationed around, but—"

"Tommy, we discussed this before. We already agreed that if there were more men, Vincent or Nicky or whoever would've spotted them and stayed away. Losing an officer's bad; I just feel lucky that we didn't lose you and Officer Wright as well."

"Someone should call Lenny Green and tell him. It was my operation; I should call."

"No, you were acting under my orders. It's my responsibility. I'll call him. Do we have any leads on the car?"

"The blue Chevy turned up abandoned where they switched cars. I don't understand it. Vincent picked her up in the blue car, and Nicky drove off in the Studebaker. Oh," Cliff said, thinking out loud, "Vincent probably switched cars. They would expect us to put out an APB for blue cars. He just drove off in another car and slipped through our fingers. The Studebaker, well, I suppose Nicky got through the towns and into the foothills before the police could react. Did you still want me to be available tomorrow?"

"I'll have to get back to you on that." There was a long pause. Cliff waited in silence; it seemed that Fitts had something to add. "Let's see if the Studebaker shows up. Let the patrol people do their job. You go home and get some rest. We're all going to be busy tomorrow."

Once the call was over, Cliff felt exhausted. He sat at his desk and stared at the blotter. His head throbbed, and he was sore all over. He suddenly remembered that his suit was ruined; he felt mildly disgusted with himself that he cared. He wondered if his hat had made it out of the car, but no matter. If it wasn't burned in the car fire, it had been wrecked by blood.

Cliff's phone rang. *Lucille?* he wondered. He picked up the receiver. He noticed dried blood on his hand.

"Cliff, this is A. J. How are you feeling? I heard what happened."

"I'm okay. I have a headache and bruises, but I'll survive."

"The fellow that you were after, he got away?"

"Yes."

"Any leads?"

"No, none."

"Maybe you could give it a day before you pick up the search. Take a day off."

"Maybe you didn't hear, but he kidnapped a civilian. He's going to kill her as soon as he gets a chance."

"How much do they pay you at the DA's office?"

"Not enough."

"That's what I thought. And you supplement your income with your private clients, right?"

"Yes."

"You could make more, a lot more, if you represented East Coast interests. It could be arranged."

The idea caught him by surprise. "What would I have to do?" Cliff asked dryly.

"Nothing. You would do nothing tomorrow. You would take the day off. Call in sick. Hell, you've been in a terrible car accident and took how many stitches? No one would blame you."

"Dorothy will die."

"Casualty of war. Can't be helped. And that Nicky fellow you're after, he'll turn up."

"What's going on?"

"They don't tell me. They just say they want you to work for them. Doing nothing for one day is the price of admission."

"More people will die. That's the real price, isn't it?"

"Don't get all high and mighty with me. You take Tony's money, and I don't see you turning yourself in. This isn't that different."

"Tony doesn't kill people. You've got to draw a line somewhere."

"Tony is small time, and you're small time. If you want to break into the major leagues and make the big money, you have to be prepared to play rough."

"I have to think about it."

"You do that. And while you're at it, ask Lucille if she wants to live in Pasadena or in Beverly Hills. Ask her if she wants furs and diamonds and a live-in maid. She deserves to be treated like a queen. Everybody has a price; don't set yours too low. You're too good an attorney to stay stuck in the minor leagues."

"I ... I have to think about it," Cliff said and hung up the phone.

Harry drove Cliff home. Lucille met him at the door. After

Cliff assured her that he had no permanent injuries, she sent him straight to their bathroom to take a shower. While he showered, she examined his suit. Surprised but grateful that Cliff wasn't hurt any worse than he had been, she threw away his suit without a second thought. As Lucille waited for Cliff to finish in the bathroom, she wondered what this fiasco would mean for his career.

Father Conti was sitting on a folding chair in the hallway when Lou stepped out of the morgue. Luigi Conti had been the priest at San Secondo d'Asti Catholic Church since 1931, five years after it was founded by Secondo Guasti, the patriarch of the town of Guasti. The church was surrounded by thousands of acres of vineyards and a thriving community of Italian immigrants. Conti, the community's shepherd, sat in silence with his hands pressed together and his head bowed as if in prayer. He looked up as Lou approached.

"Father, I believe we spoke earlier on the phone. I'm Lou Gomez, the lead detective investigating the death of Daniel Roberts and, now, of Ricardo Stralla."

Father Conti rose and shook Lou's hand. "Yes, Detective Gomez. I was hoping to speak with your partner, Williams."

"You can tell me anything you wanted to say to Williams."

"Yes, of course, but I was wondering if he ever found Ricardo."

"Found Ricardo? I don't understand."

"Williams was out to the church this evening, about five, looking for Ricardo. It must've been just shortly before Ricardo was murdered. I imagine that Ricardo hid from him. Ricardo was not strong. He was not quite ready to surrender himself.

Or perhaps Ricardo was already dead. Such a cruel and wicked act. Poor Ricardo. Too many temptations—easy money, easy women. Surely your partner has told you all this."

Lou thought back on the afternoon. A little after three o'clock, Randy said he was leaving the station to follow up on Dorothy's alibi. At the time Lou was suspicious of this sudden show of initiative and was afraid that Randy was going home to drink. Now, looking at Father Conti, Lou did a quick calculation: if Randy was in the Cucamonga area at five, he had just enough time to do a cursory search for Ricardo before going home, getting drunk, and answering Lou's call at 7:15 p.m. "I was out of the office when he called. What did Ricardo tell you?"

"I explained this to your partner. Ricardo spoke to me in my capacity as a priest. He confided in me in confession. I cannot discuss what he said."

"Well, how about hypothetically ..."

"No, Officer, no games. What Ricardo told me is off limits. But"—Father Conti looked down at the floor for a second and said yes to himself before looking up at Lou—"you may find it interesting that Ricardo's mother asked me two days ago what 'skimming' was. I learned today from a friend that skimming is something one might do in a business that is paid primarily in cash."

"Such as a casino."

"If you say so."

"Did Ricardo's mother say anything else that I might find interesting?"

"Yes. She said she was to alert Ricardo if a woman, a young woman, called for him. She also wanted to discuss mortal sins. From her level of distress, I inferred it was a grave sin, not theft, presumably. You, of course, must know all about mortal sins."

"Yes—must be a grave matter, must be committed with full knowledge, and must be deliberate." Lou closed his eyes and recalled from memory, "Do not kill, do not commit adultery, do not steal, do not bear false witness, do not defraud, and honor your father and your mother."

"Yes, exactly. How many years in Catholic school?"

"Four. In high school. I received a scholarship."

"A well-deserved scholarship apparently. You remain committed?"

"Well, on holidays and—"

"Yes, Christmas and Easter and the occasional baptism," the priest said, nodding. "The church is always open. You may find your way back more often as you grow older. And the policeman's patron saint, Saint Michael the Archangel?"

"That prayer I know." Lou smiled sheepishly.

"Intercession is real," Conti said earnestly. "Prayer from a place of true humility is powerful. Don't be too proud to pray.

"I have arranged to spend the night at a parish house here in Santa Monica. Perhaps you would be so kind as to give me a ride."

"It would be my pleasure, Father."

Driving home after he dropped off Father Conti, Lou tried to make sense of what the priest had told him. He didn't believe it was a coincidence that Ricardo Stralla and Daniel Roberts were killed in the same manner. Whoever killed Stralla also killed Roberts, so who, Lou asked himself, had the means, motive, and opportunity to kill Roberts?

Randy and Lou at first assumed that Cornero had Roberts killed because Roberts was skimming—obvious suspect, obvious motive: Occam's razor and all that. But if Cornero had Roberts killed, the murder would have been done as a punishment for Roberts and as a warning to others. The body would have been mutilated—the right hand cut off for stealing, for instance—and left where it could be easily found. Even if Cornero killed Roberts, why kill Stralla? It would require that Stralla be in on the skimming, that Cornero overcome a reluctance to kill family members, and that he be willing to have his nephew killed in front of a church. All these were possible, but none were probable. Lou dismissed Cornero as the killer.

Lou's investigation suggested that Roberts's killer worked for Lenny Green. Roberts was picked up in Green's Bugatti and was taken to Green's Malibu house where he was shot. Roberts's body could easily have been moved from the house through the trap door and onto a boat where it could be carried to and eventually dumped by the pier. Yes, Green and his boys could have done the murder, but an experienced mobster would plan a hit so the evidence pointed away from him. Here the obvious mistakes made Lou suspicious. First, using the Bugatti didn't make sense. If you were planning on killing someone, you didn't pick him up in a car that drew attention; you stole a common car and dumped it afterward. Also, why would Lenny Green let Lou walk out of the Malibu house alive? Lenny and his boys would have killed Lou if they knew he had just seen the location of Roberts's murder. Finally, why dump Roberts's body right under the pier instead of five miles out to sea where it would never be found?

If someone was trying to frame Green, then everything made sense. The killers used a Bugatti *because* it got noticed and there were only two in the area, Lenny Green's and George Raft's. Green let Lou walk out of the Malibu house because he didn't know Roberts had been killed there. Besides, as Lou proved, anyone could have gotten into the house. And why dump the body near the pier? Because the killers wanted it to be found.

Once he accepted that lots of people could have killed Roberts and Stralla, the crucial question became motive. But here Lou drew a blank. He drove on, oblivious to the familiar sights, his mind spinning. *Screw motive*, he thought to himself at last. He couldn't read minds, but he could work the problem backward: what did killing Roberts and Stralla result in and who wanted that result? Killing Roberts made Stralla head of the counting room and put him in a position to skim. But Stralla didn't skim; he went home, had a crisis of faith, and confessed something to his priest. Stralla's attack of conscience made him a liability—that's why he was eliminated.

The priest implied that Ricardo had a girlfriend who wanted him to skim. But skimming was dangerous; if Bugsy found out about it, he'd have the boy killed. Since the boy was Cornero's nephew, Bugsy would assume he was skimming on Cornero's orders. Cornero would end up on a slab beside his nephew. Bugsy would then need a new front man to insulate himself from the press and police inquiries. He would want a local mobster to front him, someone who knew whose palms to grease to keep the *Rex* in business, someone like Lenny Green or Jack Dragna, the mafia boss of Los Angeles who ran most of the gambling in town. Between Green and Dragna, Green would be Bugsy's first choice as his new front man—they were friends from the old days in Brooklyn—but Bugsy wouldn't choose Green if he was under suspicion for Roberts's murder.

Dragna was the key. He was always pressuring the smaller gambling operations like Green's. And rumor had it that Dragna put out a contract on Cornero the previous year that was rescinded only because Attorney General Warren put gambling under a microscope and made the hit too dangerous. Dragna could cripple Green's business and get rid of Cornero through one operation. He could get a girl to seduce Ricardo Stralla and convince him that Daniel Roberts needed to go. The girl could use the Bugatti and the Malibu house on Friday since Dorothy was in Mexico. With Roberts dead, Stralla would take charge of the counting room and could start to skim. Dragna would have someone blow the whistle on Stralla, and Bugsy would have Stralla and Cornero eliminated. With Cornero gone, Bugsy would choose Dragna to run the *Rex* because the inevitable police investigation would conclude that Lenny Green was responsible for Roberts's murder.

The plan could work, but there were so many moving parts. Lou doubted even Dragna was capable of such intricate planning. *But who knows?* Lou thought as he pulled into his driveway. The bastard was Sicilian, and those Sicilians grew up finding new ways to stab each other in the back. *Even other Italians think they're*—Lou paused to fish out his house key and capture the correct word—*duplicitous.*

Carlota answered the call on the first ring. She too had been waiting by the phone, waiting for a call she feared. She always worried when Dorothy went out, always waited for her until at least three in the morning. Past that time she could assume that Dorothy was staying the night with a friend. In her mind it was always a girlfriend whose parents had a spare bedroom. "Green residence," Carlota said clearly, almost accent free. She used to practice certain phone phrases with Dorothy so callers could understand her with ease.

"I need to speak to Mr. Green. Tell him that Buron Fitts is calling. He'll want to speak with me."

Fitts. The name was familiar although Carlota usually heard it as "goddamn Fitts" from Señor Green.

"Please wait." Carlota ran to the study and announced the call. Green picked up the phone in that room. Carlota rushed back to the phone in the foyer to listen in, careful to cover the mouthpiece silently with her palm. When the call was over, Carlota hung up the phone. Lenny Green was already rushing up the stairs, calling out instructions to his men. They would run their search operation from Green's office at his nightclub. Carlota did not understand exactly why but the phone lines at the club were "safer." Before they left, she heard Green's men boast that they would know from their police sources where Dorothy was before Fitts knew. As soon as Green and his men were out the door, Carlota called the one man who truly loved Dorothy, the father of her child, a man who would do anything to get her back safely. She told him everything she heard from the conversation between Fitts and Señor Green in the words they used, even if those words did not make sense.

CHAPTER 16

He pushed the car hard, weaving in and out of slower traffic. He drove almost, but not quite, recklessly. His window was rolled down, and the cool night air was sobering. As he drove, he thought about her incessantly. He recalled the first time he saw her there at the beach. He had come to the beach in Santa Monica to get out of his apartment, to get away from work, to be in the sun, and to be around other people, but not with them. He was lying on a blanket in the sand near the pier. He could hear the rolling waves, the music from the merry-go-round, and children yelling. The sun was hot, and the smell of the ocean mixed with the aroma of hamburgers was intoxicating. A shadow fell on him. When he looked up, he saw a beautiful young girl in a one-piece bathing suit that defined every curve of her breasts and slender hips on her not-quite-mature body. Her long blonde hair was swirling around her like a halo. He could tell she was still growing; she wasn't quite into her body yet. But what a body! He looked at her and thought, *Another year.*

He was getting stimulated just looking at her as she strode from the water toward him. She was silhouetted by the sun behind her, looking like a young Venus arising from the sea. He kept gazing until he turned over to avoid embarrassing himself.

"Hey, mister, is this your dog?" she asked. Randy was surprised that a young woman would address a stranger, an older man, even if it was about a dog. "The dog is hurt," she stated matter-of-factly. "Can you help me with him?"

Before responding, he reminded himself, *Too young.* "Sure, let's take a look."

They stood over the dog, a golden Labrador retriever. She was lying on her side, panting in the hot sun. Her red-rimmed eyes were watery and bulging out. She didn't have the strength to get up on all fours.

"Damn owner should put this poor dog out of her misery," the girl said. "If we had a gun, we could do it."

"We should try to find the owner," Randy suggested.

"I've already asked around. The owners dumped the dog here. You're a cop, right? You have a gun. We can take the bitch to Topanga Canyon, shoot her there, and bury her where no one could ever find her."

"How did you know I was a cop?"

"Oh, I was watching you. I saw the way you look at people. So, are you going to put down the bitch, or are you gonna do nothing and let her suffer?"

"I can do it. Do you want to come with me to see that things are done right?" Randy asked.

"Sure, but"—Dorothy looked around—"I have to tell Carlota, my *dueña*, where I'm going. And you gotta bring me back here."

As they drove up Topanga Canyon, Dorothy asked, "Do you know where there is a safe place to take care of the dog?"

"Yeah, there's a small grove up in the hills not too far off the road. We can put her down and bury her there. I have a shovel in the trunk. I've been stuck on dirt roads around here before; I've learned to keep a shovel handy," Randy explained.

At Dorothy's urging, he drove faster and faster up the twisting, deserted one-lane road until he dared not go any faster. They could overtake a slower car on a blind curve and rear-end it, or, worse yet, meet a car coming down the road head-on with no chance of avoiding it. Despite the risk, neither Randy nor Dorothy were afraid. The danger seemed to free them from any other concern in their lives; they were alive in the moment with the possibility of death around the next curve. Conversation came easily. Dorothy told of her recent trip to New York by plane and train while Randy spoke of the upcoming presidential election between Hoover and Roosevelt.

He pulled off the road and stopped the car. They both got out. Randy took his gun from the glove compartment and shoved it in his waistband. He removed a shovel from the trunk and handed it to Dorothy. Gently he lifted the Labrador from the backseat and carried her in his arms. As they walked to the grove, Dorothy asked, "While we're up here, will you teach me to shoot? I always wanted to learn. My father won't let his men teach me 'cause I'm a girl."

Randy laid the dog down. Standing in the shade of the grove, he wondered who this creature was that he'd found. Why did her father have men with guns? How could she seem so innocent one moment and so reckless the next? "Shooting is serious business," Randy said, trying to read the young woman's expression. "You should never point a gun at anyone unless you're ready to kill."

"Don't get so excited. I understand about guns."

Reluctantly he drew his gun. "All I have is a snub-nosed .38

with me. It's a gun for close quarters, when you're in the same room with the person you're shooting at."

"Show it to me." Dorothy walked over to where Randy was loading the gun so she could see the operation. She brushed against his arm as she watched each step. When the cylinder was loaded and snapped back into place, Dorothy said, "Show me how to aim."

Randy handed her the revolver. He knew she was trouble, but he couldn't help himself. He pressed up against her and put his arm over her shoulder. "Close one eye and look down the sights. Line up the rear sight, the front sight, and your target. If you have time for a careful shot, pull back the hammer till it clicks, then squeeze the trigger smoothly. If you need to hurry the shot, you can just pull the trigger, but it will feel heavier and you'll need to work to keep the sights on your target."

"I recognize the sound of a hammer being cocked. It's frightening but exciting," she said.

Randy stood there with Dorothy in his arms, breathing in her scent, growing intoxicated by her aroma. Dorothy squeezed the trigger, and the gun barked. A wood chip flew off a nearby tree.

"Let's put down the bitch."

Randy took back the revolver and aimed at the dog's chest. He fired. The dog yelped and collapsed.

"Is she dead?"

"No, not yet. She'll bleed out in a couple of minutes." The dog lay whimpering in a spreading pool of its own blood. Randy stood mesmerized, watching the rapid rise and fall of the dog's chest and listening to its wet, shallow breaths. He looked over at Dorothy. She stared intently at the dog, her eyes bright with excitement, a tightlipped smile on her face. "I'll put one in the dog's head," Randy said softly. "That'll finish her off."

"Let me." Dorothy reached out for the gun but still hadn't taken her eyes off the dog.

"It's harder to kill up close where you can see the life in their eyes go out."

"Give me the gun," Dorothy demanded as she stepped closer to Randy. She trembled with exhilaration. Randy handed over the gun. Dorothy walked over to where the dog lay struggling for breath. She looked down at the dog, took steady aim with her arm fully extended, and pulled the trigger. The shot rang through the little grove. The dog heaved and then lay still.

Randy raised his eyes from the dog to Dorothy's face. She was flushed, excited, and smiling. He found himself energized by the whole episode. He quickly scanned the ground for a likely burial spot. Locating a small depression where he didn't expect tree roots, he began to dig. Once he had a suitable hole, he dragged the dog over and dumped the body in. He covered it over with dirt and, where there had been a small depression, the area was even with the rest of the surrounding dirt. "Let's get you back to the beach."

"You're more fun than other guys," Dorothy said with a laugh. "Maybe we can get together some other time and do something special ... if you know what I mean."

Randy remembered how later they would meet in secret. How Carlota would take Dorothy to the movies, buy two tickets, and then watch as Dorothy walked out of the theater and into Randy's arms. Randy was vaguely aware that Dorothy ran with him partly because it was forbidden and partly to hurt her father, but he loved her nevertheless. Randy needed to be with her, needed her to make him feel alive. Some of his few happy memories since the war were of the times he drove with her to a remote beach, set out a blanket, and brought along some Jack Daniels. They would lie around for hours telling each other stories of their childhood, laughing, and making love. Their child together was another source of joy even if she could not be acknowledged.

Despite their twenty-year difference in age, he loved her as an equal. She loved him, in her own way, as much as she could love another person. That, of course, would not stop her from being with other men. Randy accepted that, but he took comfort in knowing that they meant nothing to her beyond the thrill of a one-night stand or as fools to be manipulated.

Randy pushed the memories back and focused on driving. He was determined to save Dorothy if he could. He was headed south on Lincoln Boulevard and was almost to Manchester Avenue. His plan was to start at the Red Onion restaurant and ask around. Some patron had to know something he hadn't told the police. Randy would get people to talk, even if he had to beat the information out of them. And he would gladly kill this Nicky character, and anyone else, to save Dorothy. He was ready: his .38 was on his hip and a shotgun was in the trunk; someone would die tonight and Randy didn't care who it was.

As Randy drove up to the Red Onion restaurant, he saw several squad cars with red lights flashing and officers in uniform standing around, but no ambulance or meat wagon. He parked behind the restaurant and asked one of the uniformed officers who was in charge. The officer pointed to Paul Lewis. Lewis was wearing his cowboy boots with a striped, blue-gray double-breasted suit. Randy was surprised to see that Lewis was about his height, perhaps taller in the boots. Lewis's suit looked boxy on his slender build. Randy inferred that Lewis was single—a wife or girlfriend would not have let him buy that suit.

"Detective, I'm Officer Williams from Santa Monica PD," Randy said, producing his badge. "Our office has an interest in the kidnapped victim in an unrelated matter."

Lewis looked Randy up and down suspiciously, noting his bloodshot eyes, disheveled suit, and the stink of sweat and whiskey that hung on him. "Well, ain't that just peachy. We can't help you here."

"Mind if I go into the restaurant and look around?"

"Suit yourself, but don't interfere with the investigation."

Inside the Red Onion, policemen were interviewing patrons and staff. Randy silently moved from officer to officer, listening to the questions and answers as the interviews continued. None of the patrons had noticed anything until a dark-haired woman rushed from the rear door, through the restaurant, and out the front. After that, all the patrons agreed, men in suits seemed to be running around in a panic. Drifting through the bar area, Randy overheard a pair of officers ask a man sitting at the bar a question that caught his attention.

"Did you see when Sam left?"

"Yeah, as soon as the ruckus started, Sam jumped off the bar stool and scrammed. He said something about catching a bus to San Diego."

"Did you see if Sam and the blonde in the red dress spoke to each other?"

"Nah, there was a line of guys that went up to her, but Sam stayed put until the cops started running around."

As soon as the officers moved on, Randy walked up to the man, flashed his badge, and said, "The boss says I gotta track down Sam and ask him a few questions. Sounds like something they can let the patrol boys do, but the boss said it has to be a detective. Hey, your glass is almost empty, can I get you another?"

"Yeah, sure. Billy," the man waved at the bartender, "a shot of Johnnie Walker. This public servant is paying."

Randy nodded his assent and waited for the shot to be poured. "I know what you told the uniforms but tell me again. Who is Sam and what does he look like?"

"He's some low-life, two-bit dope peddler. He's the one who knew the guy with the weird eyes, you know, the one they say grabbed the lady."

"What does Sam look like?"

"Sam is a short little shit. About five foot five. He always wears a cap like the Irish wear. I see him at the track all the time. He's wearing a plaid jacket, and he walks funny, like there's something wrong with his legs. Always in a hurry. He took off out of here like a bat out of hell."

"White, black, Mexican? Young, old?"

"Mexican, with bad skin. He's about, oh, I'd say in his thirties."

"Do you think he's really going to the bus depot?" Randy asked.

"Yeah, he said he's going to 'ride the hound.' Sam's got connections in San Diego."

Randy remembered that when Carlota called, she told him that Sam had called someone named Vincent and that Vincent was the one who grabbed Dorothy. Vincent passed her on to Nicky who was likely the Canyon Killer. Randy knew what he had to do: find Sam, get to Vincent, and track down Nicky. He drove to the main Greyhound bus station in downtown LA. As he drove north on Figueroa, doubts nagged at him—suppose Sam went to the substation in Long Beach, suppose the San Diego bus had already left, suppose, suppose, suppose. Randy realized that he had to assume that everything would break his way; otherwise, he wouldn't find Dorothy in time and she'd end up like the girls in the canyons. Sam to Vincent to Nicky—Tinker to Evers to Chance. It had to be that way; Randy had one chance to be right, but there were a hundred ways to be wrong.

He drove up to the bus station but couldn't find a parking place. He double-parked in front of the building and ran to the front entrance. He stopped before opening the door and caught his breath, straightened his hat, and then strolled into the waiting room. The room was half filled with waiting passengers seated on wooden benches that reminded Randy of pews. Luggage was stacked on the floor in front of its owners. He started circling the benches when he noticed in the corner near the bathrooms a man slumped down on a bench. The man wore a cap. Randy moved closer and could see the man's plaid jacket and that the man was hugging himself while rocking forward and back from the waist. Only when Randy sat beside him on the bench did he see that Sam's face was shiny with sweat even as he shivered from a chill. Sam started to slide away, but Randy gripped his right wrist.

"We got a deal, copper. That DA said I can go."

"I'm from Santa Monica PD; you don't have a deal with me. Tell me what I want to know and you can still make your bus; otherwise, I'll take you in and you can sit in a cell all weekend. That'd be about, what, sixty hours of cold turkey?"

"You don't got jurisdiction. They'd cut me loose."

Randy inclined his head toward Sam and said softly, "Maybe, but before that we'll have Vincent in custody. You two should have lots to talk about."

"I don't know nothin'," Sam protested. He tried to pull away, but Randy held him fast.

"We're going to the men's room for a little chat. You can walk, or I can drag you."

Sam knew that the bus would be boarding soon. He needed

to make a decision fast. He was sure that this detective wouldn't hesitate to hold him all weekend, but they couldn't use Vincent to scare him. Vincent was too sly to be caught by these dumb cops. The problem was that the DA might renege on their deal. Sam knew he couldn't do a five-year stretch and come out alive. "Okay, let's go."

The men walked together to the men's room, and Randy held Sam's wrist the whole time. Once inside the restroom, Randy bent down and looked under the stalls to make sure they were alone. "I only want to know one thing: what's the telephone number you called to get in touch with Vincent?"

Sam looked worse in the bright light of the restroom. Sweat had soaked his collar and had beaded up on his face. He shook like a man with palsy. "I changed my mind. Fuck you. I'm not telling you anything."

With his free hand, Randy punched Sam in the gut.

Sam doubled over and vomited on his shoes. The restroom door opened and a man started to step inside.

"Get out of here," Randy growled. "Police business." The man quickly took in the scene. Randy still held Sam's wrist. Sam was bent over and had begun to retch again. The man backed out the door. "I don't want you," Randy told Sam. "I want the man who kidnapped Dorothy. Now talk."

Sam's vision was blurred, and he felt like he might pass out. "Okay, okay, let go of my hand. I need to get something." Randy released his grip. Sam straightened up and reached inside of his coat to where the lining had become unraveled at a seam. Hidden under the lining was a small piece of paper with names and phone numbers.

Randy snatched the paper from Sam's hand and stared at it. "Which one?"

"This one," Sam said, pointing to an entry. It read "Tommy," then a number, and then "Vinny."

"I'm keeping this."

"Sure. Are we done?" Sam had walked over to a stall and was using toilet paper to clean off his shoes.

"Yeah, we're done."

"You know," Sam said with a smile, "I hope you do find Vinny."

"Why's that?"

"You'll see."

Randy wanted to leave before the LA officers showed up. They didn't appreciate other departments hunting in their territory. He drove to a drugstore where he made a phone call to the station. The station had a crisscross or reverse directory that listed telephone numbers and the corresponding addresses. The duty office was able to provide Randy with Tommy's address.

Tommy lived on Beloit, between Santa Monica Boulevard and Olympic on the west side of Los Angeles. His place was one unit in a typical court that had four separate small bungalows, two on each side of a central walkway. The court was quiet and well kept. The lawn had been recently mowed, and there was a large bougainvillea bush climbing up one side of the wall. Randy drove past the address, parked, and walked back to the court. He checked the mailboxes at the front and saw that a T. Bertolli lived in number four, one of the back bungalows. Randy returned to his car, drove to the end of the block, turned right, and went down half a block until he came to the alley that ran behind the residences on Beloit. He drove along the alley and parked at the carports for Tommy's court. Randy retrieved a pry bar from his trunk and followed the sidewalk behind Tommy's bungalow. A light was on inside. Using the pry bar, Randy forced open the door almost silently. He could hear a radio tuned to swing music. He stepped through the doorway into the bungalow's narrow kitchen, passed the pry bar to his left hand, and pulled his revolver with his right. Five steps took him to the bedroom. The only light in the room came from the kitchen. Tommy lay on the bed with his eyes closed. He was a stocky man in his thirties with black hair and a prominent Roman nose. He was dressed in slacks and an undershirt. His suit coat hung on the back of a chair, and a dress shirt and tie were draped across the seat of the chair. Black leather shoes and dark socks were on the floor at the foot of the bed. A cigarette burned in an ashtray on the nightstand. Randy walked softly up to the bed and, as he sat on the edge, he pointed his gun at Tommy's face.

The man woke with a start and sat up. The barrel of the gun was three inches from the bridge of his nose. He looked cross-eyed at it and then shifted his eyes to Randy. "What's this? A shakedown? You bastards have been paid. Get the hell out of here before I call your captain!"

"Hey, *paisan*, I'm not with LAPD. You're going to tell me what I want to know, or I'm going to paint the wall with your brains. *Capisce?*"

"The people I work for have a long reach. Maybe you should worry about your wife and kids."

"Oh," Randy said, more as a long exhalation than as a word as he lowered his gun down and to his right. Tommy smiled until the gun whipped across his face. "Now, listen, you piece of shit, I don't care about you or your guinea friends. Tell me what I need to know. Where are Vincent and Nicky?"

"Nicky? I don't know nothing about Nicky. They told me the

boys in the Outfit took Nicky for a ride." Tommy's eyes refocused on the barrel of the revolver. "Mother of God." Tommy's voice was shaking; he had suddenly realized that someone crazy enough to go after Vincent and Nicky was crazy enough to kill him. "I just pass messages to Vincent."

"You have to do better than that! Where does he live?"

"I don't know where he lives. I call his number at one o'clock or nine and pass on information and assignments. That's all I know!"

Randy's frustration was growing. Tommy was talking but not telling him what he wanted to know. "Where is he taking Dorothy?"

"I don't know no Dorothy. Vincent goes to the track and picks up broads afterward. Where he takes them and what he does to them, I don't ask."

Randy cocked the revolver and stood up.

"Wait! I know where he'll be tomorrow."

"Out with it! This ain't no time for holding back!"

"Vincent is supposed to meet some guy at the Hollywood Roosevelt Hotel tomorrow. I don't know why."

"Yeah? Who's he meeting?"

"I don't know. They don't tell me. The guy will be wearing a blue coat and carrying a copy of the LA Times in his left hand. By the pool near the diving board."

"What time?"

"Ah ... ah ... eleven thirty. Roosevelt Hotel eleven thirty tomorrow by the diving board."

"Okay, okay." Randy considered this information. Tommy, he suspected, was a one-way valve: information goes one way; nothing goes back the other way. "Who are you working for?"

"I don't know. I swear on the head of my mother. A guy named Johnny calls me at twelve thirty every day and tells me what to do. Cash in an envelope shows up every Friday. I think it's the Syndicate from back east, but I don't ask questions."

Just as Randy figured, Tommy was merely a tool, but he still had one more use. "What's Vincent's number?"

"It's there, on the paper beside the ashtray. Careful! That's flash paper."

Randy eased the revolver's trigger down, holstered his gun, and reached for the paper. Out of the corner of his eye, he watched Tommy pivot around and put his feet on the floor. Just as Tommy was starting to stand, Randy swung the pry bar and smashed Tommy in the head. A spray of blood splashed onto the flash paper and Randy's shirt cuff. Tommy fell back, his body stretched out on the bed. Randy set the pry bar on the bed, reached over, and grabbed a bed pillow. He held the pillow over Tommy's face, drew his revolver, and pressed it into the pillow before firing into Tommy's head. The pillow muffled most of the sound of the shot.

He left the way he had come, got in his car, and drove to a gas station. He called the station, and the same duty officer used the crisscross directory to furnish Randy with an address. The telephone number was to a mom-and-pop market in Venice. Randy drove down Santa Monica Boulevard to the store and questioned the owners. They confirmed that a tall, blond man used the phone almost every day at one or nine o'clock, but he never bought anything at the store and they knew nothing about him. Randy left the store and drove around Venice looking for a blue Chevy and a gray Studebaker. He didn't find either. He drove up and down the streets along the canals for two hours but decided it was useless. Nicky and Vincent were both on the run; there was no reason either would come back to Venice. Randy couldn't even be sure that either one lived nearby.

It had been a long, wearisome day and still he was left with too many unanswered questions. He decided to go home and get some sleep. In the morning he'll call Lou to tell him about the kidnapping, but not, he thought, about the Roosevelt Hotel. Randy planned to go there alone and wait for Vincent or Nicky. Lying in bed, Randy willed away images of a struggling Dorothy before drifting off to a troubled sleep.

Dorothy felt the truck coming to a stop. There was a rattle, a lurch forward, and then a jerk backward as the truck settled.

"I know you're awake," Nicky said in a silvery voice. "Have ya been plotting a way to escape?" he asked in a sweetly cajoling tone.

Dorothy listened in silence. She was frightened but also angry. She relished the thought that she and Randy would kill this bug. Randy would be looking for her; she was sure of it. Nicky got out of the truck, walked around the front, and yanked open the passenger door. When the smell of gasoline, warm rubber, and burnt oil poured into the cab, Dorothy felt her stomach giving way. She tried to hold back the eruption from her stomach but couldn't. Dorothy hung her head out the doorway and began to vomit. Nicky dragged the retching Dorothy onto the ground. Vomit splashed onto his pant legs and shoes. Red-faced with anger, Nicky kicked Dorothy in the thigh. Quickly he took the cord from around her wrists and used it as a gag. He pulled a set of handcuffs from his coat pocket and secured her wrists.

Dorothy lay on her side on the sandy ground and surveyed her surroundings. Her thoughts were still jumbled from the chloroform, and her senses recorded a kaleidoscope of sensations. She smelled oil being pumped and felt the rhythm of petroleum derricks through the ground. She heard water lapping against wharfs. In the moonlight, she could make out an ice plant with small pink flowers growing in deep sand. Cool, salty sea air told her that the beach was near, but she could be anywhere along one hundred miles of coastline. She could try to escape, but which direction would she go? She needed to recognize something, to get her bearings. Dorothy managed to climb to her feet but felt unsteady. A sudden shove on her shoulder pushed her toward what looked like a shack. She felt the handcuffs bite into her wrists and heard the sharp click of metal on metal. Gradually Dorothy was becoming more and more aware of her surroundings. She smelled food cooking, so she knew she was near civilization. Suddenly Dorothy realized where they were: Venice! It all made sense. The petroleum, the lapping water, the feel of sea air, and the faint smell that she recognized but couldn't quite place was saltwater taffy.

Nicky knew the neighborhood well. Many of the residents lived in low-rent bungalows or squatted in abandoned shacks. None paid much attention to what was going on outside. After a short walk, the two arrived at a secluded bungalow along a canal. Nicky opened the door and dragged a resisting Dorothy inside. When he started to unlock one of the handcuffs, Dorothy began to fight and flail her arms. She tried to run but was wobbly on her feet. Nicky caught her as she stumbled toward the door and slapped her across the face. Dorothy tried to scream, but the gag allowed only a guttural groan. The noise excited Nicky and spurred his imagination. As Nicky dragged Dorothy away from the door, he looked to the ceiling, trying to determine where the joists were located. But business before pleasure—he had to prepare for work in the morning. After the job was done, he would take his time with this one. She was headstrong; he would teach her humility. She would beg for death before he was done. He would … well, that was for tomorrow. For now he shackled her to a radiator along the back wall.

Before leaving the bungalow to move the truck farther away, he turned to see Dorothy struggling with the handcuffs, her face beginning to swell. "Doncha go anywhere 'til I get back now, ya hear?"

Dorothy heard the truck start and drive away. Venice, she realized to her dismay, was a good place to hide someone. Once the weather turned warm, tourists filled the Front, the walkway running along the shore between Ocean Park and Venice, but few people were willing to leave the well-lit walkway and venture around Venice's dark, unpaved streets or navigate among its swampy canals. Only someone who lived in the area would know his way around. But Randy would be looking for her, and her father would look for her, and even the police would look. Someone, Dorothy told herself, would find her before this madman butchered her.

Nicky came back twenty minutes later. Dorothy reasoned that he had moved the truck, maybe a mile away, and parked it with other cars that could stay out all night without drawing attention. He probably parked it near a pier where fishermen and crabbers would congregate.

"Listen, dollface, I gotta get up in the morning and do a job. When I get home, me and you are gonna have lots of fun. Right now I gotta get some sleep, and so do you," he said, stepping into the bathroom. He came out with a bottle of pills and a glass of water. "One for me," Nicky said before he swallowed a pill with a gulp of water, "and two for you." He forced two pills down her throat and poured some water into her mouth. Dorothy swallowed, happy to get some water for her parched throat. Nicky inspected her mouth and looked under her tongue. Satisfied that she had really swallowed the pills, Nicky took off his shoes and lay on the single bed. Soon he was asleep. Dorothy fought to stay awake, but within a few minutes she too was lost to sleep.

CHAPTER 17

Saturday, June 10, 1939

Cliff and Lucille sat in their sun-filled breakfast nook with their coffee and shared a newspaper.

"Cliffy, are you going to tell me what's bothering you?"

"I told you before—I just have a lot on my mind."

They read their portions of the newspaper in silence for a few minutes and then Lucille said, "Cliffy, you're in the paper." She folded back the page for him to look at.

Cliff looked up and glanced at the picture of his burning car. "So, am I the hero or the goat of this story?"

"They have you as the heroic fool. A fool for letting the Canyon Killer get away, but heroic for your 'death-defying chase.' It looks like Fitts kept a lid on some of the facts—they don't know who the kidnapped girl is." Lucille folded the paper and set it down. "Will they fire you?"

"Probably. Oh, they'll ask for my resignation and let me stay on for a few months. My failure is their failure, and they don't want to announce it to the world, but yes, I'm done at the DA's office."

"Well, you still have your private practice."

Cliff set down the newspaper and studied Lucille's face. He reached across the table for the cream pitcher and brushed against the back of her hand needing just to touch her. He poured a few drops of cream in his coffee and replaced the pitcher, brushing against her hand again.

Lucille met his eyes. She saw the tension in his face. "What is it? I know there's something you're not telling me."

Cliff closed his eyes and let out a long breath. "I was offered work last night. Wait, before you say anything, it's work for the East Coast mobsters, the Syndicate. It could be worth a lot of money, but it comes at a cost. They want me to drop the Canyon Killer case and not look for Dorothy."

"You can't do that; you can't let her die. I don't care what they promised you, those bastards. Don't work for killers; we don't need their blood money."

Cliff stood up.

"What are you going to do?"

"I need to call Fitts about something. Maybe I can catch him at his house."

"I mean after that."

"Take a shower and change my bandage. The wound wept into my hair last night."

"No, silly, about the job offer."

"Oh, nothing. After I shower, I'm going into work. I'll see if we have any leads to run down. I should check with the coroner about Ray and make sure someone contacted his family. Ah, while I'm in the shower, could you call the office and see if they can send someone to pick me up? I guess we should buy a new car while I can still qualify for a loan."

"What about poor Dorothy?"

"Like my grandmother used to say, 'Shed no tears until seeing the coffin.' It sounds better in Chinese. I'm going to assume that she is alive until we find her body. Nicky, if it is Nicky who has her, won't kill her quickly. That's the only thing we have going for us.

"Remember to call the office about a ride," Cliff said as he bent over and kissed Lucille on the forehead.

"Hey, Mr. Deputy DA," she said, grabbing the sleeve of his robe, "did you ever really consider throwing in with a bunch of murderers?"

"Not for a second." In his mind Cliff believed it.

Lucille released Cliff's robe. "But you asked me, not in so many words, if that was something that I was willing to do. Don't you know me by now?"

"I had to hear you say it. When I leave the DA's office, we are going to have a couple of tough years. Are you ready for that?"

"As long as we're together, I don't need anything else to be happy." Lucille stood up and started clearing the table. "Ah, not that I care, but what did the mobsters promise you?"

"Oh, you know, a home in Beverly Hills, furs, diamonds, a live-in maid. Nothing that you'd want."

"Hurry up and take your shower. Find the girl. And don't let that damn animal have her."

While he waited for a car to pick him up, Cliff called Buron Fitts's home. Fitts's wife answered and explained that Buron had left early for a meeting but was expected back in his office around ten o'clock. A few minutes later, a car arrived from the DA's office. Cliff went straight to the morgue. When Cliff walked into the autopsy lab, Ray's body was on a table. Cliff was surprised to see Dr. Yashida conducting the autopsy instead of one of his assistants. Yashida had already made the

Y incision through the chest and was dissecting the neck when Cliff arrived.

The doctor looked up and gave a small nod in greeting. Then he turned his attention back to the dissection. "Oh, this guy is good. Haven't seen this type of wound since the war. Military technique for sentry removal. Notice the trachea, torn and collapsed." Yashida motioned to Cliff to come closer and pointed out the damage to Ray's windpipe. "Sneak up on a sentry and smash his larynx by sticking your thumb and two or three fingers behind it, then give it a twist. With your other hand, you stab the subclavian artery." Yashida demonstrated the actions in the air, using his scalpel in place of a bayonet. "Sentry loses consciousness and bleeds out quickly. You catch him as he falls and hide the body. With his larynx crushed, he can't call out. It takes strength to crush the larynx and a cold disposition to stalk a man and kill him with a knife. So"—Yashida turned to look at Cliff—"was this the work of the Canyon Killer?"

"Him or his partner."

"Great team. Ah, no longitudinal cuts on the body if that means anything."

"No, not really. Our boy was in a hurry. Um, what about Ray's family?"

"I called them last night. Bad part of my job. I gave them your condolences, said you were recovering from a head injury or you would have called them yourself."

"Thank you. I ... I should have called them."

"You should have gone to the hospital. I halfway expected to see you here this morning on a gurney, dead from an occlusion. Chasing a killer half your age—that was stupid. Did you even have a gun?"

"Yes."

"Well, that's something," Yashida said with a shrug. "What's your next step?"

Cliff wiped a hand slowly across one eye. He shook his head weakly. "I don't know. I was hoping the patrol boys would come up with something last night."

"You came in through the back door?"

"Yes."

"Go back out the same way. There's a pack of reporters waiting for you by the front entrance. Oh, if anyone from the Sanchez family asks, tell them that he died quickly and painlessly. He didn't, but that's what I told them last night." Yashida saw Cliff frown. "A harmless lie. The truth would only make things worse," he said with a shake of his head.

Carlota had been up most of the night waiting and worrying about Dorothy. She managed to sleep for a few hours, but by eight o'clock she couldn't restrain herself any longer and called Randy at his house. "Mr. Randy, did you find her?"

"No, Carlota. I tracked her as far as I could and looked for hours, but there wasn't any sign of her. I have another lead, but I have to wait 'til later to follow it up. Did Green have any luck?"

"Señor Green not here. He is at his club."

"Yeah, sounds like he's still looking too."

"You find her soon, Mr. Randy?"

"God, I hope so. There are so many places she could be."

"*Quizás la bruja puede encontrarla.*"

"Yeah, whatever you say. I've got to get ready. Call me at the station this afternoon."

"Okay." Carlota heard Randy hang up. She thought about la bruja. The witch knew things. It wouldn't be a sin if it was for a good purpose. Carlota knew that the witch couldn't be an agent of God, but she could still be an instrument of God. Carlota decided to retrieve the witch's business card and call her if Randy was not successful.

Randy carefully cleaned and reloaded his revolver and then got ready to go to the Roosevelt Hotel. Before he left, he called Lou at home and informed him that he had heard from friends in the sheriff's department that Dorothy had been kidnapped, a detective on the Scott squad run by ADA Thoms had been killed, and that Thoms had almost died in a car crash. Lou told Randy about Ricardo Stralla's murder the night before and explained that the MO was the same as in Daniel Roberts's death.

"Maybe the cases are related. Could be the same guy who killed those girls in the hills also killed Roberts and Stralla, and had a reason to kidnap Dorothy," Randy suggested.

The idea that the Canyon Killer case and his case could be related startled Lou. He had gone from being certain on Wednesday night that Dorothy was involved to believing on Friday night that Dragna was behind the killings of Roberts and Stralla. Now the news of Dorothy's kidnapping troubled him; Lou distrusted coincidences. He began to question his theory of Dragna being behind the killing and was reminded that he and Randy had never verified Dorothy's alibi.

Lou asked Randy to meet him at the station. Randy said he could not make it in the morning because his car needed to be serviced and it might take several hours. They agreed to meet at the station in the early afternoon.

Back in his office, Cliff called Buron Fitts at exactly ten o'clock. The secretary told him that Fitts was not yet back from the meeting with the attorney general and that he should call back in an hour. Cliff called back exactly at eleven. The secretary was apologetic and said she would call Cliff back as soon as Fitts stepped into the office. Cliff waited anxiously by the phone. At eleven forty-five, the secretary called and whispered into the phone that Fitts had just returned. She asked Cliff to call back so she could answer the phone and announce that he was calling. Cliff called Fitts's office once more and was put through to his boss.

"Buron, I'm glad I caught up with you. I spoke to a confidential informant last night, and he implied that the Syndicate is planning something for today. He didn't know what. I know it's not much to go on, but I gather it is something big, maybe something to do with Nicky. Could Dorothy Green's kidnapping be a distraction to keep us busy while Nicky does—what?"

"Okay, Tommy, let's analyze what you have. We can start with the fact that Nicky is an elusive killer. But if he is responsible, with or without Vincent's help, for murdering four young women, doesn't that suggest that he is too unstable to be used by the Syndicate? And kidnapping Dorothy—how can that be part of a Syndicate scheme when you arranged, with no prior notice, to use Dorothy as bait? Clearly her kidnapping was a crime of opportunity and not part of an overall plan. Finally, why is this crime happening today? What is special about today? But let's say your information is correct, and Nicky will do something today. Nicky is a killer, so he will kill someone. Who will he kill? Mobsters kill other mobsters for business reasons. So the likelihood is that Nicky will kill a mob boss. A crime, yes, but I won't be losing any sleep over it. Pass your information over to the intelligence unit and take the rest of the weekend off. Monday we should meet and discuss what happened last night."

"I guess the talk won't involve a new assignment that you alluded to yesterday."

"No, Tommy, and I'm sorry about that. You were my first choice, but after what happened yesterday, well, you understand."

"If it's just the same to you, I'd like to work this weekend and see if I can clean up my mess. I shouldn't leave it for others, unless you're ordering me off the case."

"No, stay with it if you feel up to it, but you're on your own. I've disbanded the Scott-Mara squad pending an investigation. I was going to tell you about that on Monday, but you might as well know today. On the other thing, I just came from a meeting with Earl Warren at the Hollywood Roosevelt Hotel. He's planning on raiding the gambling ships and putting them out of business. He wanted someone from my office as the representative on the team he's putting together. LAPD, Santa Monica PD, LA County—we're all being brought in. The raids will happen later this month or in July. I have to keep you off the team—you're a leper for now."

"Raiding the ships? Even the *Rex*? How can he? The Supreme Court is still deciding whether the *Rex* is in local or international waters." Cliff was surprised that Earl Warren would risk incurring the wrath of the Supreme Court just to carry out his crusade against gambling interests.

"Yes, all of them." Fitts sounded distracted. "Warren wants the team in place by today so the planning can get started. He goes back to Sacramento tonight."

"Tonight? So he's here just for the rest of today? Maybe," the thought suddenly occurred to Cliff, "he's Nicky target."

"Unlikely. Tommy, I need to go into a meeting right now. Dwight will explain why Warren isn't the target. Dwight," Fitts said, handing the telephone to his assistant, "tell him about Dewey."

"Thoms, sorry to hear about last night. Buron regrets how things worked out for you. Yeah, about Dewey. We know the mob doesn't like to kill DAs because of the experience with Dutch Schultz and Thomas Dewey."

"Yes, I seem to remember the story." Cliff wondered if Dwight was Fitts's new fair-haired boy. As for Dewey and Schultz, Cliff knew the story well. Thomas Dewey was a New York prosecutor who hounded the mobster for years. Finally, Schultz went to the Syndicate's board of directors and requested permission to kill Dewey. The board refused. The Syndicate board thought that killing Dewey would bring down so much police scrutiny, especially federal interest, that it would be counterproductive to kill him. Schultz would not accept the board's ruling and had his organization start making preparations for the hit.

"Well, then you know that the mob had Schultz killed rather than risk having the FBI come after the Syndicate," the assistant explained as if speaking to a slow child. "The only way it makes sense for the mob to hit a DA is if the killer were completely untraceable back to the mob, which is virtually impossible. It would require that the killer have nothing on file: no arrest record, no picture, and no fingerprints.

"I've been waiting a long time for this, *Tommy*." Dwight spat out the name. "I'm looking forward to seeing you Monday morning. Nine o'clock, don't be late." The line went dead.

Cliff hung up the phone. "No record, no picture, and

no fingerprints." The description fit Nicky, and now A. J.'s disclosure made sense: wait one day and Nicky would turn up. Nicky would kill Warren and then the mob would kill Nicky. With Nicky dead, there would be no way to trace him back to the mob. But that meant that Nicky had to act today before Warren returned to the relative safety of his Sacramento offices.

A sudden pang of compassion for A. J. Barnes took Cliff by surprise. Did A. J. know he was a cog in a murderous machine? Yes, he must, assuming he even thought about it. The trick for most people would be not thinking about it. But if A. J. allowed himself to think about it, would he, Cliff wondered, try to extricate himself? Probably not. Cliff knew that Fitts was right; once you've crossed the line, each step forward was easier. The unspoken corollary was likewise true: reversing course was almost impossible. A. J. didn't deserve anyone's compassion. He put on blinders and started walking forward, crossed the line, and kept on going.

Standing in his office, Cliff knew two things: first, Nicky would try to kill Earl Warren that day, and second, he would not be able to convince Fitts to act on that fact. Cliff decided to contact Warren's head of security directly.

Lou got to the squad room about ten in the morning. Waiting for him was a report from officers who had interviewed fishermen on the Santa Monica pier the night before. The officers talked to two Friday night regulars who remembered a speedboat with either three or four passengers roaring up to the pier from the north about eleven o'clock the previous Friday. The boat was under the pier briefly before a man and a woman disembarked onto the landing at the west end of the pier and walked toward town. The speedboat went back the way it came. Neither man said he could identify the people who walked off the pier except to say that the woman was tall and loud.

Lou made some calls and determined that the couple could have caught a Red Car to Union Station and made the 12:10 a.m. express train to Mexico. It would take only a minute to lower a body over the side of a boat and into the water. Lou was convinced that the tall, loud woman was Dorothy, but Randy and he would still have to break her alibi.

"Roosevelt Hotel, how may I help you?"

"This is Assistant District Attorney Clifford Thoms from the LA County district attorney's office. I want to speak to the head of Attorney General Warren's security," Cliff said, trying to sound every bit the pompous bureaucrat.

"I'll put you through to Mr. White's office."

"This is Jerry White, Mr. Thoms. How may I help you?"

"I've been contacted by a confidential informant who has proved reliable in the past. This informant now indicates that the attorney general's life is in danger. The person we believe will make the attack has many aliases, but often goes by the name Nicky. He is approximately five feet seven inches tall, one hundred sixty-five pounds, and thirty years old, with black hair, brown eyes, and a New York accent. He may be working with another man who goes by the name Vincent, approximately five foot eleven and also about thirty years old, with blond hair and a New York accent. Both should be considered armed and extremely dangerous. Both appear to have connections with the East Coast Syndicate. Our information is that the attack should be expected today."

"Thank you, Mr. Thoms, for the information. I'll put extra precautions in place," the security chief replied and hung up.

Cliff was left holding the phone, surprised that White did not ask follow-up questions, did not inquire about the source of the information, and did not ask anything about the nature of the attack. The more Cliff thought about the conversation, the more he was disturbed. Gradually he realized that what bothered him most was not what White said or failed to ask, but his tone of voice and his attitude of unconcern. It was likely that White was already aware of the planned attack and knew more about Nicky and Vincent than Cliff did. That would account for White's lack of any sense of urgency. Still, Cliff couldn't shake a feeling of uneasiness. He decided to go to the Roosevelt Hotel himself although his main motivation, he had to admit, was his desire to confront Nicky and try, if it was still possible, to save Dorothy.

Randy drove to the Hollywood Roosevelt Hotel about nine thirty. He circled the block several times looking for someone or something that was out of place. He looked for florist deliverymen walking around with flowers, but not looking for an address; he looked for men leaning against buildings holding newspapers, but not reading them; he looked for cars parked on the street with their drivers sunk down in their seats. After he was satisfied that there were no obvious lookouts, Randy parked two blocks away from the Roosevelt Hotel and walked over to the building. He walked around the block several times. The second time he passed the doorman at the hotel entrance, he was careful to take off his suit coat and tie, which he folded over his arm, and carried his hat in his hand. He walked with a young woman and struck up a casual conversation as they passed the doorman. The doorman, who was in uniform, didn't seem to notice him, but stared glumly at the checkerboard tile on which he stood. Randy entered the hotel grounds through the back, off Hawthorn Avenue, and walked through the pool area. This area was enclosed on all four sides by a two-story building that was separate from the main, twelve-story structure that faced Hollywood Boulevard. Randy noted the lounge chairs and tables with umbrellas surrounding the pool. He made a mental note to return at eleven o'clock with a newspaper and sit at the far end of the pool area, away from the diving board, and watch for the man with the blue coat.

Randy put his coat and tie back on and entered the lobby. He found his way into the Blossom Room, a large Spanish-style banquet room designed to look like a courtyard with arches on the ground floor and second-story balconies that overlooked the open area. The room's ceiling had a grid of large, exposed wood beams with a delicate lattice of small wooden cross pieces. When not used as a banquet hall, radio shows and dance bands were broadcast from the room. It was most famous as the site of the first-ever Academy Awards ceremony in 1929.

Randy returned to the lobby and bought a newspaper and a pack of cigarettes. He sat down where he could watch the front door, the check-in counter, and the hallway to the elevators. He expected to see wealthy tourists and show-business types— maybe even the occasional movie star—but what he saw surprised him. City and county officials and the upper ranks of law enforcement came and went. He nearly bolted when he spotted the Santa Monica chief of police, Charles L. Dice, walk from the elevators, through the lobby, and out the front door. Randy, like most city employees, knew that Chief Dice was hanging on to his job by his fingernails. Corruption in the force had become a problem during Charlie L's tenure, so much so that folks swore that the L stood for "loaded." Most insiders thought Dice would be out on the street by the end of the year and the mayor would bring back Old Man Webb who had been chief of police from 1921 to 1936.

At 10:55 a.m. Randy got up and ambled over to the pool area. He dragged a chair into a patch of shade and settled in. His location gave him a clear view of the diving board and the few people swimming in the pool. He thought about Dorothy and their child. When the child was a toddler, she had carried around a picture of Randy for weeks. The photo was crumpled, and the image was misty from a coating of saliva. Dorothy was going to destroy it so her father wouldn't find it, but Randy said he would take it home and burn it. He kept it in a drawer beneath his undershirts.

Randy reread the sections of the paper he had already scanned for an hour in the lobby in between glancing at his watch and looking over the top of the paper at the diving board. At exactly 11:30 a.m. a man in a blue coat with a folded newspaper walked up to the diving board, stood there for few seconds, and then retreated to a narrow band of shade against the wall of one of the buildings around the pool. Randy tensed up but stayed in his seat and continued to watch. Seconds later a blond man, about six feet tall, walked up to the man in the blue coat. Randy folded his newspaper, stood up, and dropped the paper on the chair. As he did so, a gray-haired man in a brown suit walked quickly up to him.

"Hotel dick, where you going, buddy?"

"Santa Monica PD, get the fuck out of my way," Randy said

as he flung open his coat and reached for his badge. The open coat exposed the snub-nosed revolver at his waist.

"Gun," blurted the hotel detective.

Almost simultaneously Randy heard footsteps behind him, but before he could turn around, he felt a crushing pain at the back of his head.

When Randy came to, he was on a couch in a small office. The hotel detective was sitting behind a battered wooden desk with Randy's badge in one hand and a telephone receiver in the other. "Yes, sir, I'll ask him; he's awake now." The hotel dick hung up the phone, glanced at the badge, and tossed it to Randy. "That was your boss. He wants to know why you're hunting in LA."

"I'm working on a murder investigation. My captain knows that I follow the leads wherever they take me and—"

"Wait, wait, not your captain. I was talking to your big boss, Chief Dice. This ain't some flophouse; this is a first-class joint. We got presidents and prime ministers staying with us, not to mention movie stars and studio chiefs. Hell, we got the attorney general himself on the fifth floor. You're lucky we got to you before Warren's security chief spotted you. He would have shot first and asked questions later.

"If you're following a suspect, come to me first and let me know what you're doing. We get a lot of crazies wanting to bother their favorite movie star. We keep a close eye on our guests and protect them. We were watching you for an hour. Bet you didn't see us, eh?"

"Nope," Randy admitted reluctantly. "But did you have to have your guy sap me?"

"Sorry. I saw your gat before I saw your buzzer. What would you have done?"

"The same, I guess."

"Sure. So everything's jake?"

"Yeah, sure, everything's swell." Randy stood up. The room spun a bit, and he sat back down. "Say, do you ever get any trouble boys around here? I saw a six-foot blond talking with the man in the blue coat. He matches the description of a mobster from back east that I've been tracking."

"If he was talking to the guy in the blue coat, he can't be a mobster. The guy in the blue coat was Mr. White, Warren's security chief."

"Okay, must be a different guy then. Well, I think I've had plenty of your first-class hospitality. I'm going home and putting my head in a bucket of ice."

Both men stood up. The hotel detective extended his hand. "I'm Bill Murphy, by the way. Put in nearly thirty years with LAPD. Left as a lieutenant in burglary. The boy who sapped you is my nephew, also William Murphy. Goes by Will." Murphy still had his hand out. "So, no hard feelings?"

"No, you were doing your job." Randy shook hands. "Ah, is there a men's room around here? I could do with a splash of water on my face."

"Yeah. Through the lobby in the hallway near the elevators."

"Thanks." As Randy walked through the lobby, he thought, *Gat? Everything's jake? Buzzard talks like he's twenty-five instead of sixty-five.* He passed the elevators. When he reached the door of the men's room, he stopped abruptly and looked back the way he had just come. No one had followed him. He walked over to the elevators and waited. The doors opened. Randy stepped in and told the operator, "Fifth floor."

When Randy got off the elevator, he hung his badge from the breast pocket of his coat and began walking the hallways. When he came upon a knot of men in suits huddled together discussing something in hushed tones, he approached them and said, "Excuse me, gentlemen, Mr. White is expecting me, and I seem to have misplaced his suite number."

"You found the place. Right here." One of the men gestured with his thumb at a door. "Don't knock, just walk in," another volunteered.

"Thank you." Randy opened the door and strolled in. Just inside the door a woman sat at a table. She had a list of names in front of her. Randy gave the woman a smile and said, "Hello, darling, I'm Detective Williams from Santa Monica PD. I talked with Mr. White about eleven thirty. He asked me to come up." Randy then bent down and whispered to the woman, "I forgot his first name. Help me out, hon."

The woman giggled and whispered back, "Oh, it's Jerry." Then, in a normal voice, the woman said, "I'll let Mr. White know you're here." She stood up and walked into another room.

"Thanks," Randy said to the woman's back. He was left alone in the room. He removed his revolver from its holster and held it against the small of his back where it would be hidden from view when White walked in the room. Randy heard White and the woman approaching.

Before they entered the room, Randy could hear White denying that he had asked anyone to come up. "But he asked for you by name," the woman replied impatiently.

The woman entered the room and walked back to her chair. White stopped in the doorway and gave Randy a hard stare. With a thrust of his chin, White asked brusquely, "What do you want?"

"Vincent sent me." White's eyes opened wide, and he reached for the gun in his shoulder holster. Randy brought his gun to bear on White and shouted out, "Where's Dorothy?"

In his haste to draw his gun, the muzzle of White's big semiautomatic got caught up in the lining of his coat. White fired and shot away part of the coat freeing the gun. He swung his gun in Randy's direction, but he rushed the shot and fired low and to Randy's right, narrowly missing the woman sitting at the reception table.

Randy fired once, and White let out a grunt. A bloodstain appeared on his shirt, and White collapsed to the floor, his head against the doorframe. Randy walked over to White and screamed down at him, "Where is she? Where is she?" White looked up at Randy, his eyes showing no comprehension. In a rage Randy fired two shots into White's head.

From another room Randy could hear running footsteps and a man shouting. Warren's bodyguard was leading the attorney general to a back hallway that led to a flight of stairs. As soon as the two men entered the hallway, Nicky fired at them from the dark stairwell. The bodyguard, leading the way, staggered from the gunshot but was able to turn around and push Warren out of the hallway and back into the suite of offices from which they came. The bodyguard was hit twice more in the back before he collapsed in the hallway.

Randy ran up to Warren and shouted, "Which way?" With a shaking hand, Warren pointed to the doorway that led into the hall. Randy ran into the hallway, hopping over the bodyguard slumped on the floor. He could hear footsteps on the stairs. He ran down the steps but couldn't gain on the shooter. The door on the first floor opened and light briefly flooded the stairwell, then the stairwell went dim again as the door swung shut. Randy reached the ground floor and ran outside just in time to see a dark-haired man wearing a white coat dash into the parking lot behind the main tower, jump on a motorcycle, and head north on Orange Drive for Hollywood Boulevard.

Randy ran the two blocks to his car and drove north to Hollywood Boulevard. Once at the corner, Randy stuck his head out the window and listened for a motorcycle. No motorcycle sounds rose above the constant drone of traffic. He could not determine whether Nicky had turned east or west, continued north, or doubled back going south. He realized that Nicky was dressed as a messenger and other drivers would allow him to pass, assuming he was on the job. Randy was startled by a car horn honking. He looked in his rearview mirror and saw a line of cars waiting behind him. Discouraged, Randy turned west on Hollywood and returned to his apartment in Santa Monica.

Cliff arrived at the Roosevelt Hotel just after noon. He could hear police sirens as he walked up to the front door. The doorman stepped into his path to stop him, but Cliff pulled out his badge. The doorman stepped out of the way and waved him in saying, "Fifth floor."

Holding up his badge, Cliff walked up to the counter clerk who wordlessly pointed to the elevators. An elevator waited with open doors; it was empty except for the operator. The operator looked at Cliff's badge and said, "Five?" Cliff nodded. The operator closed the doors, and the elevator began to rise. Clearly agitated, he turned to Cliff and said, "We heard gunshots. What's going on?"

"Uniformed officers are on their way. What have you heard?"

"Ah, just the shots. Someone said the attorney general's guards got shot, but the AG's okay, and some cop is chasing the shooter."

The elevator stopped and the doors opened. Cliff had hung his badge from the breast pocket of his coat and had slipped his pistol from its holster into the coat pocket at his hip. "Which way?" The operator pointed to the right. Cliff poked his head out of the elevator and looked right and then left before charging into the hallway.

The operator cautiously stepped one foot into the hall and called out, "Suite five twenty-one." He watched as Cliff rushed down the hallway, head down, body leaning forward, left arm swinging freely, and right hand jammed in his coat pocket. The operator muttered under his breath, "You're a better man than I am, Gunga Din," as he closed the doors.

When Cliff walked into the suite, the hotel detective stood talking with a pale Earl Warren while his assistant sat and comforted the receptionist. "I'm Clifford Thoms, Deputy DA, LA County. Are you Jerry White?"

"No, that's Jerry," Murphy said, pointing to White's body crumpled in the doorway that opened to a suite of offices. "I'm Bill Murphy, the house detective. This is the attorney general, Mr. Warren."

"Thoms? Fitts spoke of you. Why did you want to speak with Jerry?" Warren asked.

"I called him a half hour ago and warned him that there might be an attempt on your life today. We think that one or two men working for East Coast interests were sent to kill you." Cliff surveyed the room. "What happened here?"

"Someone tried to shoot Mr. Warren, and another man, a detective from Santa Monica—"

"Detective Williams," the receptionist interjected. "I wrote it down."

"Okay, Detective Williams shot and killed Jerry White. We're not sure why. Maybe over a woman," Murphy said.

"Dorothy. That man asked White, 'Where is Dorothy?' Jerry shot first. He almost killed me. Not on purpose. See where the bullet hit the table?" The receptionist stood and pointed at the damaged table. "Jerry shot twice, and then the detective shot him. And then, and then ... it was horrible! Williams was yelling about Dorothy, and then he shot poor Jerry in the head. Two times. In the head. Oh my God! The blood. You can see where it's soaked into the carpet. Brains too. Horrible." Murphy's nephew put his arm around the receptionist and led her back to the couch.

"You warned Jerry about an attempt?" Warren asked incredulously.

"Yes. I said that he should expect an attempt on your life today and that we had two suspects, Nicky and Vincent. I gave him descriptions of both," Cliff said. He could see that the back of White's head had been shattered by the two gunshots and bloody brain matter had oozed onto the carpet.

"Vincent!" the receptionist blurted out. "Williams said something about Vincent." She tried to stand, but the younger Murphy held her tight at the elbow.

"Williams said White was meeting someone by the pool. I saw him. Didn't look like no mobster I'd ever seen—and I've seen plenty," Murphy said, glancing at Warren.

"Six foot, blond hair?" Cliff offered.

"Yeah. Yeah." Murphy suddenly sounded old and tired.

"This doesn't make sense. If Williams was in on the attack, why didn't he shoot me when he had the chance?" Warren asked.

"He wasn't working with the mobsters. Dorothy was kidnapped last night by Vincent and his partner, Nicky. It sounds like Williams was trying to find Dorothy, but ..."

"Williams said he was tracking a mobster from back east. Guess that mobster was Vincent," Murphy said, shaking his head.

"Searching for Dorothy wouldn't be something his office would undertake," Cliff said. "My office is handling that matter."

"Oh, it was personal. That Williams fella *loves* Dorothy." The men stared at the receptionist. "Well, a woman can tell," she added defensively.

"What happened to Williams?" Cliff asked.

"He took off after the bastard who killed"—Warren stopped to rein in his emotions—"killed my bodyguard. We were trying to get away from the gunfire and went down a back hall. Someone was waiting for us and opened fire. Mike was killed defending me." Warren was visibly shaken by the memory.

"A setup?" Murphy speculated.

"Likely. White probably would have come up with a pretense to have you go into the hall first, sir," Cliff said, addressing Warren.

"And then White would kill the shooter. Be the hero. Get a medal for doing it, I bet." Murphy sounded bitter. Just then a half dozen LAPD patrolmen rushed into the room, all with their guns drawn. "Settle down, boys," Murphy shouted at the officers, the senior man back in charge. "All the excitement is over. Don't contaminate the crime scene. Get the lab boys up here."

"I should be going," Cliff said, watching the patrol officers mill around.

"Thoms, a word." Warren waved him over. In a low voice, he asked, "Were you here to save me or the kidnapped girl?"

"Both," Cliff answered after a pause.

"Don't let the oil from your gun ruin your coat." Warren pointed at Cliff's coat pocket. The right side pocket, weighed down by the gun, hung lower than the left.

"A pleasure to meet you, sir." Cliff extended his hand.

"Likewise," Warren said. They shook hands and Cliff headed back to his office.

CHAPTER 18

"I lost him in traffic. I'm so sorry, Carlota. I don't know what to do."

"*Pobrecito.*" It felt strange to Carlota to call Randy "poor little one," but she had never known him to despair before. "*Voy a llamar a la bruja. Ella puede ayudarnos.* I call the ... the lady. She can help. I call you back."

"Call whoever you think can help us. I'll wait for your call."

Carlota rushed to her room and pulled Zoe's business card from a drawer. She returned to the phone in the hallway and called the business line. She let the phone ring ten times and then hung up. There was a second number, Zoe's home number; Carlota hesitated briefly before calling that number.

"Woolfolk residence."

As soon as she heard the young man's voice, Carlota realized she hadn't planned what she was going to say in English. "I want to speak"—should the word be *to* or *with*?—"to Mrs. Woolfolk." Twenty-five years in the United States, she thought, and still English prepositions baffled her.

"May I say who is calling?"

Is he asking for my name? Carlota thought and then answered, "Carlota Gonzalez."

"Just a moment."

Carlota heard the phone being set down and then snatches of a distant conversation.

"Hello, Carlota. How may I help you?" Zoe spoke sweetly into the phone, knowing that Carlota must be in a panic if she was calling la bruja at home.

"Miss Dorothy kidnap, yes? By a man, Nicky; he kill her soon. You"—what verb, what verb?—"can know where she is, yes?"

"Possibly. You must bring me something that Dorothy has worn recently or that she carries with her. Don't clean it! Carry it to me in a paper bag if possible. Can you do that?"

"Yes. I take to your office?"

"No, bring it to my house. I'll give you the address. Do you have something to write with?"

"Yes, ready."

"Fifty-one Navy Street, Ocean Park."

"Thank you, thank you." Carlota hadn't planned for this. "Ah, I send a man with Miss Dorothy's clothes, yes?"

"That's fine, dear. I'll be waiting." Zoe hung up.

As Zoe walked back to the dining room where her family sat, Margie, Bobby's girlfriend, leaned over and whispered in his ear, "Aren't we in Venice?"

"Yeah, but Ocean Park is a posh address, and it's only two blocks away."

Mama Lou was waiting for Zoe to return before saying the lunchtime prayer. When Zoe entered the room, Clarence and Mama Lou had their hands folded, and Clarence's head was already bowed. Zoe would have to poke him so he would know when the prayer was over.

Bobby and Margie watched, questioning with their eyes, as

Zoe took her seat. "So, Mom," Bobby began, unable to contain his curiosity, "was that a new client?"

"A man is coming to see me. He'll be here in a few minutes. He's"—Zoe sensed the flood of emotions coming from the man—"very determined."

After the prayer, Bobby and Margie ate and chatted. Zoe ate in silence, listening to the young couple. Zoe looked over at her son's girlfriend. Margie worked as a model at I. Magnin. She was still a little young, just barely twenty, but a true beauty. Zoe wondered when they would announce they were going to marry. Maybe they didn't know themselves that they would marry, but Zoe knew. Bobby had had other girlfriends, but the second time Bobby brought Margie to the house, Zoe had a vision of her in a white satin wedding dress with a lace bodice. The dress was lovely; Margie's mother would help her pick it out. True, Zoe hadn't seen Bobby in her vision, but the groom being in shadow was evidence enough that he was the groom. And she hadn't seen grandchildren, but that meant little. With Marie, Joanie came as a surprise, although Zoe had a glimpse of Caroline early on and knew that Marie would have another child after the war. The war, another few months and ... Zoe caught herself drifting through time.

Past, present, future—her gift demolished their boundaries and made time a seamless whole. Here she was indulging in Saturday afternoon woolgathering when there was work to be done. Zoe shook her head at her foolishness and fought to focus on the here and now. It was the man coming to see her; somehow his agitation had stirred her mind and emotions. As she turned her attention back to the meal, a sudden wave of emotions crashed through her consciousness and swept away her thoughts. "Bobby, he's almost here. Go to the door and let him in."

Bobby made eye contact with Margie and smiled. Then, wordlessly, he got up from his chair, walked to the front door, opened it, and looked out. Nothing. "False alarm, Mom. No one ... oh, someone just drove up."

Randy bounded up to the door with a paper bag in his hand. "I'm here to see your mother."

"Hello, Officer, welcome back. Have a seat." Bobby gestured to the couch. "I'll get her." Bobby walked back to the dining room. "Mom, he's in the living room."

Randy sat down on the old couch and sank low in the cushion. He rose when Zoe entered the room and extended his arm to hand her the paper bag he carried. Zoe recognized him as one of the detectives who had tried to shake her down days before. Zoe took the bag with mixed emotions. Last week he had wanted to arrest her for fraud; this week he came to her for help. She set the bag down on a lamp table; the merest touch of the bag brought a burning anguish to her hand. What was Dorothy to him that he felt such emotions? Zoe opened the bag and drew out a cream-colored silk scarf, wrinkled in the corners where it had been knotted. Zoe stroked the scarf; it was slick between her fingers. Images and emotions trickled out from the fabric. They had used the scarf as a restraint in their sexual games. Dorothy had left it at his apartment. Their relationship was not just sex; they had a bond, sick and tangled, twisted from each one's depravities, and yet ... Oh! They have a child—boy or girl, she wasn't sure—whom they love. Their capacity to love a child was unexpected. Zoe looked up into the detective's eyes. "I'm sorry; I've forgotten your name."

"Randy Williams. I'm, ah, sorry about last week. We don't have much time. He'll kill her."

"Let's sit down. The information comes at its own speed. I can't rush it." Zoe sat in the upholstered chair, and Randy returned to the couch. Zoe laid the scarf on her lap and stroked it with her right hand. She closed her eyes and let the images wash over her. Dorothy was in a small house. Near the ocean. Canals? Venice? She'd been drugged and knocked about. There was a radiator and a dirty floor. Outside, what did she see outside? The front door opened for an instant. Yes, the Animal came through the door, but behind him, parked on the street, what? A red pickup. Rounded fenders, spare tire on the running board, fairly new but dirty. That's all. No, there's more. Randy drove by the house last night. *So close*, Zoe thought to herself and smiled.

"What? What did you see?" Randy leaned forward, his eyes imploring.

"She's in a small house in Venice near a canal. You drove by it last night. There is a red pickup truck parked in front. The truck is fairly new but dirty. She's still alive. The man who has her, well, kill him as soon as you can."

Both stood up. Zoe handed the scarf back to Randy who dropped it back in the bag. Randy took Zoe's hand in both of his and pumped her hand. "Thank you. I hope Carlota's right about you. I didn't know what else to do."

Zoe watched Randy rush to his car and drive away. His touch revolted her. She knew he had killed recently with those hands. She went straight to the bathroom and wiped her hands on a towel, trying to remove the greasy feeling of death. After twenty seconds of desperate rubbing, she got hold of herself and hurried to call Cliff at his office. Zoe explained that the Animal was holding Dorothy in a bungalow on a canal in Venice and that Officer Williams was on his way to rescue her.

Cliff confirmed details of the location, hung up the phone, and started to call the Venice substation of the LAPD. Abruptly he hung up the receiver. How would he explain the source of his information? A psychic? An astrologer? And his position? Head of a special unit that had been disbanded and was under investigation. Cliff called the Santa Monica police station and spoke with Lou Gomez. His message was simple: Williams was going after Nicky, and presumably Vincent, on his own. Williams had killed a man on the attorney general's staff less than an hour before by shooting him once in the chest and twice in the head. And Williams was likely the lover of Dorothy Green, the daughter of Lefty Green, the mobster. Cliff gave Lou as much information on the house in Venice as he had and told Lou that he would be there in fifteen minutes. Cliff ran downstairs to the car pool and signed out a car with a siren. He took off, going west with the siren screaming. Cliff's assigned driver, sitting behind the wheel of an old county car, barely had time to look up and see Cliff's car disappearing down the road as traffic parted before it.

Nicky felt the wind on his face as he steered his motorcycle through the traffic on Hollywood Boulevard. He had been riding around for thirty-five minutes. By changing directions every so often, he made tracing his route almost impossible. He was dressed as a deliveryman in a stolen jacket and hat. Other drivers gave him room, allowing him to weave quickly through traffic. Nicky smiled as he thought about the deliveryman whose clothes he took and wondered how long he had before the man was found. Nicky pulled into the parking lot at Sears and Roebuck and motored over to his stolen truck. As he dismounted and took off his messenger's bow tie and cap, he saw two teenage boys eyeing the motorcycle. He called to them, "I'm quitting this damn job. Can you help me out? Could you drive this cycle back to the Mercury Messenger Service on Wilshire and tell them I quit? The name is Buron Fitts. Do you know where the messenger service is?"

"Sure, mister. We go there all the time."

"Oh, you better wear the jacket and hat or they won't let you in the parking garage."

"Thanks, mister. We'll go straight there."

"I'm sure you will." Nicky smiled and waved as he watched the youngsters ride off on the motorcycle. *Fitts*, he thought. *Nice touch.*

Nicky climbed into the truck and drove to Venice, careful to obey every law. He parked near a construction site a little over a mile away from the abandoned bungalow where he had left Dorothy shackled. He walked along the residential streets of Venice where people were enjoying the early summer weather until he was sure he wasn't being watched, and then he went directly to his house. Once inside, Nicky saw Dorothy still handcuffed, lying on the floor. "How are you, my dear? Need to use the toilet? I don't want you pissing on me once we get started."

Dorothy heard him but couldn't answer. She leaned up against the radiator with her head on her chest. She was awake but weak and confused from the cumulative effects of alcohol, chloroform, and sleeping pills, in addition to being struck and deprived of food and water.

Nicky unhooked Dorothy from the radiator. When he started to move her, he saw that she lay in a puddle of her own dark urine. Nicky dragged Dorothy to the center of the room and started stripping off her dress. At this, Dorothy revived, sat up, and begun to fight back. She managed to punch Nicky in the face, but this served only to enrage him. Nicky punched through Dorothy's outstretched arms, striking her on the cheek. Her head swiveled sharply and she fell back to the floor. Dorothy tried to sit up, but as soon as she lifted her head, Nicky punched her again, bouncing her head off the hardwood floor. Dorothy was knocked unconscious; blood trickled from her nose and mouth. Nicky stood and surveyed his work. Dorothy lay still, barely breathing. Satisfied that Dorothy would not continue to struggle, Nicky stepped onto a chair and proceeded to batter out two holes in the ceiling on either side of a joist with a claw hammer. Working up a sweat in the afternoon heat, he climbed down from the chair and picked up Dorothy. Her body was lax and unresisting, an unwieldy dead weight that Nicky found difficult to handle as he hung her from the beam by the handcuffs. Nicky was fatigued but exhilarated at the prospect that Dorothy would revive and react once he started cutting.

With an explosion of splintered wood, the door flew open and Randy burst into the room with his gun drawn. He was stunned by what he saw. Dorothy's naked body, pale and limp, hung from a ceiling joist. Her face was bruised and bloody. Was she dead already? Randy wondered. In that instant of hesitation, Nicky took cover behind Dorothy and drew his knife. Randy's mind raced. He had a fleeting regret that he didn't fire when he had the chance. He made a mental note that the man he faced must be Nicky, the shorter, dark-haired one. He wondered whether Vincent was here at the house and was lining up a shot. Whatever the risks, he realized that there was no retreat, no second chance, no stalling for time hoping the cavalry would come to the rescue. Pointing his revolver where he guessed Nicky's head might appear, he shouted, "Police! Throw down your knife and get on the ground!"

"I'm going to cut her throat, and you can watch her die, copper." Nicky pressed his knife against Dorothy's neck.

Beyond his fifth grade education, Nicky had studied only two things: weapons and anatomy. He knew by cutting down and inward, he would sever the carotid artery where it fed from the aorta—then nothing could be done to save Dorothy.

"Whatcha gonna do with that knife? She won't scream for you," Randy said as he angled for a head shot. "You can't torture her. Dorothy's already dead."

Nicky, worried that he might have hit her too hard, brought the mirrored side of his knife under Dorothy's nose. He was relieved to see the blade fog from her shallow breath. "Oh, so it's Dorothy. Dorothy, my love," Nicky sang out in falsetto. "Ain't that sweet: a copper dizzy with a dame, a chippy at that."

Randy needed a clear shot; he couldn't risk hitting Dorothy. Slowly he circled at the edge of the room looking for an opening. Nicky moved to keep Dorothy between him and Randy. As they moved in unison, Nicky got his foot tangled with a chair leg. He fell to the floor, his body outstretched. His knife skidded along the floor and bounced off the wall near the front door. Randy ran back toward the door to block Nicky from retrieving his knife and to get an unobstructed shot. When Randy stepped clear of Dorothy, he saw Nicky lying on his side and firing a revolver at him. The shot hit Randy in the ribs on his right side; a bullet fragment exited his ribs on the left at sternum level. He felt all his breath pushed out, as if he had been punched in the diaphragm. He dropped his gun, staggered a step, and then collapsed in the doorway.

Nicky got up and calmly walked over to Randy. He squatted down beside him, opened up Randy's coat, and examined the wounds. "Through both lungs. Probably tore up the plumbing inside too. Ten minutes tops. You'll outlive the bitch, anyway." Nicky stood up, picked up his knife, and stepped over to the detective's gun. He picked it up and dropped it in his front pocket. "Thanks," he said with a nod. "Okay, copper, watch this," Nicky said as he walked over to Dorothy. With one swift motion, Nicky savagely slashed Dorothy's jugular vein. A spurt of blood soaked his shoulder. Nicky stepped back and stared as a sheet of blood descended across Dorothy's chest. "God, isn't it grand? *Bellissimo!*" Nicky turned, his face beaming, and locked eyes with Randy. "Think I'll go out the back. Guess we'll all meet up in hell; you and the chippy can give me a tour when I get there. *Ciao.*"

Two minutes after Nicky left the house, Randy heard a car screech to a stop and somebody run up to the front door.

"Randy!"

"Hey, Lou. Figured you'd come."

Lou stepped over Randy and into the house. He knelt beside his partner and looked up at the figure in the center of the room. "Jesus, Randy, *she* was your girl?" Lou gestured with his chin to Dorothy's naked body dangling from a ceiling joist, her blood bright red against skin so white it gleamed like snow.

"She is my girl, always will be." Randy closed his eyes and rested his head against the doorframe.

"Randy"—Lou gave him a shake—"wake up. You want to be awake when the ambulance shows up. I radioed for one on the way here, you know, just in case."

"Yeah, yeah." Randy smiled weakly as he chuckled. Pink foam appeared at his lips. "You know, Dorothy is amazing. She does whatever she needs to do to ... to get what she wants. Fuck 'em, kill 'em, whatever."

"One's more pleasurable than the other."

"Yeah, but you can't kill them all."

"No, I meant ..."

"Oh, right." Randy nodded weakly.

Lou cradled Randy's head and dabbed his handkerchief at the foam on his partner's chin. "You should have been there last night."

"Yeah, well, I was busy killing Ricardo."

"Guess so. Fred's sister, you know, the one married to the rummy, is like a fortune-teller."

"Yeah? So what did the rummy's wife say?"

"Oh, that we'd fought in wars together in past lives."

"Figures."

Lou probed Randy's wounds with his finger. Neither hole was big enough to create a sucking chest wound. There was nothing he could do for his partner except keep him awake, comfortable, and upright until the ambulance arrived. "I keep thinking about Ricardo—one in the heart, two in the head. Why?"

"That's the way she wanted it. Just like with Roberts."

"Dorothy wanted Roberts to skim?"

"Yeah, but he wouldn't play ball, so we killed him." Randy paused to catch his breath. "Ricardo took his place."

"But why? For the money?"

"Nah. Dorothy wanted to get the *Rex* for her father. To prove to him that she could do what he couldn't."

"And Roberts was in the way."

"That's about the size of it."

"So why *did* you shoot Roberts three times?"

"I only shot him twice. Once in the chest, then Dorothy wanted a turn, like with the dog."

"What dog?"

"It's not important. Anyway, with Roberts, she was so excited that her hand was shaking, and she shot him in the jaw." Randy had to take a couple of deep, wet, wheezy breaths before he could continue talking. "I took the gun back and finished him off with a shot to the head. She liked it. That's how she wanted Ricardo done—one in the chest, two in the head."

"How about White?"

"Who?" Randy's eyes were closed again, and the pink foam had built up at the corners of his mouth.

"The security guy at the Roosevelt," Lou said as he dabbed away at the foam with his handkerchief.

"Oh. I was mad." Randy managed to open his eyes, but they were hazy and unfocused. "The guy was working with Vincent. The son of a bitch deserved to die. I didn't even realize I shot him three times." The bloody froth at Randy's mouth had gone from pink to bright red. "Is the ambulance coming?"

"Yeah, it's on its way."

"I'm not gonna make it, am I?" The question was more of a statement. Randy fought to keep his eyes open. With what little strength he had, Randy tilted his head back, looked in Lou's eyes, and asked, "Kill Nicky for me, will you?"

"Yeah. With pleasure."

"I'm gonna sleep now. Wake me when you're done." Randy's head dropped to his chest, and he closed his eyes.

"Sure. You get some rest. I'll be back soon." Lou laid his partner's head against the doorframe and arranged his sleeping body so it sat upright. Lou knew Randy's chest was filling with blood and that he would drown if he lay down. Lou got up and realized he'd given Nicky an extra four minutes on his head start. For an instant he despaired of ever catching Nicky, and then he heard gunshots. Lou jumped up and ran out the door. He headed toward the sound of the gunfire.

Cliff cursed himself as he drove toward Venice. Vincent and Nicky had been miles ahead of the police for months. Even as the Scott squad was closing in, first Vincent and then Nicky had disappeared like ghosts. Cliff assumed that Nicky would slip by Williams and Gomez. Then what? He would go to his car, drive someplace where he could hide or dump the car, and then walk to a flophouse where, Cliff assumed, Nicky had paid in advance. He probably had two or three lined up. No doubt he had switched cars by now, but where would he leave the car? He would not park too near the Venice house—it was likely that a cop or a resident would notice a strange car in the neighborhood. But he wouldn't park too far away either, maybe within a mile of the house. So where would he park? Cliff had to admit that this Nicky was sly. *Sly*. The word triggered a dim memory, something from his childhood. His old Chinese grandmother had a saying for every situation—and then it came to him: "A sly rabbit will have three openings to its den." Nicky would park where the car wouldn't be noticed, and more importantly, he'd park where there were several escape routes open to him: the traffic circle at Windward Avenue. Five or six roads converged on it, and the WPA was building a new post office between Windward and Main. There would be plenty of strange cars parked around the site; no one would give another car a second thought.

Cliff drove to the building site on the traffic circle and slowly cruised toward the canals, looking for Nicky hurrying on foot. He took Main south to Venice Way and went east. He turned south on Riviera Way—the only street coming directly from the canals to the traffic circle. He parked on the street just north of Mildred Avenue. From there he could see the length of Riviera where it crossed the canals and also had a view both ways down Mildred, which ran east and west. As he had done the night before, Cliff sunk down in the front seat so he could look through the steering wheel and over the dashboard. He pulled his Colt pistol from its holster and put it on his lap. Then he waited.

There were people strolling on the street through the neighborhood of slightly shabby homes in the warm, late spring afternoon. One man was in a hurry. He walked north on Riviera, sometimes in the street to overtake a knot of slower pedestrians on the sidewalk. The man looked down the cross streets as he passed and occasionally looked over his shoulder. As he drew closer, Cliff could see that the man wasn't tall, had dark hair and a stain of some sort on one shoulder, and, yes, he matched the composite drawing of Nicky. As he approached the intersection of Mildred and Riviera, Cliff jumped out of his car, pointed his gun at Nicky, and yelled, "Stop where you are and get on the ground!"

Nicky darted to his left and took cover behind the corner of a house. Cliff fired and a chunk of stucco landed on the dirt near Nicky's foot. Nicky popped his head around the corner and fired. A hole appeared in the windshield of Cliff's car. Cliff crouched lower to put more of his body behind the car's hood and waited for Nicky to expose himself to another shot. Cliff was unhappily aware that his pistol's heavy trigger pull and rudimentary sights made accurate shooting beyond thirty feet difficult. Nicky's gun, like Cliff's, had a four-inch barrel, but it could be fired with a light, single-action trigger pull and had better sights. Both gave Nicky an advantage in accuracy, but his revolver had only six shots and was slow to reload. Cliff knew that he couldn't shoot it out with Nicky from a distance. He had to move to Nicky's side for a clear shot, and he had to keep Nicky in sight. Nicky could be circling the house and on his way to his car while Cliff hid behind his car.

Cliff hopped in his car, slid down in the seat, and drove through the intersection. He pulled even with the side yard south of the house on the opposite corner and saw Nicky backing away, firing at the car. The passenger window exploded and glass shards landed on Cliff, who returned fire. In the distance he heard sirens approaching. With equal parts irritation and amusement, Cliff marveled at the fact that it had taken half a dozen shots for neighbors to realize there was a shootout going on in their front yards. Nicky had taken cover behind the back of the house. Cliff pointed his gun where he expected Nicky to appear, wondering if he could wait it out now that the police were on their way. Nicky must have kneeled down to take his next shot because he appeared just for an instant and two feet lower than Cliff anticipated. The shot went through the passenger door and struck the steering column just inches from Cliff's chest. Cliff scrambled out the driver's door and took cover behind the engine block. Hugging the fender of his car, he fought to maintain self-control. Sheet metal wouldn't stop bullets; he knew that. He had seen enough cars where bullets had entered one side of a car and gone out the other. Inside the cars was usually blood-soaked upholstery.

Impulsively, Cliff ran north to the intersection to cut off Nicky's route to his car. Nicky just then poked his head around the corner of the house, and Cliff fired three wild shots. Nicky retreated, and Cliff rushed to the corner where Nicky had appeared. As he ran, Cliff frantically tried to count his shots. One across the intersection, one—or was it two?—when Nicky was in the side yard, and now three more shots. Five or six so far. He had one or two left. Reload now or chase Nicky down? Chase. Cliff ran behind the house and saw Nicky turn the corner. Cliff went around the next corner and was now in the side yard, facing his own car. Cliff shot at Nicky's back. The bullet hit the car with a thump.

Nicky stopped, turned around, and raised his hands. "Ya got me, copper," he said, a little out of breath.

"Throw down your gun and get on the ground!" Cliff yelled. He watched as Nicky flicked his gun to the dirt. He looked at it with relief; the chase was over. Then he realized that the gun on the ground was a snub-nose. Cliff looked up and saw Nicky, smiling broadly, holding his revolver, the one with the four-inch barrel, the one he had used to pistol-whip some Chicago mobster a lifetime ago, aimed at Cliff's head. "You cops sure are dumb. I got the other cop the same way. Oh, yeah, seven shots; you ran dry, copper. Say sayonara, Charlie Chan."

Cliff pulled the trigger of his gun and heard a click. Seven shots. He closed his eyes and waited for the impact; in that instant he longed for Lucille's caress.

CHAPTER 19

The .45 slug tore a ragged gash in the side of Nicky's neck, and before he could clamp his hand over the wound, an arcing spray of blood erupted. He turned and saw the red fountain splash on the dirt. He stood briefly transfixed by the sight of his own blood in a puddle on the ground. Then he panicked. He dropped his gun and ran, not purposefully, but wildly. The motion only caused him to bleed out all the faster. He collapsed on the ground and lay on his side, wound uppermost. Lou ran up and watched the blood pulse between Nicky's fingers, which were covering his wound. The flow gradually decreased until it ceased altogether. Nicky went limp and rolled unresisting onto his stomach, with his face in the dirt, soundless and still.

"Thanks," Cliff muttered. His mouth was dry; he could hardly breathe.

"Yeah, no problem." Lou continued to look down at Nicky.

"Was Dorothy Green found?"

"Yep. She's hanging from a rafter in a house a few blocks from here. Her throat's cut."

"Oh," Cliff said in a long exhalation. "And your partner?"

"Dead by now. He was bleeding out. Nothing I could do. He confessed to me."

"Confessed to what?" Cliff asked, holstering his gun. His hand was shaking.

"That he and Dorothy killed Daniel Roberts and he killed Ricardo Stralla."

"Who's Stralla?"

"Some kid from the sticks, Tony Cornero's nephew or cousin. Probably the only time the kid got some first-class pussy and it gets him killed."

"So that's three. He killed Jerry White at the Roosevelt Hotel today."

"Yeah. He said that White was working with Vincent. Wasn't White Warren's security guy?" Lou looked up at Cliff. Lou's face was ashen. His hand trembled slightly as he put his gun back in its holster. The police sirens were very near now.

"It looks like White was bought off. As best we could figure, there was a plan to assassinate Earl Warren. White was probably supposed to get Warren to walk down the hallway where Nicky or Vincent would kill him. Then White would kill the shooter. We think Nicky and Vincent were button men for the Syndicate, but we can't definitely tie them to the East Coast boys." Cliff shook his head weakly. "If the Syndicate gets rid of Warren, the drive to close down the gambling ships dies with him. Risky, but if it works, the mobsters keep making, hell, who knows, tens of thousands of dollars each month.

"Did Williams tell you why he killed Roberts and the Stralla fellow?"

"Yeah, 'cause Dorothy wanted him to," Lou said bitterly. "She wanted to make a gift of the *Rex* to her father. It had something to do with skimming, but Roberts refused to skim, so they killed him. I'm betting that they thought Stralla was close to cracking, so Dorothy sent Randy to kill him."

"You said Dorothy and Williams killed Roberts, but I picked Dorothy up at the airport on Sunday when she flew in from Mexico."

"We never confirmed her alibi that she was in Mexico all weekend. Stralla could have driven the Bugatti down the coast and picked her up in Mexico or, more likely, San Diego and got back in time for Dorothy to pick up Roberts Friday night. He was killed at the Green's Malibu house, but we'll never prove it now."

Three police cars had arrived almost simultaneously. Six officers, with their hands on their guns, got out of their cars and nervously inspected the scene. The sergeant in charge recognized Lou. "Hey, Gomez, did you already call for an ambulance?"

"No, Sarg, this one needs a meat wagon. Gentlemen," Lou announced with a wave of his arm, "meet the Canyon Killer."

"The chink?" asked a voice from the back.

"No, stupid, the stiff on the ground," the sergeant said, pointing to Nicky's body. "Gomez, who's in charge here? Venice is LAPD territory."

"Deputy DA Thoms is the ringmaster of this circus, right, Thoms? Doesn't the Scott squad have priority over regular operations in the county?"

"I don't want to be stepping on anyone's toes," Cliff said, nodding to the sergeant. "This homicide should get processed through regular channels. Gentlemen," he said, addressing the officers, "I should be getting back to the office to confer with the district attorney. He wanted to be informed right away when we got the Canyon Killer.

"Detective"—Cliff took Lou by the elbow—"could I have a

word with you?" The pair walked over to Cliff's car. "I imagine that you heard that one of my detectives was killed last night and that Dorothy Green was kidnapped during my operation."

"Yeah, some operation."

"I thought you should know—the Scott squad had been disbanded. I expect that Fitts will ask for my resignation on Monday."

"I should be glad, but I figure I'll be looking for work come Monday too. This train wreck is too big to hide. When it comes out that Randy and Dorothy knocked off two people right under my nose, well, Chief Dice is gonna have my badge.

"This your car?" Lou asked, pointing at the shot-out window and bullet holes in the door.

"County car on loan."

Lou laughed softly. "For a fixer, you sure fucked up everything you've touched lately. Better hope your radio works. With that slug in the steering column, you ain't driving this bus back."

Cliff's phone was ringing when he returned to his office midafternoon. It was Fitts on the line. "Christ, Tommy, I don't know whether to fire you or congratulate you. Bowron's office has been on the phone hounding me about you. Lenny Green has been working the phones. He wants your head. He heard about his daughter—strung up like a side of beef and murdered. And that Santa Monica detective shot through the lungs. He was dead when the ambulance got there. But you and that other Santa Monica detective got the Canyon Killer." Fitts paused, feeling conflicted. "That was good work. I heard you chased the guy around until the detective shot him—gutsy. And what the hell happened at the Roosevelt? Jerry White and another bodyguard are dead? Jesus, Tommy, this is a hell of a mess!"

"I'll write you up a report and have it to you Monday morning."

"No, you'll write up a summary and have it to me in two hours. I need to know what happened so I can protect you—and me—as best I can. You know Bowron wants me out of office; hell, he wants me in jail. Two hours, Tommy, and don't talk to anyone, not even Lucille, until I give you the word. Understand?"

"Loud and clear." The line went dead, and Cliff was left with the phone in his hand. Yes, the mayor did want Fitts in jail. Cliff recalled that when Fletcher Bowron was a judge, he had pressed a grand jury to indict Fitts for perjury and bribery in thirty-four. Fitts was acquitted in thirty-six, but the bad blood between Fitts and Bowron remained.

Cliff called Mary at her house and asked her to come in to help him with the report. Then he sat down and began to make some notes. He called the Venice substation lieutenant and asked that a car be sent to the post office building site to look for Nicky's car. They agreed that the vehicle and the bungalow had to be searched and secured for evidence. Both understood that the press had to be kept away. As soon as he was off the phone with the Venice lieutenant, the police captain from Santa Monica was on the line.

"Thoms, did you recruit my men without going through me? Williams is dead, and supposedly you and Gomez got the Canyon Killer. What's going on? Why are people telling me that Williams killed Earl Warren's bodyguard? None of this makes sense."

"Sorry to hear about Williams, but Fitts told me not to talk about it. I have to have a report on his desk in less than two hours. Have your chief call Fitts; maybe they will let us work together to sort it out. Oh, and no, I didn't recruit your detectives. I did call Gomez to let him know that his partner was chasing Nicky on his own, but he sure as hell wasn't working for me. He saved my ass, you know. I ... I guess I owe him one."

"I'll talk with Dice and suggest he call Fitts. Dice is the boss; I suggest and he does what the hell he wants." The captain sounded bitter. Cliff heard the captain's chair squeak. "Is it true?"

"Is what true?"

"That you were chasing the Canyon Killer with an empty gun?"

"It wasn't empty when I started."

"Chinaman's chance—hell—twice. I hear that this Canyon Killer fellow almost killed you last night as well."

"That's me, lucky *and* good-looking."

"Yeah, luckier than Williams. I'll talk to Dice and see what he says."

When Mary arrived, Cliff started dictating the report. They were interrupted after a few minutes by a call from the Venice lieutenant. "Thoms, it's the damnedest thing. We found Nicky's truck. It had some clothes for a taller man and a wig and, we think, some lifts, you know, what you'd wear in your shoes to be taller. Your office put out a description for Nicky's partner, ah"—Cliff heard some papers rustling—"Vincent. So this Vincent fellow was supposed to be six feet tall and blond or wearing a blond wig. Looks like we have the wig and some of his clothes, but what do you make of the lifts? And what happened to Vincent?"

"I don't know. I'll have to get back to you." Cliff hung up and wondered. The lifts were most likely for Nicky. The composite sketches did make it seem like Nicky and Vincent looked alike. No one saw them together. No witness who saw Nicky also saw Vincent. Could it be? Cliff remembered that Zoe said that Nicky worked alone.

The phone rang again, and Mary answered it. "Yes, sir. He's right here." Mary handed the phone to Cliff and silently mouthed, "Fitts."

"Yes?"

"Something to add to your report. The LA city coroner went through Jerry White's pockets and found two wallets, one for White. The second one contained a California driver's license for another person. The name is, well, maybe Romanian. The thumbprint on the license matches Nicky. It has his address. Sheriffs are over there now going through his stuff. The boys say the place is filled with anarchist literature. I heard that you and the house dick over at the Roosevelt thought that White and Vincent were working together. If that's right, then your speculation that Nicky was supposed to kill Warren and that White would then kill Nicky makes sense. White plants the wallet on Nicky, and we find the apartment with the anarchist stuff. Do you still think the Syndicate is behind this hit?"

"Yes. Nicky was the perfect button man. No arrests as an adult, no fingerprints on file, not even a picture. There's no way to tie him to the Syndicate. Once Warren was dead, the pressure, I mean the pressure from Sacramento, to close down the gambling ships would disappear."

"Why was that Santa Monica detective at the Roosevelt?"

"He confessed to his partner that he was Dorothy Green's

lover. They had planned to get control of the *Rex*; that's why they killed the accountant on the *Rex*."

"The accountant?"

"It's complicated. Williams, the detective, was looking for Dorothy Green and saw Vincent with White. Williams killed White and then chased Nicky to the house in Venice."

"What happened to Vincent?"

"I'm not sure there ever was a Vincent. He may have been Nicky wearing lifts and a wig. We need to coordinate with Santa Monica PD. Luis Gomez can fill us in on his investigation. I'm afraid that Williams was dirty. None of us are going to come out of this looking good."

"Finish your report and leave the press to me. I have Warren crying over his dead men and their families, and now Dice is going to want to save what's left of his reputation. And Lenny Green, he has friends in high places. They can make trouble for all of us. Ah, no Vincent?"

"Not that we can verify."

"Okay, Tommy, get me your report and stay home tomorrow. Don't go out, and don't speak to anyone, especially the press."

CHAPTER 20

Pasadena, California
Sunday, June 11, 1939

Lucille let Cliff sleep in. She could see that he was exhausted from the activities of the previous day. In the morning she carefully read the newspaper's account of the attack on Earl Warren. This was what Cliff wouldn't tell her. She surmised that things went badly. The story was surprisingly sketchy; the police must have kept a lid on the scene and the witnesses. Lucille asked Cliff about the attack once over breakfast and again later in the evening over cocktails. Both times Cliff refused to discuss what he knew.

He had submitted his report to Fitts about nine the previous night—well beyond the two-hour deadline—after a series of phone calls in which Fitts had called for clarification about the Scott squad's investigation. It was apparent to Cliff that Fitts had a team working on the case, tying up loose ends.

In the evening, Fitts called Cliff at home and told him to be at the Blossom Room of the Roosevelt Hotel the next morning by 8:50 a.m. for a nine o'clock news conference. "Wear a nice suit" were Fitts's last words. Cliff knew he would leave the room either in glory or in handcuffs. The awful possibilities and his consciousness of blood on his hands, of Sanchez, of Dorothy, and even of Williams, made for a restless night.

Monday, June 12, 1939

A uniformed officer in a patrol car picked up Cliff at 8:10 a.m., drove to the Roosevelt, and parked in an area reserved for the police. The parking lot was full. Men and a few women were making their way to the Blossom Room. Inside on a podium, a lectern covered in microphones had been set up facing several rows of chairs. On either side of the lectern was a large table with chairs. Cliff stood against the wall where he could watch people file in. Technicians were making adjustments to the microphones. Reporters were taking their seats. Cliff spied Fitts standing against the back wall talking with a small group of men. One looked to be Dwight Carpenter, Fitts's newest favorite assistant. Yes, Cliff confirmed, he did see Chief Dice and Attorney General Warren. What did they know about Cliff's envelopes of cash from Tony the Hat's bagman? Was the Fresno Kid here ready to spill his guts—"Yeah, I'm the Chinaman's enforcer"—for a chance to get back into the fight game? God, he couldn't bear the shame if Lucille found out about the corners he'd cut. As Cliff contemplated his possible legal defenses, he felt a tug at his sleeve.

"Tommy." It was Mary. Her eyes shone with excitement. "Isn't it wonderful? They sent me to find you. They want you to take your place at the table. The one on the right. Your spot is marked."

As Cliff walked up to his spot, he saw Lou Gomez walking toward him. Cliff nodded a greeting.

"Any idea what's going on?" Lou whispered into Cliff's ear.

"I was just told to be here. Nothing else."

"My captain is here, and so is Dice."

Cliff looked around at the dignitaries taking their seats. Everyone had a lot to lose. Earl Warren was the man who could go places, certainly the governor's mansion and maybe even a national office, but now his political future was in danger if it became public that his trusted security chief had thrown in with the Syndicate. And maybe it was true; maybe Warren wanted White's family to get his pension, which they might lose if White was revealed to be a felon. Then there were the boys from Santa Monica: Chief Dice and the captain. The stink of corruption already hung on Dice; the city was looking for a way to push him out the door. Both would certainly lose their jobs if people found out that Detective Williams, working directly under them, had killed Daniel Roberts and the Stralla kid as part of a conspiracy with the daughter of a mobster to muscle in on a gambling ship. Being the father of Dorothy's bastard child, conceived when she was underage, was merely an embarrassment. Of course, statutory rape by a police officer wouldn't sit well with the society ladies of Pasadena, but then, Cliff thought, neither would his own transgressions. And then there was District Attorney Buron Fitts. Yes, murder cases against the well connected seemed to disappear when he was in charge, and his family did seem to profit from questionable business deals, but he had survived worse fixes than this. After all, what had Fitts done? He had approved his trusted deputy DA's harebrained plan to use a civilian woman as bait to catch a mad-dog killer. Sure, the killer had been caught and killed, but only after he had killed the civilian and two officers, had almost killed the attorney general, and had killed the AG's bodyguard and maybe a few others along the way. The mayor wanted Fitts out of office and into a cell, and this disaster of an investigation gave him the perfect opportunity to get rid of Fitts and all his lieutenants. Someone had to take the fall. Cliff wondered whether they would handcuff him and Gomez separately or together.

Fitts stepped up to the lectern at exactly 9:00 a.m. The room fell silent. "Gentlemen ... and ladies, thank you for coming today. The Los Angeles County District Attorney's office, the LA County Sheriff's Department, and police departments throughout LA County yesterday ended a crime spree perpetrated by anarchists determined to tear down the criminal justice system in California and terrorize the people of our great state. Two shadowy men, Nicolae "Nicky" Antonescu and Vincent Popa, anarchists from Romania, have been positively identified as the individuals who kidnapped and killed Mary Scott and Anna Mara, whose deaths were previously attributed to the so-called Canyon Killer, as well as Helen Burke and Virginia Reed, the victims in the Baldwin Hills murders. We now believe that these kidnappings and murders were an attempt to sow panic among the people of California. In the course of our investigations, we uncovered a connection between these four deaths and the murders of Daniel Roberts and Ricardo Stralla. Nicky Antonescu and Vincent Popa, working with Stralla, concocted a plan to kidnap and coerce Daniel Roberts into diverting untaxed money to finance their plan to assassinate Attorney General Earl Warren. When Roberts refused to cooperate, Vincent shot and killed Roberts. Vincent's gun has been conclusively tied to that murder as well as the subsequent murders of coconspirator Ricardo Stralla and Thomas Bertolli, a suspected dope peddler.

"Nicky and Vincent were thwarted in their attempt to assassinate the attorney general through the brave efforts of detectives from the Santa Monica Police Department. The case was cracked open through the risky, although ultimately successful, gambit of drawing out the anarchists and attempting to lure them into a trap on Friday night. This effort was aided by the selfless sacrifice of Dorothy Green, the daughter of well-known businessman Leonard Green, who provided crucial information to our detectives and allowed herself to be used as bait in the police trap. As has been publicized, the trap failed to capture the anarchists and resulted in the death of Detective Raymond Sanchez. But this tactic did serve to flush out the anarchists and ultimately led to the foiling of the assassination plot against the attorney general.

"We have incontrovertible evidence that following the attempted assassination, Nicky killed and disposed of the body of his coconspirator, Vincent, before returning to his hideout in Venice where he had taken Dorothy Green. Detective Randolph Williams of the Santa Monica Police Department single-handedly tracked Nicky to the hideout where the two men shot it out. Williams was fatally wounded, and Nicky, before making his escape, inflicted a fatal wound on Dorothy Green. Clifford Thoms of my office, despite having received a serious wound the previous night in his relentless pursuit of the Canyon Killer, cut off Nicky's escape and shot it out with the anarchist at the risk of his own life. Detective Williams's partner, Luis Gomez, joined the pursuit and finally shot and killed Nicolae Antonescu.

"This investigation, while it achieved its goal of ridding our streets of a group of killers, came at great cost. California lost several brave police officers and, of course, the life of one extraordinary young woman. Attorney General Warren"—Fitts turned his head and spoke to Earl Warren—"I believe that you have a few comments you want to make."

"Yes, thank you, District Attorney Fitts." Warren stood up and walked over to the lectern as Fitts sat down. "Ladies and gentlemen, while I may have been the object of the attack on Saturday, make no mistake, the true target was the criminal justice system of the state of California. These foreign elements, these anarchists, have as their goal the destruction of the social order of our state and our nation. Even with detectives hot on their trail, those two anarchists—who are no better than common criminals—chose to carry out their planned attack on me. In the course of that attack, two brave law officers, Jerry White and Michael Robinson, died. I owe my life to the sacrifices that Jerry and Mike made, and I will do everything in my power to see that their families receive the financial benefits that were paid for by the blood of those two fine officers. Thank you." Warren sat down. The audience gave him a round of applause.

"Thank you, Mr. Attorney General." Fitts was back at the lectern. "Now I believe that Charlie Dice, Santa Monica Chief of Police, Charles L. Dice, has a few words to say. Charlie?"

Dice walked over the lectern, grabbed it with both hands, and looked across the audience. "A lot of people say that cops are crooked." He looked across the audience again. "They say that politicians are crooked. I know that in the past people made some pretty wild charges against our district attorney, Mr. Fitts. Well, we know what happened when those charges were tried in a court of law—Fitts walked free like the innocent man he is. And a lot of people have thrown some scurrilous charges at me. Well, I have broad shoulders; I can carry that burden. But what makes me mad, really mad, is when anonymous voices make unsubstantiated claims against my officers. People said some nasty things about Randy Williams; they weren't true, of course, but those same people would then pick up the phone and ask Randy to run down to their neighborhood and put his life on the line. Randy Williams was a fine officer and a dedicated public servant who gave his life trying to get scum like Nicky and Vincent off the streets. He didn't ask for special favors; hell, he didn't even know Dorothy Green, but he risked his life to save her, and for that, this county should be eternally grateful. I just want to say one more thing: I'm proud of the way that Randy Williams and Lou Gomez contributed to this investigation, and I'm proud that it was my man, Lou Gomez, who did what needed to be done and killed that son of a bitch, Nicky." Again the audience applauded but with a little more enthusiasm.

Dice returned to his seat, and Fitts returned to the lectern. "We have one more speaker. We've heard from law enforcement officials memorializing fallen officers, but there was one civilian who also made the ultimate sacrifice. Let us welcome her father, Leonard Green. Mr. Green?" Fitts took his chair and looked over at Lenny Green.

Green had his head down and was staring at the table. After several seconds, he got up from his chair and walked slowly to the lectern. Green held some note cards in his hand but didn't look at them. He stared straight ahead, over the heads of the audience. He spoke in a tired voice. "My daughter's dead. This is the worst thing that's happened to me since her mother died eighteen years ago. When I first heard the news, I was mad at the police and that Nicky guy." Green paused, seemingly to gather his thoughts. "Yesterday I had a long talk with DA Fitts. He told me things about my daughter that I never knew. It's funny; you can live with your kid for twenty, twenty-three, years and not really know her." Green turned his head and glanced at Fitts. He turned back and resumed speaking over the heads of the audience. "I found out that she knew those girls who got killed in the Baldwin Hills. She called the cops and offered to help. She agreed to be the bait in the trap. I guess I should be proud that she was brave, but I just wish I had her back. That's all I gotta say." Green walked slowly back to his chair and sat down.

Fitts walked back up to the podium. "We have time for a few questions. Yes, Agness, with two S's," Fitts said with a smile and a wink. "Ladies first."

"Agness Underwood, *Los Angeles Herald-Express*. Originally we were told that the Canyon Killer deaths were not related to the Baldwin Hills murders, but now you say that the same people committed them. Why the change of story?"

"When the Baldwin Hills victims were found, the bodies were in poor condition, and it was assumed that they were shot rather than stabbed. The coroner later determined that they were killed in the same manner as the Canyon Killer victims. Once we realized that there was a connection, it was apparent that this was part of an effort to terrorize the people of the county of Los Angeles, and we refused to play into the anarchists' hands. Leaving the mistaken information uncorrected allowed us to sort through the false confessions a case like this generates. You can't imagine how many people we had confess to shooting those two girls in the Baldwin Hills.

"Yes, in the second row."

"Jim Burton, *Daily News*. Previous speculation was that one group of mobsters was trying to take over the *Rex* from another group. Are you saying that there was no mobster connection to the Daniel Roberts murder?"

"That's right. Nicolae Antonescu and Vincent Popa were not affiliated with mobsters, either here on the West Coast or on the East Coast, and I defy anyone to prove otherwise. In fact, neither had a police record of any kind. They were also not affiliated with any known anarchist group. That lack of a record and lack of affiliations was what allowed those two to remain undetected for so long, despite the effectiveness of the intelligence capabilities of the LAPD developed under former Chief Davis.

"We have time for one more question. Yes, Jim?"

"A follow-up. The rumor going around the DA's office was that you were going to sack ADA Cliff Thoms for the fiasco on Friday. Any truth to that rumor, and if not, what are your plans? Does he stay on?"

"The rumors that Cliff was to be sacked are absolutely untrue. It's always easy to criticize after the fact, but consider the situation. We had four horrific murders and no suspects. Dorothy Green's information, which we received only this past ..." Fitts paused and looked over to Cliff.

"Wednesday night," Cliff said softly.

"Wednesday night," Fitts continued, "was the first time we put a name to the Baldwin Hills murder victims and their kidnapper. Yet, within three days, both Nicky and Vincent were dead. Yes, the trap on Friday night was a gamble, and yes, it had a high price, but it achieved its ultimate aim of removing the killers of four young women from society. Conventional police work might have taken weeks or months to track down Nicky and Vincent—we couldn't wait that long. Desperate times call for desperate measures.

"As for your second question"—Fitts glanced quickly at Cliff—"I wanted dearly to keep Cliff Thoms on my staff, but after nearly being killed two times in as many days, Cliff, with some encouragement no doubt from his wife, has tendered his resignation effective the end of September. Cliff"—Fitts turned and faced Thoms—"I'd like to take this opportunity to thank you for all the great work you've done for me and the people of the county of Los Angeles, and to wish you the best of luck in your private practice. I know you'll be a terrific success." Fitts walked over to Cliff and extended his hand.

The men shook hands. Cliff forced a small smile and muttered, "Thank you."

Fitts returned to the lectern. "That's all we have time for. The attorney general has a train to catch, and the rest of us need to get back to our offices to carry out the people's business. Thank you for your attendance."

Several newspaper reporters jumped up to be the first to the phones to call in their story. Earl Warren and Buron Fitts moved away from the lectern and table and conferred briefly before Warren left. Cliff stood a few feet back, waiting while the conversation was in progress, but stepped forward quickly before others could command Fitts's attention.

"Remind me, Buron—when did I decide to resign?"

"About the same time the bodies started piling up from that stunt on Friday."

"You said yourself that that 'stunt' achieved its ultimate aim."

"Tommy, you should read Gomez's report. It was pure luck that Warren wasn't killed and that Williams found Nicky. How did Williams find Nicky, anyway? Gomez doesn't know, and your report just says something about an anonymous tip."

"That's right, an anonymous tip."

"That was called into your office on Saturday afternoon?"

"The public can be very helpful."

"Well, it didn't happen that way. We rewrote your report. You recruited Gomez and Williams on Tuesday night, and the three of you coordinated the capture of Nicky on Saturday. Williams got to the hideout ahead of you and Gomez, and was killed, but you and Gomez worked together to kill Nicky. It wouldn't do either of us any good to have it known that you were standing there with an empty pistol in one hand and your dick in the other hand waiting for Nicky to fill you with daylight."

"No, I guess not."

"Tommy, you're a good man and a bright attorney, but you've become a liability. Warren, Dice, Green, and I worked it out so that everyone is protected. The only people taking the fall are already dead; no one is going to complain."

"That's not quite true. What about Ricardo Stralla? You're going to leave his family with that burden? I talked to Gomez. I can imagine what his report, his original report, said. Ricardo was used and discarded; he was a country kid who was in love and in over his head. He went to his priest to confess his sins, for God's sake. Don't we owe it to his family to tell the truth?"

"The truth? Tommy, the truth hurts everyone else; this fable is best. I feel as sorry for the Strallas as anyone, but their boy is dead, and nothing will bring him back. The truth won't help them now."

"Ah, what did you say to Green to get him to go along?"

"We had Williams's dying declaration that he and Dorothy were behind the scheme to take over the *Rex* and that they killed Roberts together. And my investigators turned up evidence that Dorothy did get on the plane to Mexico on Thursday night but got off in San Diego and had Ricardo pick her up in the Bugatti. A gas station attendant in Oceanside remembers the car. They don't get a lot of Bugattis there. Guess Green didn't want his granddaughter growing up knowing that her mother was a murdering floozy. Better to have Dorothy remembered as a heroine."

"Yes, better that way."

"You and Dorothy ... you didn't—?"

"No, there was nothing improper going on between us. We met, and she furnished us with invaluable information. She was a heroine ... in a way."

"All right. Get back to the office, and sign your report. Don't forget to backdate it."

CHAPTER 21

Summer 1939

"Tommy, I'm interviewing all of the senior attorneys in the office. Warren is as mad as a wet hen. Cornero's men were waiting for us with the water hoses. Warren says that someone had to have tipped them off."

Fitts stood up and limped to the window overlooking the city. He worked his bad knee while staring out at the horizon. "What was it—eight, nine, days? The press is having a field day. They're calling the standoff 'the Battle of Santa Monica Bay.' We had sixteen boats and two hundred fifty or more men from half a dozen agencies. The planning, the expense! Sure, we shut down the other gambling ships, the *Tango*, the *Texas*, the ... the other one, but the *Rex* was the prize, and we looked like fools out there." Fitts turned and faced Cliff. Cliff was surprised to see that Fitts wore a small smile. "I've got to hand it to Cornero; throwing bottles of rum down to the boatloads of reporters was a great way to get good press." Fitts sat back down at his desk. Cliff had never seen him so restless. "Sheriff Biscailuz's office swears that no one in their office said a word. Same with Dice's office. Everyone's pointing the finger at this office. You know there are rumors that you're a little too close to A. J. Barnes and"—Fitts glanced quickly at Cliff before dropping his eyes—"maybe have a connection with Cornero himself."

"Buron, you know I wasn't working on preparations for the raid. That was Dwight and his people. I don't need to tell you that Dwight doesn't share information with me. Sure, A. J. and I socialize from time to time, but how could I pass along information I didn't have? Maybe Dwight let something slip without realizing it."

"Okay, I'll talk to Dwight." Fitts was standing again as Cliff rose to leave. "Tommy, did you see what Cornero said to the press, why he surrendered? He said he needed a *haircut*. What a character! I'm almost going to miss him."

Earl Warren's planned raids on the gambling ships in Santa Monica Bay had been delayed following the attack on him in June. By late July, he was ready to try again. Without waiting for the California Supreme Court to decide whether the gambling ships anchored in Santa Monica Bay were in international water and therefore legal, Warren declared the ships a public nuisance and ordered them to close down. When they refused, he launched a raid against the ships on August 1. Three of the ships allowed police officers to board and destroy all gambling equipment by dumping it over the side of the ships. The crew of the *Rex*, led by Tony Cornero, refused to allow the officers to board and forced them away by spraying them with fire hoses. Eventually Cornero relented and, after making arrangements with a lawyer and a bail bondsman, surrendered to the police. The gambling equipment from the *Rex* was dumped into the sea.

Richard Woolfolk and many of his coworkers from the gambling ships were out of work. Jobs that paid a living wage were scarce. Rich had a wife and two children who needed to eat and have a place to live. He was able to find some temporary work, but the tough times of the Depression dragged on.

Early in September, Zoe had her family over for a Sunday dinner. Robert and Margie were there, as were Richard and his wife, Marie, and their two children. During lulls in the conversation following dinner, they could hear the seagulls screeching as they swooped down to pick up the remnants of food left by visitors to the beach two blocks away. While the others talked, Richard was silent. He was restless, rootless, and despondent; he had no work or ambition. He was haunted by the death of Danny Roberts and the change of fortune of many of his friends. The company of his family seemed stifling. After dinner he walked alone along the Front. He stepped into his favorite bar, where he ordered a drink and joined his friends and acquaintances. They told jokes, played games, and made bets. It was a little like old times when he was employed and could afford a few indulgences.

Richard suddenly needed a pack of cigarettes. His face turned hot; sweat appeared on his forehead. He became angry, overwhelmed with shame: he had no money for a pack of Lucky Strikes. His shaking hands couldn't hold his glass without spilling the whiskey. His throat burned; he could feel his heart pounding. He had to have a smoke. Richard stumbled outside and continued walking along the Front past a drugstore. He was captivated by a cigarette display in the window. The cardboard woman seemed to be calling him, beckoning him to come and get his cigarettes. Richard walked to the side of the path, picked up a brick, and hurled it at the plate glass window. The noise caused people to stop and stare as Richard walked through the shattered window, picked up a carton of Lucky Strike cigarettes, and calmly sauntered away, unaware of the havoc he'd left behind.

Richard pled guilty to reduced charges and was sentenced to one year in the Honor Rancho. Marie and the children were forced to leave their home and move in with her mother and her brother, Fred Tsheppe.

In mid-September, Zoe invited Cliff and Lucille to her home for dinner with her family. After dinner, Zoe, Cliff, and Lucille stayed in the dining room to talk while Clarence went into the living room to finish up some paperwork for Tony Cornero's businesses. Zoe was concerned for her friends and wanted to know what Cliff planned to do after the end of the month when his resignation from the DA's office became effective.

"Oh, Zoe, I'm not worried. I already have a few private clients, and once I hang my shingle, more will come. It will take a while, but business will build. I have contacts. I'd prefer not to do criminal defense, but I guess I'll have to take what walks in the door until I'm in a position to pick and choose my cases. I'd like to focus on representing business clients ..."

"What are you thinking?" Zoe asked, seeing Cliff hesitate.

"Well, this war ... how long will it last? If the United States is pulled into it, there will be lots of businesses that will need representation. It's just that I hate to profit from destruction."

"The war will last far longer than most people think. We won't be directly involved for a while, but"—Zoe had a faraway look in her eyes—"so much death."

Marie walked into the dining room carrying her eight-month-old child, Caroline. Her toddler followed behind at her heels. "Zoe, the girls and I are leaving now. Thank you for dinner."

"Yes, it's getting late. You should be going," Zoe said, barely looking up.

"Oh, let me hold her for a minute," Lucille said, standing up and reaching out to Marie.

"Joanie, come here and ride on Uncle Cliff's horse." Cliff held a hand out to the older child. Joanie, a beautiful, towheaded three-year-old, was small for her age but bright and talkative. She ran over to Cliff and straddled his leg. He held both her hands, her arms outstretched, as she balanced on his bouncing knee. Cliff looked over at Lucille and said softly, "If only we had met ten years earlier."

Cradling the sleeping baby in her arms, Lucille nodded. "We could have done a lot with another ten years together," she said without taking her eyes off the child.

CPSIA information can be obtained
at www.ICGtesting.com
Printed in the USA
LVOW10s0029110517
534091LV00001B/50/P

9 781491 789582